Victim
Impact

Mel Bradshaw

RendezVous
Crime

Cover design: Vasiliki Lenis/Emma Dolan

LE CONSEIL DES ARTS
DU CANADA
DEPUIS 1957

THE CANADA COUNCIL
FOR THE ARTS
SINCE 1957

We acknowledge the support of the Canada Council for the Arts for our publishing program.

We acknowledge the financial support of the Government of Canada through the Book Publishing Industry Development Program (BPIDP) for our publishing activities.

RendezVous Crime
an imprint of Napoleon & Company
Toronto, Ontario, Canada
www.napoleonandcompany.com

Printed in Canada

12 11 10 09 08   5 4 3 2 1

Library and Archives Canada Cataloguing in Publication

Bradshaw, Mel, 1947-
        Victim impact / Mel Bradshaw.

ISBN 978-1-894917-70-4

        I. Title.
PS8603.R332V52 2008   C813'.6   C2008-905621-3

For my friends

Oh, membranza sì cara e fatal!
Oh, memory so fatal and so dear!
—Temistocle Solera
(libretto of *Nabucco*, opera by Giuseppe Verdi)

Prologue

As late as mid-afternoon, Ted Boudreau thought he had plenty of time. He lingered over waxing and polishing the painted surfaces of his second-hand Yamaha. He replaced the spark plugs. Then he found he had a burned-out headlamp and had to go back to the shop. He still would have been in good time if he hadn't, at the last moment, had to remove and patch a tire. On the first motorcycle-riding day of the 1998 season, he was to attend a recital at the Royal Conservatory of Music.

This disorganization was not like Ted, but then neither was it like him to be looking forward to an evening of Beethoven cello sonatas. Bill Nikolic's son Dan was playing the piano accompaniment, and Bill had heard from Dan that the cellist was pretty. Ted had been in town nine years, as graduate student and lecturer at the University of Toronto, and had dated intermittently over that time. Currently, though, he was between girlfriends—as his colleague Bill Nikolic well knew.

Once the wheel was back on the bike, Ted had to shower and dress. His parents owned a dry cleaners in Montreal, in which Ted and his siblings had all at one time worked. None had escaped with an indifferent attitude to clothes. What, Ted wondered, would a cellist playing at the Royal Conservatory be wearing? He thought back to pictures of the Queen in floral print dresses with matching jackets and feathered hats. That called at the very least for grey flannels and a blue blazer. It was

1

only March, however, and he was riding a motorcycle, so Ted settled on dress chinos, a turtleneck sweater and a ski jacket.

The recital was well begun by the time he arrived, and he was asked to wait outside the auditorium till intermission. All the printed programs had by this time been handed out. Ted prowled the Conservatory halls pretending to look at the hanging photos of past directors.

When the doors opened, Ted spotted Bill by the piano in conversation with a young man still seated at the keyboard and a breathtaking red-haired being from another planet. Pretty didn't begin to cover it. Why, Ted wondered, was everyone in the room not staring at her? It couldn't be that the first half of the recital had already given them their fill. Maybe they were just too polite to deny her a break from non-stop admiration. He tried to rise to the occasion and go meet her. She was wearing a full, floor-length black skirt and a sleeveless, high-collared gold lamé top that fastened somehow in the back and made the most of her trim figure.

Introductions were made. Introductions were repeated. Ted took in nothing the first time, so busy was he apologizing for being late. To get over his nervousness, he half-seriously remarked that Beethoven was his favourite classical composer after ABBA. Unfortunately, ABBA was the serious half.

Karin looked him over with cool green eyes.

"Which Beethoven do you particularly like?" Dan asked.

"Oh, everything. The lullaby, *The Barber of Seville*..."

Bill came to the rescue by taking some photos with his digital camera. Dan and Karin made an attractive pair. To avoid feeling extra, Ted offered to snap the other three. They put Bill in the middle, his head rising above the musicians' like a snow-capped mountain peak, and Karin laced her arm through his. Ted liked the way these pictures turned out when he checked them on the screen.

Lights in the auditorium and corridors were flicked on and off a few times to signal that the recital was resuming. The room was high-ceilinged but narrow and intimate, with rows of wooden chairs in place of fixed plush seats. Bill had saved Ted a chair and lent him his program. Sonata No. 3 in A Major, it seemed, was to be the featured work of the second half.

For Ted's taste, it got off to a slow start. The long first movement was marked Allegro, ma non tanto. He guessed he'd have liked tanto better, though every so often there were passages of higher energy, interludes he began to look forward to. At the same time, the sound of Karin's cello—an instrument he'd never paid any attention to—was stealing into his gut and setting up home there. Not doing much yet, just announcing its presence.

The second movement, Scherzo (Allegro molto), was more like it. Red hair was starting to fly around the soloist's face. Ted thought he had a handle on Beethoven now. Wasn't Beethoven the one that always gave you a storm if you waited long enough? Now the interludes were the slow bits, and here the rumbling strings could really churn you up before the tune raced off again in all directions.

In the end, though, the most memorable thing about this movement was not that in these five minutes Ted became a cello fan. It was, rather, that some ass three rows in front of Ted set off a camera flash in Karin's face. Her attention was diverted momentarily. Her eyes narrowed. Soundlessly, she mouthed a word, which Ted from where he sat was sure was "prick". At the sudden light and his partner's movement, Dan looked up from the keyboard. Neither musician what you'd call allegro—molto or otherwise. It could have been a disaster. True performers that they were, however, neither one missed a beat. Ted squirmed nonetheless. He would have considered the interruption adequately dealt with if only Karin had been staring down the shutterbug when she said what she said. But, dazzled and distracted as she'd been, Ted was sure she hadn't found the right face in the crowd, and the offender had not suffered the sting of her disdain. The man didn't take any more flash photos of Dan and Karin, but that was more likely because he had what he wanted than because he had any consciousness of what he'd done.

The sonata's third movement again featured alternating tempi, but for Ted the music passed in a blur. At the recital's end, he borrowed Bill's camera and armed the electronic flash while threading his way between slower audience members to the door. Once there, he turned. It was perfect. The shutterbug was struggling into his overcoat. He was a big man in a tight suit, and tall. He grimaced as he pulled the tight Burberry over his broad shoulders. The camera caught an unflattering expression.

He lumbered forward, still not entirely into his coat. "What did you take my picture for?" he demanded.

"For the Conservatory," said Ted. "They're compiling a gallery of boors. You know, so they'll know who not to admit to future recitals."

He considered snapping off one more shot of the hot, angry face at close range, but the point after all had been made.

"Bite me," bleated the man, attracting scowls from the departing music-lovers.

He looked ready to push Ted down, but Ted slid out of the way and back to Bill, Dan and Karin. When he showed them the photo, Karin laughingly said, "That deserves some recompense."

She sat and drew her honey-coloured instrument between

the the folds of her full, black skirt. Then she tossed off a few bars of "Chiquitita".

Ted felt he'd been blown a kiss.

*   *   *

When Karin told her violist friend Nancy that she had met a guy, they were strolling to The Coffee Mill after a lecture at the Conservatory. Nancy Malik *née* Gallo—a clear-skinned Rubenesque goddess, peerless authority on men, and recent bride—naturally wanted to know what he was like.

"Kind of short," Karin answered. "Well, my height, actually. Short for a man."

"Cute?"

"Yeah." Karin dragged the word out and gave Nancy a "well, duh" look. Would she be telling her about Ted if he weren't cute?

"So? What's he like?"

"Okay." Karin's hands started moving, as if she were conducting a group of Ted's features, bringing each one in when required. "Nice hair—wavy, brown. Slightly cleft chin, not too much. Great smile—reserved, but warm. I mean, his eyes are this mysterious taupe colour, but they really look at you. Rides a motorcycle, without all the leather. Quiet dresser, well-pressed. Nice flat gut."

"Musical?"

Karin touched the tips of her middle finger and thumb to make a zero. "A potential listener."

"I can't be hearing this." Nancy raised her arms and eyes to the heavens. "Funny?" she ventured.

"He has a mischievous side."

"Dare I ask his age?"

"Unimportant."

"Uh-oh. Older or younger?"

"Nance! Would I waste my time with teenagers? He's a prof or assistant prof of criminology, so I figure with that and the way he looks, he has to be around thirty. That's only six years' difference. Hey, you know that book I was reading on Chinese astrology for westerners? I'd say he fits the Tiger profile much better than I do, even if the calendar says he's a mild-mannered Sheep."

"A quiet dresser in orange and black? That would be a stretch, even over a flat gut." Nancy's hoots of laughter turned heads on both sides of Bloor Street. She enjoyed razzing Karin, but was happy for her as well. Her new husband was an academic also, so she couldn't take too hard a line in that area. "Criminologist, eh? What's his specialty?"

"He tells me he has a number of irons in the fire."

"Huh, man of mystery. As you say."

Chapter 1

Ted looked at the chalkboard a little longer than usual on his way to the table the hostess had picked out for him. Most weeks he just had to confirm that the Friday night special of barbecued Atlantic salmon with snow peas had not changed, but today was Thursday, and an unfamiliar dish was posted. Toulouse bean casserole.

He had the server explain that to him—navy beans, pork rinds, leg of goose, a few carrots, garlic sausage—before Karin arrived. The printed menu was the same as always, but there seemed to be a new wine list, with even fewer whites by the glass. And most of those Chardonnays. Quirk wouldn't be pleased about that.

The first time he'd heard it, at the Beethoven recital, he had thought her name was K-a-r-e-n, but when he'd written down her phone number, she'd taken the pen from his hand, darkened in the loop of the e, and added a dot over top to make it an i. "It's a quirky spelling," she said with a grimace of embarrassment he hadn't seen on her face in the eight years since. She later told him she had been irrationally afraid he wouldn't like her.

The server asked Ted if he'd like a drink. He thanked her, no. He always said no, because one glass was all he ever managed in an evening, and he preferred to wait for Karin before starting in on it.

While waiting, he enjoyed the familiar surroundings. Aside from the fact that there were fewer diners at seven on a weekday, the view from the usual table was as usual. The bistro had a steeply pitched cathedral ceiling, from which bright floral-patterned banners hung. Posters of lavender fields in Provence punctuated the yellowy, rough-plastered walls, and each table sported a vase containing a fresh white carnation. The scene was set, Ted reflected; bring on the star!

Then he saw her. Karin was standing at the lectern where they kept the reservation book, talking to the hostess. His sense of anticipation quickened. He watched the woman he loved toss her head of red-gold hair, saw her smile blossom into a laugh, watched her long, lean body sway a little as she shared the joke with the hostess. Ted liked her friendliness, believed—with arrogance he readily forgave himself—that happy people like Karin and him ought to spread their joy. He waved at her, but she didn't see. She had turned to speak to one of the servers. Fine, fine. Now she could come laugh with him. He didn't want to lose another moment. While she was turned, Ted admired her from a distance. *Quirk,* he thought, not for the first time, *has a sweet butt.*

He realized his lips had been moving. Lately he had caught himself saying this mantra aloud, and he looked around to see if anyone was within earshot. No, his reputation for sanity was intact.

Here she came, in a yellow sundress showing a lot of cleavage and shiny red sandals. Ted sprang to his feet to kiss her. Her lips were warm, the skin around them moist with perspiration. He was glad they had nothing planned for after dinner—except that he'd have to spend a half hour reviewing his notes for tomorrow's panel discussion.

"Did you hear?" said Karin. "Giovanna's come top of her year in Commerce."

"Was that the girl you were just talking to?"

"No, Ted, that was Fairuza. Giovanna's the one that serves this table."

He wondered how she kept them straight. The servers didn't even wear name tags. They were identified on the checks, of course, in print and sometimes in a signed hand-written thank-you accompanied by a smiley face. Perhaps Quirk went through his wallet when he was asleep.

He passed her the diminished wine list without comment and braced for a change in her mood. About some things—housework, for instance—she could be bohemian enough, letting matters slide then pouring effort into a mammoth, occasional cleanup. She was invariably flexible and downright classy about sudden developments in Ted's life. His volunteering to fill in for a colleague at the conference over the long weekend, for instance, and the consequent change in their weekly dinner at the Bouquet Bistro. But there were spheres to which her tolerance did not extend. She had a passion for precision in string playing, for punctuality at lessons and rehearsals. And, a recipe for frustration this, for consistency and continuity in her urban environment. There would be no point in Ted's saying the proprietors might have found that most Bistro patrons liked oaky Chardonnay. Public taste shouldn't be pandered to, she had shot back at him in similar circumstances; it should be educated. Didn't Ted believe the same thing, after all, in the matter of capital punishment? At this point, Ted would likely say something conciliatory. He wasn't the champion of market forces so much as of economy of emotional effort. The writing, teaching, and administration work of an academic career kept him as occupied as he wanted to be with external issues. A compact circle of family and friends soaked up another block of his energy. The bulk of his passion, all that remained, was reserved for Quirk.

"We could order a whole bottle tonight," he offered. "There's a Chablis they don't do by the glass."

"Only if you had a really rough day and can drink it all yourself. I'll have Perrier."

Giovanna—a short, solid girl with shiny black corkscrew ringlets—was back hovering over their table. "Are you guys ready to order, or would you like another couple of minutes?"

In the bustle of congratulating the server on her marks and getting the drinks ordered, the significance of what Quirk had said hadn't quite sunk in. Then Karin and Ted enjoyed a private chuckle over the possible adverse effect of bean casserole on the evening's erotic potential and decided on steak frites all round. It was only when Giovanna returned with the green Perrier bottle and Ted's usual glass of Beaujolais that suspicion started to dawn. Ted's eyebrows crept up as he studied Karin's face. He didn't dare ask, but she was nodding.

"Hot damn!"

"I was wondering how long it would take you," she teased.

"'Take us', you mean." Three years of the in vitro song and dance, he reflected, and the four years before that trying everything but.

"To figure it out, silly."

"Good thing intelligence comes from the mother."

"This mum says it would be smart to keep it quiet for a while. It's only two weeks—if you can imagine knowing so early. Lots can still go wrong."

She must have seen from the way Ted was looking around the Bistro that he was dying to tell all the Giovannas and Fairuzas. But her words settled him. He stared at her wondrous, lightly freckled face. "Yippee," he whispered.

"So, did you book our flight to St. Vincent today?"

Damn. For over a week now, Ted had been promising to

make arrangements for their Boxing Day to New Year's getaway. Today, the conference had distracted him, but he really had no excuse.

"Yep," he said. "All set."

"You did not, you goof. You forgot."

"Not at all."

"Show me the tickets then," Karin playfully demanded.

"They're paperless tickets. I booked over the Internet."

"Pants on fire! You've never bought so much as a CD over the Internet."

"I'll get them tomorrow."

"I'm not swallowing that one either, Ted. You and I will go together to the travel agent on Tuesday. You know, if anyone ever actually believed any of your lies, I'd haunt your dreams." She must have noticed that that made him smile, for she added, "And not in a nice way."

By the time they started home, Ted had already made up his mind to go downtown early the next morning and do his conference preparation then. A ten minutes' walk brought them from the Bistro to the house, their second in this west Mississauga neighbourhood. It was bigger than their first, a vote of confidence in their future family, and was situated on a street that wound quietly to a dead end. It had more rooms than they needed, than they had needed up till now. The master bedroom seemed almost too big for two. They had joked about having a duty to leave clothes strewn around the floor so the place wouldn't look so empty. Ted found himself wondering where they'd put the crib. There was room on either side of the queen-size bed.

Karin got there first and slipped under the duvet while Ted was still brushing his teeth. Before joining her, he fed some Schubert into the CD player. Piano Trio in E-flat, Op. 100, it said on the box liner. His non-musical memory continued to struggle with these keys and numbers, but he knew the piece. The second movement in particular was a favourite of theirs. With the piano beating time in the background, the cello introduced the melody. Slow and catchy was how Ted described it in his offhand way. Karin had better words—dark, intimate, stirring, otherworldly—but what she did with it on her instrument was more communicative than any of them. She had yet to make good on her promise to record her reading, so they were going to make do tonight with Leonard Rose on cello.

Ted waited for the opening bars so he could adjust the volume. Then he slid in beside Karin, and around her, and it astounded him yet again how perfect every square millimetre of her skin felt against his. Soft, yielding, resilient, firm, warm, caressing to whatever part of him caressed her. How could anything on earth be this perfect? And within her now another her, another him. Quirk was already pulling him on top of her. He supposed in a few months, they'd find it more convenient the other way up. He looked forward to the swelling of her sweet, perfect belly above him.

He moved slowly but still came ahead of her. Extravagantly, joyously, but silently. Quirk was so quiet in bed that he always suppressed his own urge to cry out. When he rolled off to her right side, he slid his hand between her legs and helped her to her own mute convulsions of bliss before they breathed their tender goodnights and let sleep take them.

*   *   *

Karin and Ted thought of themselves as Torontonians and would have identified themselves as such in Moscow or Beijing. Ted's department was at the downtown St. George

Campus of the university. Karin taught at the Royal Conservatory of Music. In point of fact, they lived just to the west of Toronto in Mississauga. Their neighbourhood had a clean, safe, spacious, suburban feel, which they liked—though not so spacious as to make them indifferent to the charms of cottage country.

The couple had planned to spend the Labour Day weekend with Karin's father in Muskoka. On Wednesday, when Ted was asked to fill in at the "Punishing Homicide" conference, he urged Karin to carry on with the original plan. It was still hot in the city. He would not be able to spend any time with her anyway, and Markus would enjoy her company. Ted had been perfectly sincere in this suggestion. He got on well enough with Markus himself, but Markus had a playful tendency to turn encounters with Ted into manly jousts, with Karin left only to applaud from the sidelines. It would be just as well for father and daughter to have some unhurried hours alone together. Things would be said on both sides that wouldn't have come up in his presence. Markus had been a widower for some years and seemed to be managing well. Still, health questions could be gone into, questions of diet and hours of work. For all his twinkling smiles, Markus was an intense, lonely man, capable of using reckless activity to keep himself from brooding. Karin understood this yet put up some resistance at being pushed off to the lake while Ted batched it in the city. On Friday morning, in view of her news, Ted wished she had resisted more, and that he'd given way. He wanted her with him so they could go on savouring the long-awaited pregnancy. This was not the weekend he wanted her letting down her hair with her father. But by now Markus would have done his weekend shopping, and it was too late for him to invite anyone else.

Karin had lessons to give at the conservatory in the morning and a rehearsal of her chamber group in the afternoon. The octet. The way that gang went on, it was anyone's guess when she'd get started on the one and a half hour drive to the lake. Two and a half on a summer Friday evening. Sometimes Ted thought the string quartet and the opera orchestra should be enough in addition to her teaching, but the clarinettist had a pretty decent studio in his basement and had promised to help her make a demo to send around to record companies.

They parted in the driveway.

"Can I drive you downtown?" Quirk's cello was safely stowed behind the two seats of her gas-electric hybrid, as was her portfolio of scores. It was a sticky thirty-two degrees, and barely five minutes out of the air-conditioned house her face was shimmering above the collar of her white sleeveless blouse. Sweat had pasted strands of red hair to her cheek. "You could take the train back and a taxi from the station."

Ted said he might be late that night; he wasn't sure there'd be a taxi.

"Car-pooling is doomed," she laughed. "The two of us can't even do it."

"See you Monday night." He was waiting for her to go before he backed his second-hand Corolla out of the garage.

She had her keys in her hand as she threw her arms around him. "No need to tell you not to wait up," she said over his shoulder.

"Wake me."

They faced each other. How beautiful she was! This was the worst time for a weekend apart. They kissed hungrily.

Ted knew this was making it harder. In their marriage, he'd slid somehow into the rôle of timekeeper. He'd balked at first, pointing out as an example of his own unpunctuality his extreme lateness for the recital where they'd first met. Karin laughed at his protest. What had ancient history to do with them now? She disliked wearing a watch—especially if she were playing or practising, but at other times too—disliked the feel of metal around her wrist. No, Ted was to be the sensible one. It was up to him, she said, to know night from morning, the lark's song from the nightingale's. And he indulged her, no matter that he had never heard either bird.

Usually being sensible was easier than this. Their lips parted. He kissed her again on her unbearably sweet lips, but lightly.

"See you Monday," he said again.

*   *   *

After Karin left, Ted drove to the Clarkson GO Train station. Plainly, many regular commuters were starting their September holiday weekend early: there were dozens more parking spaces available in the south parking lot than was usual for a weekday, and more seats on the upper level of the second last coach. He'd found this railcar tended to be the least crowded. The trip took just under half an hour, barring mishaps, and this morning he spent the time reading the paper. He usually did—although he had had occasion to correct colleagues who supposed there would be nothing but industrial wasteland to see out the windows anyway. While Mississauga might still fall a blossom or two short of Arcadia, this rail corridor was for the most part a leafy green, interrupted only by the very occasional school or commercial enterprise. The factories, rail yards and graffiti-spattered abutments didn't begin till you were into Toronto proper.

He spent the morning at his desk in the University of Toronto's Department of Criminology. He was late with his peer review of an article a lecturer at Simon Fraser had submitted to one of the learned journals, but he had time to give it only a passing glance at present. It dealt with the Mafia and had been sent to Ted because someone had reported he was interested in gangs. The report had some foundation, but Ted didn't consider it safe to be known as a mob expert. Besides, the subject of this paper wasn't one of the criminal organizations he was collecting data on. More urgent this morning was the tweaking of an unpublished article of his own on young offenders into something he could deliver at one of the conference's workshop sessions on Sunday. And his first duty was getting ready to moderate a panel discussion on sentencing at seven o'clock that evening.

The conference proper, a symposium on punishment, was open to registrants only, mostly academics with positions at universities as far flung as Hong Kong, Cape Town and Helsinki. Proceedings would be launched with a keynote address tonight at eight thirty by a big cheese from the Australian Institute of Criminology. His subject, according to the program that Ted now retrieved from a drawer in his desk, was to be "Life Sentences as Overkill: the Need for Evidence-based Penalties." A good, progressive topic without being really provocative to the criminological community.

The panel discussion, open to all comers and featuring politicians and social activists as participants, had been publicized as a gesture of goodwill and inclusiveness towards the larger community. It had been organized also—Ted suspected, although this goal had been less explicit—as an opportunity for the academics to see how unenlightened the masses really were on the subject of sentencing and hence how vital it was that there be criminologists to straighten them out.

Shortly before noon, the man he was substituting for at the conference dropped by. Ted heard the rackety approach of the hard plastic wheels on the rolling suitcase before Graham Hart's tall frame filled the doorway.

"Lend me a blank DVD, Ted?" The suitcase was quite small for all the noise it made. Graham parked it in a corner and leaned on the back of a chair. He wore a buckskin jacket with fringe.

"Sure." Ted opened his top desk drawer and groped around.

"Some soc prof at Lakehead is going to let me copy his whole dossier on the Ojibway."

Ted's hand came out empty. "I could have sworn I had one." A quick check showed it wasn't in any of the other drawers either. "Sorry. Say, shouldn't you be on your way to Thunder Bay by now?"

"The airport limo's waiting as we speak. So just a quick heads-up on what to expect tonight. There's a victim of violent crime—suggested by our department chair, who knows her somehow. There's old Kerr, the happy warrior from U. of Calgary. He was your idea, wasn't he? And I dug up a fire-and-brimstone Toronto city councillor and a Brampton-based Crown counsel to round out the bear pit." Graham dropped an annotated list of names on Ted's desk. "As for topics, be prepared for concurrent versus consecutive sentences, conditional sentences, the faint hope clause. Capital punishment probably won't come up."

"The hang-'em-high crowd has had to do without since '62," Ted observed. "I guess folks get discouraged."

"More than that, there've been too many wrongfully

convicted. It's one of the universe's little jokes that obtuse juries have done more for progressive penology than acute criminologists."

"Do the Ojibway do a better job selecting members of their sentencing circles?"

"Ask me Tuesday," said Graham and clattered off. He'd been trying to get a first-hand look at how aboriginal communities dealt with crime for more than two years, and yesterday without warning an accused and his chief had agreed to let the white scholar attend. An opportunity not to be missed.

Ted looked over Graham's notes. He thought the tone he should strike as moderator would be imperturbable good humour, evinced by a tolerant smile and a willingness to interrupt when panellists and questioners weren't letting each other be heard. The main work remaining was to make sure he could pronounce the participants' names. A couple of phone calls established that both Cesario and Szabo started with an S sound.

*   *   *

Karin didn't get back to the house until seven thirty. She would have left the rehearsal early without scruple, but the music had absorbed her, and she had lost track of time. It still shouldn't be a problem. Unlike Ted, Markus was a night owl. She'd just have to warn him not to keep supper for her. In the shower, she remembered she had meant to pack her bag Thursday night. Hearing the results of the pregnancy test had driven all such thoughts from her head. Well, she needn't pack much: she was sure she had some cottage clothes up there. The worst of it was she was bone tired, in no condition to thread her way through hours of snarled traffic and to make allowances for other drivers' weary irritability. On her way to the basement to pick up her knapsack, she stopped by the range to put on water for a quick cup of tea.

The basement was full height, which—as the real estate agent had delighted in pointing out—they'd appreciate if they ever decided to finish it, or to sell the house. In the meantime, the correspondingly numerous basement stairs were one of Karin's pet hates. She imagined builders overdue at their next job slapping together scraps of wood and tacking on a thin railing with sparse supports. Never had she seen stairs so cheap, steep and flimsy. And the low basement floor, far from being a plus in her eyes, only increased the odds that someone ascending or descending with less than full concentration would someday come to grief.

Hand on rail down. Knapsack. Hand on rail up. Kettle boiling. Tea bag in mug. Water in mug. Tea bag out. Carry mug of tea and knapsack back to bedroom. Pack. Dress. Slurp down tea. Phone Markus.

He wanted to know where she was calling from and chuckled when he heard.

"Still at home? My goodness, Ted's timetables have slipped for once."

"Ted's conferencing, remember? It'll just be me and you this weekend."

"Maybe I'll ask that movie star on the next lake to come over and keep you company."

Her answer came a beat late. "I'm bringing my cello. There may not be room for him in the bed."

"You sound tired, Karin. Why not drive up tomorrow morning?" No banter now.

She said she was looking forward to a midnight swim and

rang off quickly. She didn't want to be here in the city when Ted got back and have to go through the parting scene again Saturday.

Her father made his living by counselling and could be expected to be sensitive to fine shades in voices, but she was supposed to be a performer, and it irritated her that she hadn't been able to sound more upbeat for the space of a brief phone call. Her tea bag was already in the recycling bin, but not touching anything gross. She wiped it off and popped it into a mug she knew would fit in the holder by the driver's seat of her car. Wine for her dad? She opened the fridge and found a bottle of Sauvignon blanc to stuff into her knapsack between the underwear and her toilet case. As soon as the kettle was back at the boil, she was ready to go, knapsack on her back and tea mug in her hand. She pulled the front door to and tested it. Firmly locked.

Gas? No, she'd filled the tank Tuesday at Meryl's gas bar, and topping it up at one of the highway service centres would give her an excuse to break up the trip. She'd taken less than an hour at home on the turnaround, so she'd be at the cottage by eleven or a little after. The tea was starting to perk her up, and perhaps even more so the feel of the steering wheel in her grip. Karin liked driving. It was absorbing, with life and limb dependent on how you performed, but the demands—unless you were a NASCAR or F1 race driver—were looser than in the world of classical music. Karin believed her driving was "good enough for jazz," and jazz was fun.

When she pulled onto the northbound 400, she called the cottage again and left a report of her progress on Markus's machine.

An hour later, she was yawning her way through a bumper-to-bumper stretch of highway and having much less fun. Impatient drivers were cutting in front of her with millimetres to spare, while the four-by-four behind her was practically climbing her little Honda's sloping hatch. She began to think of car seats, wondering how often they had to be changed as an infant grew into a toddler. There'd be the home to childproof too. Before long, she and Ted would be stuffing protectors in every electrical outlet and fencing off the heads of the stairs. Fine, every danger would be provided against in time—no need to work herself up right now. Except...

Except that the suspicion was also beginning to gnaw at her that she had left something undone at home tonight. Not something inconsequential either. She had locked the door, and every last window as Ted had asked, and turned down the air conditioning, even though the house would be stifling when he got home. She had turned off the water in the shower and hadn't left the toilet running. What else could it be? Her eyes dropped down to her empty tea mug. That was it. She might not have turned off the element on the stove top after the second boiling. She'd lifted off the kettle, poured and placed it to cool on the unused small back element. But she had no memory of reaching over to switch off the heat in the large one. She looked across the median. The southbound traffic was light. If she could get across, she'd be home by ten fifteen. She could call Markus again and take him up on his suggestion that she drive up tomorrow. She could spend one more night with Ted. Was she just looking for an excuse?

It wasn't like her to worry this way. She believed she had a good memory for the things that mattered. Then again, Markus liked to twit her on little duties neglected, and there was always the possibility—when she was tired as she was tonight—that she'd forget something not so little.

If she had left the element on, she wasn't just wasting electricity. There was a kitchen cupboard above that element.

The heat could cause the paint to blister and perhaps fall off onto the red-hot metal. Flames would shoot up. The wood would get dryer and hotter, until their house would be on fire. Maybe she had turned the element off and didn't remember it. Yes, that was more likely. She was ninety-five per cent certain. But no, she couldn't take the chance. Just ahead, a bridge carried a county road across the highway. An exit lane was opening up to Karin's right; she committed to it.

Chapter 2

The conference was being held in the various lecture halls of University College, but the panel discussion was to take place across King's College Circle in the seventeen-hundred-seat Convocation Hall. It was routinely used now for first-year psychology lectures as well as for graduation ceremonies, and the enclosed circular space could be almost as hot and humid at this time of year as the inside of a clothes dryer.

Ted dropped by the athletic centre for a swim and a shower in the late afternoon before heading over to the hall. He'd brought a freshly pressed golf shirt to change into, leisure wear that had become the work uniform of everyone from burger flippers and supermarket checkers to library technicians and massage therapists, and would—he hoped—be accepted as suitable for an unpretentious academic as well. In keeping with the folksy tone, Ted and the panellists sat at their places, chatting pleasantly as members of the public filed in. By 7:05, the hall was a quarter full. As it was little more so by 7:10, Ted tapped his mike and got proceedings underway. After a few standard remarks, he asked the first speaker to introduce herself and her position on the question, "Is Canada soft on crime?"

In appearance, Rose Cesario suggested a beach ball, short and round, with a lack of neck, a surplus of chins and a gleam of sunlight in her brown cap of hair. A well-fitted pale grey summer suit nudged her back in the direction of seriousness. Her eyes were outlined severely in black. And any hint of frivolity was forgotten when she began to speak.

"As councillor for one of Toronto's western wards, I have worked tirelessly to get more police officers on the streets and to cut down on response times to 911 calls. Much as I've been able to accomplish, however, the real power to fight crime is in Ottawa, and that is why I will be running in the next federal election as the Conservative candidate in Etobicoke Southwest."

She proceeded to deliver a harangue stuffed with the sort of statistics that make listeners' eyes cross. The number of felons on day parole that commit fresh acts of violence, the number on full parole, the number on statutory release. Eventually she got on to something a little easier to connect with, the so-called "Truth in Sentencing" issue. Up to a point, Ted sympathized with her: the state was attempting to implement advanced concepts of penology while posing as guardian of the old-time religion of punishment—and the disguise had become transparent. Of course, the populist politician expressed herself somewhat differently.

"The state," proclaimed Rose Cesario, "implements trendy new ways to coddle criminals while pretending to uphold time-tested standards of justice. What a hoax!

"The *Criminal Code* section 235(1) says in black and white: 'Everyone who commits first degree murder or second degree murder is guilty of an indictable offence and shall be sentenced to imprisonment for life.' Imprisonment for life— what could be clearer? But then our Correctional Service tells us that someone that commits first or second degree murder can get out on parole and still be serving a life sentence. That person is serving his or her sentence 'in the community.'" The speaker reinforced her disdain for the phrase by drawing quotation marks in the air. "Well, I don't want Clifford Olson or Paul Bernardo serving his sentence in *my* community, thank you very much. A sentence served in the community is not a sentence of imprisonment. The community is not a prison. It's where we live. So let's stop fooling ourselves. Let Parliament say nothing about life imprisonment unless they mean it. Let judges say when passing sentence for second degree murder, 'You will spend a minimum of ten years behind bars and then be granted parole if you are found deserving of it.'

"One final proof that we are soft on crime in this country is the practice of passing concurrent sentences. Commit one murder or a dozen, the sentence will likely be the same. Multiple killers get a volume discount: only the first victim's pain is given any weight by the justice system. A serial predator can be punished for several rapes simultaneously and be back on the streets in no more time than if he had offended only once. If we don't want to be soft on crime, let the criminals pay for each one of their crimes, and serve consecutive sentences rather than concurrent ones.

"When I look around this room, I see people whose hearts would I'm sure go out to the victims of crime. Let's be soft-hearted to them, the sufferers of wrong, not to the wrongdoers, the people that choose to hurt and kill."

Robust applause for this rather impersonal stump speech. Ted estimated the median age of the audience at thirty-eight—retirees in the front rows, fit twenties with bicycle helmets on their laps in the back, a few curious academics of all ages sprinkled around the edges. Queues were already forming at the audience mikes, but Ted announced that he wanted to get each panellist's position on the record before opening the evening up to questions from the floor.

Rose Cesario's final words about victims of crime were, deliberately or not, an appropriate cue for Martha Kesler. She was a grey-haired woman with dark pouches under her eyes, so physically slight as to look somewhat lost in her shiny wheelchair. The mention of her name, however, elicited a broad smile from her. Two rows of even teeth shone as brightly as her Indian cotton white blouse. Her voice was clear and strong, and she spoke perhaps half as fast as her predecessor, the emphatic deliberation of her delivery sounding every bit as confident as Cesario's rapid fire.

"As you may know, someone's finger on the trigger of an unlicensed firearm put me in this chair. As a crime victim, I'm very grateful for that heartfelt sympathy Rose spoke of. Anyone that expects me to second her call for tougher sentences, however, will be disappointed. I'm much more inclined to the opinion of Oscar Wilde, who wrote, 'A community is infinitely more brutalized by the habitual employment of punishment than it is by the occasional occurrence of crime.'"

Drop the word "infinitely", Ted thought, and the nineteenth century wit could pass for a twenty-first century criminologist.

"Believe me," Martha Kesler went on, "I know where those punitive thoughts come from. Four years ago, I was crossing a mall parking lot when I found myself on the ground with a bullet in my spine and that dumb tunnel of light everyone talks about opening up in front of me. Well, I had an eight-year-old daughter at the time, and I can tell you I wasn't ready to get sucked up any tunnel of light. Coming back, though, was no picnic. Pain wasn't the worst of it. I was prey to flashbacks, and I had what they call a 'hyperactive startle reflex', when what I needed to deal with a preteen daughter was two good legs and nerves of steel. Violent crime leaves you feeling powerless. Would I have changed places with my attacker—who probably never was *my* attacker, just a hit man with a poor aim? Would I have taken from him the use of his legs—even if I couldn't have had back the use of mine? I'm not proud to admit it, but I surely would.

"Before long, however, I knew that my appetite for power was much bigger than that, and wouldn't be satisfied by such a small and pointless result. If I wanted to feel strong, I had to do something beneficial. That's how I came to train as a grief counsellor. And that's how I became involved through my church in the Restorative Justice movement. Tyler, stand up, please."

The young man who had manoeuvred Ms. Kesler's wheelchair onto the dais rose awkwardly from a seat in the front row. He turned slowly to let all audience members get a look at him. A look at everything, Ted noticed, except for his large hands, which were balled into fists and hidden behind his back where they were visible to the panel alone. Ted surmised what was coming next.

"Tyler," said Martha Kesler, "has bravely given me permission to tell you that he is serving a conditional sentence for burglarizing parked cars. For those of you unfamiliar with the term, a conditional sentence is one served 'in the community'— there's that phrase again that Ms. Cesario so dislikes. Really, though, it's not so scary. To be eligible for such a sentence, an offender must satisfy a judge that he will not threaten anyone's safety and that he will comply with rules and conditions imposed by the judge. It has been my pleasure and honour to give Tyler the opportunity to earn the means to compensate the people whose stereos he stole. To get tough on crime by putting him behind bars would do nothing to repair the damage he's caused."

Ted thanked her.

"Just one more thing, Mr. Moderator, if I may," said Martha Kesler. "I need to make it absolutely crystal clear that

Tyler had nothing to do with shooting me. That party has never been found. And this is the point: Canada is not so much soft on crime as clueless. I say find the criminals so we can help them not to be criminals."

The clapping was louder than for the first speaker, accompanied by a few whistles from the younger spectators at the back. The crowd was warming up.

"May I go next?" the man immediately to Ted's left asked him as soon as he was confident of being heard.

Lionel Kerr, a Maritimer if Ted remembered correctly, wore cowboy boots and a blue cowboy shirt with silver buttons, presumably out of loyalty to his present employer, the University of Calgary. He'd been a criminological institution for longer than Ted could remember, and Ted remembered when Lionel's straight, silver hair had been golden yellow to the last strand.

"A propos of what Martha Kesler has been saying, my friends," he began, "let's try an informal survey right here in this hall. How many of you believe that harsher sentences will deter violent criminals from reoffending? Don't be shy. Stick up those hands if you believe more jail time will cut down on recidivism rates."

A minority of hands shot up.

"Come on now," Kerr coaxed. "There must be more of you than that."

Encouraged by his broad and welcoming grin, more of those seated closer to the stage raised their hands hesitantly, and a sprinkling of those behind followed their lead until there was a bare majority indicating they favoured tougher sentences.

"That's more what I'd expect," said Kerr. "Well, you're wrong. Studies in both Canada and the U.S. show time after time that people contemplating violent crime don't think about punishments because they don't expect to be caught. And they're ninety-six per cent right. According to the Canadian Centre for Justice Statistics, in the year 1996, for every one hundred offences reported to police, only four offenders were sentenced. In other words, so few criminals are actually sentenced that from a deterrent point of view it doesn't matter what penalties the law applies. And it's not as if we have to keep convicted murderers locked up to prevent their killing again. Whatever you may think, my friends, that's not something most murderers do. Unlike break and enter artists, for most murderers, once seems to be enough."

Ted heard a heavy exhalation from his right, and out of the corner of his eye saw that Rose Cesario was close to boiling point.

"Now let me ask you another question," Lionel Kerr was saying. "Suppose, what I take to be the case, none of you lives with or knows any murderers. What risk do you think you run in this country of being killed by a stranger as you go about your business? Come on now, let's hear some numbers. One in a hundred? One in a thousand? What happened to Martha here is dreadful. She could have been killed if that bullet had gone through her heart. Thinking about that, will you feel less safe as you cross the mall parking lot? What are the chances of being killed by a stranger in Canada? Yes, sir, top row, what do you say?"

A boy wearing a No Fear T-shirt and sprawling across three seats at the back called out, "One in a hundred thousand."

"Half that," said Kerr. "Since 2000, Canada's murder rate has been hovering below two per hundred thousand, but in nearly half the cases the killer is a member of the victim's family; in nearly a third, it's a friend or acquaintance that'll off you; and less than a quarter of all murder victims are killed by strangers. The plain truth is that people that worry about crime are as irrational as people that buy lottery tickets. Your odds of being a crime victim are as long as your odds of winning the jackpot."

"Dr. Kerr," Rose Cesario erupted, "I have before me a publication of the Correctional Service that claims, and I quote, 'In 2000, only seventeen per cent of solved homicides were committed by strangers.' I underline that word *solved*. When the killer is not known to the victim, that killer is much harder to catch, and so the statistics give a skewed idea of the frequency of stranger killings. We don't have far to look to put a human face on this fact. Martha Kesler has just told us that her assailant has never been apprehended. If his bullet had killed her, her killing wouldn't have been taken account of in the statistics."

"My dear lady," said Kerr with a courtly nod, "do you really think that if you could have your way, if you could lock up a few bad actors and throw away the key, that you or I would be one whit safer walking the streets?"

Ted knew he had to jump in. Silver hairs notwithstanding, Lionel Kerr wasn't old enough to have made an innocent mistake in using the patronizing word *lady*. And it was plain from the daggers flashing from Rose Cesario's dark eyes that she took it in the spirit intended. "I didn't hear Ms. Cesario say anything about throwing away keys. Her position, I understood, was that conditional release from prison should be earned, not automatic, and that we should not miscall release 'imprisonment'."

"Vengefulness," said Lionel Kerr, considerable steel in his voice, "is a primitive, unlovely emotion, however human—"

"Let's save the debate until after we've heard from our last panellist." Ted had actually reached his hand out to cover

Lionel Kerr's mike, but managed to avoid turning the evening into a brawl by changing the action into a gesture towards the man on Kerr's left. "Eliot Szabo has the floor."

"Sorry to be the cause of controversy," said the lawyer. "Although that's not an entirely new experience for me, it usually doesn't happen till after I've opened my mouth."

A gust of laughter rustled through the hall. The tension eased.

Szabo wore a grey, chalk-striped suit and managed to do so without the appearance of perspiration. His tie was loosened and the top button of his white shirt undone. He sat sideways in his chair. An amused expression played over a clever, smile-wrinkled face. He had a mannerism of patting his forehead, which was already high and seemed to be making gradually for the nape of his neck. Tufts of mouse-coloured hair stuck out around large jug-handle ears.

"I feel certain," he said, "that members of the public have been lured here under false pretenses tonight. From the lineup, it looked as if they'd be getting three panellists who'd be tough on crime, and one criminologist. What they got was, first, a populist politician—no swindle there. Second, a crime victim, but not someone to argue that the only justice for victims is stiff penalties for the criminals. Instead of a Hammurabi, you got a return-good-for-evil Christian. Am I right, Martha?"

"Afraid so, Eliot," Martha Kesler replied.

"Third, the criminologist. Well, you know what they're like. Some of us Crown counsel think they're a bit of a soft touch when it comes to crooks. Criminologists are basically sociologists, and that—like any science—is a pretty deterministic business. Science is big on cause and effect, and not much into blame. Lionel will fill in the finer points for us in a minute, but what he's already said tells you which side of the question he takes.

"The kicker, fourth and last, is that even your prosecutor isn't quite the crusader against evildoers you may have been hoping for. I've spent most of my working life in the defence bar. Those scumbags the public would like to see locked up? I worked my butt off for twenty years trying to keep them *out* of jail. Last year, I crossed over to the other side—for the money as much as anything. The state may lock too many people up or lock the wrong people up, but at least it pays its legal bills. When I saw that last salary settlement negotiated by the Ontario Crown Attorneys' Association, I knew which side of the courtroom I belonged on.

"So, Martha is soft on criminals because she's a Christian and wants to forgive them, Lionel because he's a determinist and thinks they can't help it, and me—well, I sympathize with criminals because they're the people I know and work with. I don't know many victims. Call it the Stockholm Syndrome if you like. Or think of it as something like a zoologist put on the bat project who ends up sympathizing with bats. Call me a bat-lover or call me just plain bats, but I can't see that punishment does anyone any good. The public loves it, but it looks like an unhealthy addiction to me.

"I'll tell you one thing, though. If you want to see crooks punished, mandatory minimum sentences may not be the way to go. Why? Because the Crown gets to decide who will be prosecuted. If we think the mandatory minimum is more than is warranted, we will simply prosecute a lesser included charge. Or not proceed at all and let the accused walk. That may sound high-handed, but it's based on our knowing that if the penalty seems excessive, judges and juries won't convict. If we take those cases to trial, we're just wasting the time we could have spent getting a conviction against some other chump on some other charge."

Again Ted was quick off the mark. Before the audience could get their hands together, he pointedly thanked Lionel Kerr as well as Eliot Szabo so that the former would not feel he was the only one to get no chance at being applauded. Before the clapping had quite subsided, a new voice came softly and insistently over the sound system.

"Now that the panellists have all had a chance to state where they're coming from, I'd like to ask a question."

There were long queues at each of the two audience microphones now. The speaker was an underfed young man with large glasses and short hair.

"Which panellist is this question for?" To Ted's right, his peripheral vision picked up an extra attentiveness in the posture of Rose Cesario.

"For the three 'enlightened' panellists. That is, every one but the first."

"Fire away."

The boy shuffled his feet and read his question from a small blue notebook. Wooden seats creaked as audience members turned to look at him.

"Ms. Kesler, Dr. Kerr, Mr. Szabo, I'd like you to think of the person now alive that means the most to you. Please think of the person whose injuries would cause you the most pain. Would the murder of that person change your view of how a murderer should be treated?"

"I just don't know," Martha Kesler replied promptly. "To forgive those that've trespassed against our loved ones is without doubt harder than to forgive those that've trespassed against us. My daughter, for example, is much more bitter about my injuries than I am. Now if she—if Cara—were murdered... That's no small thing you're asking. I scarcely have the courage to say the words. I just pray that I would be up to the challenge."

"I put it to you," said the questioner, "that if your views did change, we're wasting our time this evening listening to people that don't know what they're talking about. And if your views were not changed by such an event, you would not be human."

Eliot Szabo pulled his microphone towards him.

"It's better to be human than inhuman. But when we're at our most human, we're not always at our most lucid. You pose an interesting dilemma—what's your name?"

"My name is Tom. What's your answer?"

"My answer is that if someone I loved was murdered, my views likely would change, but that the vengeful way I'd think then would be wrong and that the way I think now is right."

"You attach no importance," the questioner insisted, "to people having the courage of their convictions?"

"Sure I do, Tom. But you can't judge the truth of an argument by the moral strength or weakness of the arguer."

This was the point at which Ted had to bite his tongue to keep from jumping in. He understood what Szabo was saying about the fallacy of ad hominem attacks—and yet wondered whether, if a philosophy consistently failed to stand up in the crunch, it was indeed a philosophy for human beings. Recollecting his responsibilities, he asked if Lionel Kerr would like to respond.

"If Tom has been listening," said Kerr, "he'll realize that the likelihood that anyone in this room, let alone anyone on this panel, would lose a loved one to murder is negligible."

Ted wanted to ask if Tom himself had lost someone he loved to murder, but the boy had moved away from the mike and was nowhere to be seen.

The panel discussion wrapped up shortly after eight to leave time for the professionals to get over to University College for the conference keynote address. The evening ended with a reception at the Faculty Club, where Ted reconnected with Lionel Kerr. Years ago, they had done a paper together on victim precipitation of assault and how within certain subcultures a disdainful look, let alone a disrespectful word, had to be considered an act of violence and a mitigation of any aggressive response. Since then Ted had done work on the ethos of criminal organizations, and he had some questions for Lionel about Daniel Wolf's seminal study of bikers in Alberta.

"All Niagara labels, I see." Lionel ran his eyes over the bottles on the bar. "Which would you recommend, Ted?"

"Karin's the wine expert in our house. She'd steer you towards the Riesling, which seems to be dryer than the average in Europe. I find it refreshing—which is as technical as my wine vocabulary gets."

"That Rosie the Riveter on your panel was some hothead. You did well to keep her from running away with the show." Lionel put the glass of straw-coloured wine to his lips. "Yes, very pleasant."

"She can run, but she can't win," said Ted. "Not in Etobicoke Southwest. The Liberals had a margin of victory of over twenty thousand votes there last time. And it would take a major cataclysm to make law and order the ballot question. The riding is divided between young families interested in affordable day care and aging baby boomers worried about the future of medicare."

"You're thoroughly informed," Lionel chuckled. "Live there?"

"My father-in-law."

Kerr wore a large wristwatch, on which Ted couldn't help reading that it was five to ten. He ought to head for the subway soon if he wanted to catch the 22:43 commuter train westbound from Union Station. Departures were only once an hour at this time of night, and he'd have to be back on campus early tomorrow morning. Before excusing himself, Ted diplomatically—though not without genuine interest—gave Lionel an opportunity to report on the progress of the investigations he was conducting in partnership with a microbiologist. Looking not for a crime gene exactly, but possibly a virus, something treatable ultimately with pharmaceuticals. Kerr's enthusiasm, once whipped up, was hard to rein in. In the end, Ted made his train only by hailing a taxi on Spadina Avenue.

Chapter 3

He was one of the last to board the westbound Lakeshore GO Train during its six-minute stop at Toronto's Union Station. Fortunately, there were no crowds to fight. The Blue Jays baseball team were looking for some payback against the Red Sox in Boston that evening, while the Canadian National Exhibition had a station of its own.

On his way upstairs to the top level of the railcar, Ted took in the back of a lone woman in one of the aisle seats on the mezzanine or landing. These seating areas, one at either end of a car, could accommodate fifteen or seventeen passengers each. In a sparsely populated train, they could be a good place to be alone. Ted paused at first because there was something familiar about the woman's pale grey suit jacket and blond-streaked brown hair. He stepped towards her when he saw her shoulders shake and heard from her a pair of gasping sobs.

"It's Ted Boudreau, Ms. Cesario. Is there anything I can do?"

She looked up at the feel of his hand on her shoulder. Her dark eyes were brimming over, without making her eyeliner run. Ted later thought it must have been tattooed on. Her mouth was open and remarkably square, like a tragedy theatre mask. She nodded slightly and gestured to the seat beside her. Before he sat, Ted cleared from it the City Hall papers she had spread there. Meanwhile, Rose Cesario closed up the laptop she had been working on and drew an old-fashioned, lacy cloth handkerchief from her sleeve. A whiff of violet toilet water was released. Exposure of a side of her so at odds with her battleaxe image left Ted wanting to offer sympathy and not knowing what to say.

"Look, Professor Boudreau," she said, hoarse, but recovering her poise. "I wouldn't want you to think it was the panel discussion that upset me." She paused to clear her throat. "I mean, it was, but only indirectly. I've had plenty of experience with the rough and tumble of debate—at the municipal level—and, believe me, I'm looking forward to plenty more in Ottawa if I'm elected to the House of Commons."

"I understand."

"It was that boy, Tom."

"Yes?" Ted too had found the boy unsettling, though not to this degree.

"I know him," Rose went on. "I used to be an emergency room nurse. His mother brought him in twice with a broken arm. Said he got them playing football. Did he look like a football player to you?"

"Not really," said Ted, reflecting that boys often try sports they are physically unsuited for.

"No one investigated. Then one day, it was Tom's younger sister who was brought in—by the father this time. And believe me, he is a bruiser. That child had multiple traumas, including a severe skull fracture. All supposedly caused by a bicycle accident. She just wouldn't wear her helmet, dad said. We couldn't save her."

Neither passenger spoke. The only sound was the metal wheels clicking over the track. Black windows reflected the railcar's relentlessly cheery fluorescent lights back inside.

"Were police notified?" Ted asked at last.

"The father served four years for manslaughter. Tom testified about the beatings both kids had received, but the assault charges added nothing to the sentence. The mother,

Tom, and there was an even younger child—they all had to go into hiding when the father came out."

"That's rough," said Ted. Now wasn't the time to ask what counselling the father had received as part of his sentence and what assessments had been done of his likelihood to reoffend, even though these were precisely the questions Ted's training had ensured would be top of his mind.

"Very rough," Rose Cesario agreed. "Seeing Tom tonight in a public gathering made me wonder if he was safe even now. His father promised to get even with him for testifying. Also…"

"Yes?"

"Well, seeing Tom awakened my feelings of guilt and regret that I didn't blow the whistle before a young life was lost."

Ted nodded. He realized he'd been wrong to think of Rose as seizing on the crime issue purely for political gain. But then she rather spoiled the effect by climbing back on her soapbox.

"And then what Tom said… It's so true! You have no right to decide how much punishment is enough until you can really put yourself in the victim's place. Who has the right to indulge their Christian feelings of forgiveness by going easy on the killer of nine-year-old Eva? Who should be allowed to put absolving words in the mouth of the dead?"

The train came to a stop now at Exhibition Station, and the car filled up with families and their stuffed-animal trophies from the Midway. On this last weekend of the fair, nearly everyone seemed to be a winner. The interruption gave needed time for the rhetorical temperature to drop. When the journey resumed, Ted made this remark:

"I wonder, Ms. Cesario, whether the living have any more right to punish in the name of the dead than to forgive."

"Thank you for listening," Rose Cesario said in a businesslike voice, taking her papers from Ted and stowing them in a pocket of her computer case. "I know my way is not the current academic way of thinking about crime. I don't despair of bringing you around, but it will take something more than words. In panel discussions or in railcars."

At Long Branch, the politician got out, and Ted was left to glance over his own papers. He didn't take the time to reflect on what she meant by "something more".

*   *   *

His Toyota was one of the last dozen cars in the south lot. He drove straight for the exit, diagonally over all the solid white lines. Five minutes more brought him home. He wasn't exactly bursting with energy, but not tired either. A little lazy. The work of the evening was over, and it had gone well enough.

He left his car in the driveway rather than taking time to open the garage. A freshening wind was tossing Karin's rose bushes around, but there was no rain in the forecast. He further rationalized that the beat-up Corolla out front made the house look occupied. The triangular Alarm Protection Service decal in the sidelight window struck him just as forcefully as it always did when he came in by the front door after dark. The porch light, which turned on automatically at dusk, fell directly on the sign and reminded Ted that he had yet to have the alarm system reactivated and an account set up in his name. Each time, he made a resolution to rectify the situation: it had been more than two years now since the previous owners' subscription had lapsed with the sale of the house. Karin's cello alone was worth sixteen thousand dollars. But in the light of day, he never seemed to remember. When asked by outsiders about APS, he always pretended to be a satisfied customer, and wondered if the pretense plus the spotlit sign might not offer as much protection at no cost.

Tonight, though, he actually scribbled a memo to himself on the palm of his left hand. A baby was coming. There was even more to protect.

He unlocked the front door and entered briskly, as if he had a system to disarm by punching in a number code within the time permitted. The house was warmer than the night outside, though not quite as stuffy as Ted had expected. Perhaps Karin had left the central air on low. The first summer after moving in, they'd conserved energy by turning up the thermostat and just opening upstairs windows in summer. As their store of treasure grew, however, they had started closing and locking everything whenever they left the house.

His mouth still dry from the Riesling, Ted went to the kitchen for a club soda. The light on the answering machine was flashing. Three messages. The first was from a carpet cleaning company, the second a resort on Georgian Bay. The third was puzzling.

"Hi, Karin. It's Daddy-o. Got your message from 400 and Finch and reckon you should be here pretty soon. If not, you're going to miss that midnight swim. I've called your cell and there's no answer, so I'm thinking you and it aren't in the same place. Like maybe it's in the car and you're back in the house. Ted's phone is turned off, so he's no help. Clue me in if you're staying down overnight, and I'll stop listening to the radio station with that jolly joe that reports the traffic pileups." The time stamp was 11:15 p.m., just before Ted had got in.

He put down his drink and listened to the empty house. The reference to a midnight swim suggested Quirk had told her father she'd be arriving late. She usually answered her phone, even when driving, but she could have left it in the car while she stopped to grab a tea. Markus's voice contained the hint of a smile that seemed inseparable from his soft Scandinavian accent. He wasn't overly anxious yet. Still, the combination of circumstances was unusual enough that Ted couldn't blame him for wondering.

Ted crossed a vestibule cum basement stair landing between the kitchen and the garage. When he opened the door to the garage, there was Karin's blue Honda Insight. So, after starting for the cottage, she had indeed come back. On the floor, in front of the passenger seat, lay her knapsack and in the back of the car her cello, ready to go. Ted thought first of illness. He raced back through the kitchen into the front hall and took the stairs two at a time up to their bedroom. Empty. Bed apparently unused since he had made it this morning. When Karin made the bed, she spread the duvet over the bottom sheet, while Ted left it folded at the foot, as it was now. The door to the ensuite bathroom stood open.

"Karin? Karin!"

He looked inside and saw nothing but an expanse of tiles, with a few water drops on the floor of the shower stall. No longer afraid of waking her, he blundered about the second floor, his senses barely registering, seeing nothing but Karin's absence, hearing nothing but his own voice calling her name.

Ted stopped to think in the upper hall, hands on the rail as he stared down the curving stairs to the front hall. How to explain this? Karin had for some reason aborted her trip without telling Markus. Maybe the battery in her cell had run down and, rather than get off the highway and find a public phone, she'd come straight home. When she'd pulled into the driveway, she'd happened to see one of the neighbours. And, after an exchanged word or two, accepted an invitation to go over there for a drink. "I'll just pop the car in the garage first," she would have said. Which neighbour? Ted knew a name or two. Karin would know more; she always did. He'd look for her address book. But wait. She would have called Markus first, wouldn't she, if it were just a matter of a friendly nightcap? She'd have unloaded her cello. Maybe the neighbour had noticed she was unwell, rushed her to the emerg. This would be bad, but not as bad as if Quirk were still lying untended somewhere in the house.

That's as far as Ted got when he noticed the fresh wad of chewing gum on the dark blue stair runner. He knew immediately what this was from his research. It was a tag, a territorial marker that said, "This is no longer your space; it's mine."

Ted charged down the stairs and from room to room, flicking on lights as he ran. Living room, nothing. Dining room, nothing. Family room, the same. In his study, there was a hole where his new computer had been and his disk library had been ransacked. Instantly he feared that the disk the intruder had wanted was the one in his briefcase labelled Family Photos, the one that contained the dirt on the Dark Arrows. No Karin here, though, so he didn't stop. He was hoping now that, when she came in from the garage, she had heard that there was someone in the house and had got out again before being found. She could have run next door or to Meryl's twenty-four hour gas bar and convenience store two streets over from the end of the crescent. Ted just had to check the basement first.

He returned to the landing from which another door led into the garage, and a third to outside. The fourth side of this cubicle had no door but opened directly to the head of the steep, gerry-built basement stairs Karin hated. When Ted flicked on the basement light, it showed her lying at the foot of them.

On her back on the cement basement floor, feet towards the bottom step, dressed for the cottage, eyes open, and deathly still.

He picked up a splinter from the railing in his haste to get down to her. Her skin was cool rather than cold, but he couldn't find a pulse. He ripped his cellphone from its pouch on his waist. Never had it taken longer to boot up.

When the young male 911 operator asked what service Ted wanted, he said ambulance and police. His voice rasped. His throat felt tight and dry.

"Is there a medical emergency?"

"Uh-huh," Ted croaked. "Yes." He started to give his address.

"One moment, sir. I'm going to start you off with the ambulance."

Ambulance. The word carried hope. Ted tried to be patient, take things in order. It was going to be all right. It had to be. He bent closer to Karin.

"Quirk, you're going to be all right," he stammered.

While the 911 call was being directed, his gaze fixed on her hair. The red strands on the top of her head were pulled up, straight out from the scalp. He reached out to smooth them, but pulled his hand back. Crime scene, he thought. Don't touch.

He swallowed hard, managed to moisten his tongue enough to speak.

"I have a woman here on the floor with no pulse," he blurted out as soon as he sensed someone on the other end of the line.

"Is she breathing?" The call taker's voice was female. It sounded as if she'd asked this question a thousand times before.

"I don't think so."

"Do you see her chest rising?"

"No. Absolutely not."

"Can you put your face down by her mouth and feel if there's any breath coming out?"

Ted put his left ear to Quirk's dear lips. Nothing. Was he just too numbed by shock to feel the puffs of air? Yes. No. He believed both at once.

"Sir? Sir? Are you there? Do you feel any breath?"

"None. Can you please send an ambulance? 19 Robin Hood Crescent."

"Is there anyone there with you?"

"You mean—"

"Besides the woman on the floor."

"No, no one else."

The words echoed in the still house. Ted had too much voice now. He was a hair's breadth from saying one or more things he'd be sorry for.

He stared at the freckles on Karin's thin, straight nose. He couldn't admit the possibility that it was already too late. He had to look away—anywhere—at the studs of the unfinished basement wall opposite. He noted distractedly that the window in the upper part of that wall was broken. It sounded as if the operator was following a script, not trying to be an insensitive jerk. It was hard, though, and slow. Every second felt like five.

"What happened to her?"

"I think she's been assaulted," said Ted. "There's been a break-in."

"Assaulted with a weapon?"

"I don't know."

"Did you see a weapon?"

"No. Send the paramedics, please."

"How many assailants were there?"

"I don't know."

"Are any of them still in the house?"

"No." Ted didn't know this for sure, but was afraid no paramedics would come into a house where they ran a risk of attack. The word assaulted—which Ted had believed potent to speed help to Karin—was instead inducing caution.

"How many assailants did you see?"

"I didn't see anyone."

"What makes you think she was attacked?"

"Stuff has been stolen. She—I think she may have interrupted a burglary in progress."

"Does she have any injuries?"

"I can't see, but I've already told you I don't think she's breathing."

"So you can't—"

"Look, I need an ambulance here for my wife. And she's carrying a child."

Until this instant, Ted would never have called an embryo a child. And if Karin hadn't been pregnant? He'd have been no less desperate to save her. At the same time, he felt he had to throw anything he could at this disembodied functionary, anything to raise the stakes enough above the routine to engage her energies.

The operator said the ambulance was on its way. Ted dashed upstairs to unlock the front door as she requested, then returned to Karin.

"Stay on the line now while I transfer you to the police."

He had to answer all the same questions again. Mercifully, a kind of automatic pilot kicked in. Worse by far was seeing Karin lying there on the floor and believing that, if he took her in his arms as nature prompted, he might be injuring her spinal cord. A cocoon—so it seemed to him—protected him from thoughts that it might no longer matter. He touched the back of his fingers to Karin's cheek as gently as he could. He could do so little. The paramedics would between them be able to lift her without twisting her neck, to immobilize her on a stretcher, and to get her safely to hospital.

And then—but then what would become of the evidence? Maybe there was something he could do for her after all. He used his cellphone to take pictures of the way she was lying in case the police photographers didn't show up in time. He zeroed in particularly on the way her hair stood straight out, not tousled as it would have been if she had fallen. It was as if someone had grabbed her by the hair.

*   *   *

Uniformed officers of the Peel Regional Police arrived at the same time as the ambulance. Or, though Ted didn't like to think so, perhaps the ambulance had been parked and waiting for the police cruisers. The ambulance service would have a duty to protect their personnel, the personnel a right to safe working conditions.

The paramedics found that Karin had sustained blunt trauma to the back of her head. They pronounced her vital signs absent. Ted told them Karin was two weeks pregnant. They said they'd pass that information on to the doctors at Credit Valley Hospital, which was where they now had to take her. Ted wanted to go with her. The paramedics discouraged this impulse and so, more emphatically, did the police. Someone from the hospital would be in touch later. Ted made sure the paramedics had his cellphone number.

"Her name is Karin Gustafson," he said. He had to keep spelling it out. "No, mine is Boudreau."

Karin's sassy little summer purse lay on the basement floor a metre or so from where he'd found her. He handed her health insurance card to the paramedics and her driver's licence to the police to copy from.

Meanwhile, police constables called in police sergeants, who gave orders to establish a perimeter with yellow tape and to secure the crime scene. The entire house and yard, in effect. Was there a neighbour's house Ted could go to? The only neighbours Ted knew weren't answering their phones, so he was asked to wait in the back of one of the cruisers.

He hunched forward on the bench seat, hugging himself for warmth. Alone with his sensations for the first time since placing the 911 call, he found he was cold in his short-sleeved shirt, actually shivering—although nothing he could see, nothing in the way officers and onlookers were standing around on either side of the yellow tape, suggested that the temperature had dropped. Ted's slacks beneath his thighs felt clammy with sweat, none of it absorbed by the synthetic leather upholstery. The back seats of police cruisers, he reflected, had to be moisture-proof, easy to wipe clean.

He wished he had not asked for the police. They were only doing their job, but they were keeping him from Karin, separating what ought to be together. Ought to be, even if in fact Karin were dead.

There, he'd admitted it. That proved he wasn't in denial, didn't it? And yet he couldn't imagine that tonight's facts would still be true tomorrow and all the tomorrows for the rest of his life. He didn't picture the two of them back at the Bouquet Bistro next Thursday or Friday evening, preparing for a night of love. But he wasn't yet able to picture a future weekend when that wasn't going to happen.

While waiting in the back of the police car, Ted listened to

48

Markus's message on his cellphone: "My little girl hasn't shown up. Do you know what's going on? It's after eleven, by the way." Markus had to be called. Ted watched his fingers select COTTAGE on his phone's speed-dial menu. He didn't know what he was going to say. He didn't plan how to say it. *My little girl.* The news would hit Karin's father hard, but he'd have to take it the way it came out.

Markus picked up on the first ring. "Yes, Ted."

Ted summarized flatly how he'd found Karin and what the paramedics had said before taking her away.

"Is she going to pull through?"

"It doesn't look good."

Markus cursed, at length. He used the pronoun *it,* not *you.* Still... Ted picked up the implication that he himself was in some way at fault, as he believed he was, although Markus didn't know the real reason, was just expressing a father's distress.

Ted let him finish.

"Which hospital?" said Markus, regaining control. His breathing, deep and measured, could be heard now over the phone. He wasn't going to let himself fall apart while he was alone in Muskoka and his only child was in lying in an ER two hundred klicks away.

Ted felt neither in control nor falling apart—more like an automaton.

"Credit Valley," he said.

Markus got Ted to give him the nearest intersection and told Ted to call his cell if he heard anything in the next couple of hours.

"I suggest you wait till morning to drive down," said Ted.

"I'll come now," said Markus and hung up.

Plainclothes investigators were called in from the local police division. Thinking he was at last in the presence of someone with real authority, Ted made the mistake of calling them detectives. The investigators set him straight. Their inferior rank didn't prevent their asking questions. He tried to show them the photos he'd taken with his cellphone, but rather than look at these amateur offerings, they grilled Ted on how with his wife grievously injured, he could have been cool enough to take pictures more properly left to Forensic Identification Services. He pointed out that Karin had been taken to hospital before any FIS personnel arrived. He still could see no one with a camera. The investigators showed surprise at his use of a short form like FIS. He told them he was a criminologist. They received the news warily, as if they thought it much more likely he was a ghoul.

These non-detectives proceeded to ask Ted a lot of questions about his and Karin's movements and about what signs he had found that the house had been broken into and burglarized, questions that had already been asked by the uniformed officers and were to be repeated by the detectives when they arrived.

By this time, someone had brought Ted a cup of hot coffee, and he was feeling less chilled. He didn't want to meet more functionaries. He just wanted to be left alone. It seemed the best way to be with Karin if he couldn't be at her bedside. Dearest Quirk...

The detectives introduced themselves as James Nelson and Tracy Rodriguez from the Major Crime Unit. They wore dress slacks, golf shirts and fanny packs. The man was tall and black, the woman well-muscled with dark, rippling hair. Both sporty—basketball and track respectively would be good fits— but not jockish. They'd got Karin's and Ted's names from the patrol officers, so Ted didn't have to spell them out again.

Ted changed his mind about being alone. These were the people, he thought, to ask if he could go to the hospital now.

"We just need to ask you some questions first," said Nelson, busy at the computer terminal in the front seat.

"It shouldn't take all that long," said Rodriguez.

After an initial interrogation in the close confines of the police cruiser, Nelson suggested they adjourn to an interview room at the divisional station.

Ted refused. He was going to Karin. While the detectives were bargaining with him for more time, his cellphone rang. A Dr. Hassan at the Credit Valley Hospital already had doom in his voice while identifying himself and confirming that he had Mr. Boudreau. Still, Ted waited until the words had actually been spoken. Karin was dead.

"I'll be right over," Ted blurted out, as if his prompt arrival would make possible some transplant of vitality from his body to Karin's.

The detectives exchanged glances. Ted was certain they had already heard, but not told him.

"I'll have your wife laid out in a room then," said the doctor, "instead of being taken to the morgue right away."

"Which—?" The simple decency of this provision undid Ted. No more words would come.

"Just ask at the information desk, Mr. Boudreau. Have me paged if I can be of any further help." Dr. Hassan now plainly wanted to get on to his next patient, with luck a live one.

Ted stammered a thank you and ended the call. The cruiser's back seat had no inside door handle.

"Let me out of here," he said. "I have to call my father-in-law. I'm meeting him at the hospital."

"I got it." Nelson sprang out of the front seat and opened the door.

"We'll have someone drive you over," said Rodriguez, on her feet now too and beckoning the nearest uniformed officer.

"No, thanks. I'm good to drive."

"We really don't think that's a good idea, sir. We're sending a constable anyway. It's no trouble."

"Am I under arrest?" Ted asked.

Nelson raised his open hands. "No, sir! Which car were you planning to take?"

Ted glanced at the Corolla in his driveway, inside the perimeter of yellow tape.

"That vehicle is part of the scene. It can't be driven anywhere until it's been processed."

Before Nelson finished speaking, Ted had spotted an empty taxi among the onlookers' cars and was making for it. The driver, wearing a white beard and purple turban, caught his eye and nodded.

The two detectives kept pace at Ted's side.

"We understand Ms. Gustafson's father has a local residence," said Rodriguez. "Would you be able to spend a few days with him?"

"I don't know. We haven't discussed it." Ted gave the hospital name to the driver, who slid behind his wheel.

Nelson leaned casually against the middle of the passenger side of the cab. With him there, neither front nor rear door would open.

"Could we have your father-in-law's name and city phone number?" Rodriguez asked.

"Markus—with a K—"

Ted got no further before Nelson interrupted.

"Not Markus Gustafson, the anger manager?"

"You know him?"

"I was at a workshop he did last spring." Nelson was smiling at the memory, but quickly recovered his sense of decorum. Moving away from the taxi, he took down Markus's contact information in his notebook as well as Ted's cell number. "We'll get your witness statement on tape tomorrow. We'd just ask you not to say anything to the media before that. Sorry for your loss, Mr. Boudreau. We'll be in touch."

∗   ∗   ∗

Slumped against the back seat, cellphone in his hand, Ted barely heard the cabbie's questions as to what had happened that night at his house, questions to which he did not respond. He was trying to feel Karin's arms wrap around him the way they had this morning, yesterday morning. She: *No need to tell you not to wait up.* He: *Wake me.* He begged Karin to deliver him from the nightmare of her death—but woke instead to the need to share the nightmare with Markus.

When Markus answered his cell, Ted asked where he was.

"The 400, south of Barrie. What is it?"

"Pull off and call me back."

Ted's ringtone sounded the instant he ended the call. Markus wasn't pulling off.

"Talk to me," he said.

"A doctor phoned to say Karin's dead."

"I don't believe it."

Ted didn't argue. Lucky Markus if what he said were true. Ted's own beliefs were cloudier, vacillating and inconsistent, painfully confused, yet profoundly despairing.

"What kind of doctor is that?" Markus barked.

No answer was going to help him. Still, Ted felt that sooner or later he had to say something. "An ER doctor. He sounded kind."

"Kind? Christ, Ted!"

"My taxi's just pulling into the hospital. I'll see you when you get here."

53

*　　*　　*

At the hospital, Ted was directed to a private room, where Karin was laid out on a bed. A uniformed policeman, who had been sitting by the window, rose when Ted came in. The constable asked that Ted not touch the white bandage encircling Karin's head, then went out to wait in the corridor.

Alone with Karin's body in that clinical room, Ted seemed to forget for a moment how to breathe. He put a hand out to the door frame to steady himself, then let himself slide to a sitting position on the floor. What were you supposed to do to keep from fainting? Sit with your knees up, your head down between them, he distantly recalled. He did that and didn't faint.

There was an armchair by the head of the bed. Ted climbed into it. After the chair got feeling safe, he tried looking again at Karin. His darling. He leaned over and kissed her cold lips. He sat by her side holding her hand in his until he had warmed it with his own. He was just starting to think he was going to keep himself together when sorrow hit him like a wave, and he bent double under its weight. A sense of loss and waste overwhelmed him. This wasn't how it was supposed to be. Ted had imagined his final parting with Karin when they were both in their nineties. Whichever one of them wasted away first, it would have been too soon.

But this—death untimely and unnatural. The killing of a woman of thirty-two, still at the height of her loveliness. Karin had so much promise unfulfilled—as artist, mother, lover. Now she lay cold with a cold embryo inside her. Because of a crime committed in her own house, where she had most right to expect shelter.

Ted let go Karin's hand and staggered blindly towards the

door. Somewhere down the night-lit halls he found a washroom where he splashed handful after handful of cold water on his face. What was he to do? Ted had generally thought of himself as navigating life's waters on an even keel, cool and contained. Others spoke of him this way. He simply didn't recognize the foundering, leaky barque he'd become. Coping mechanisms would have to be invented from scratch. Short hours ago, he'd have considered his present condition shameful. Now, though, he was too panicked to feel shame. He didn't dare look in the mirror.

At length, he took himself out into the summer night to find a patch of grass where he could sit and let his eyes dry under the stars. He tried to focus on what had to be done. Discouragingly, however, all he could think was that he had to break the news to his own father and mother, who had four children and no grandchildren. Tomorrow would be soon enough.

*   *   *

Ted was back in the room on a stool by the window when his father-in-law arrived. It was going on two thirty a.m. A nurse had looked in at some point and turned the lights down. Ted let his eyes close. He opened them to see Markus in the doorway, his beard standing out in blond spikes while his eyes remained in the shadow of his jutting forehead. He wore blue jeans and a denim vest over an olive T. He'd once earned his bread as a performing musician and taking command of a stage still seemed second nature to him. He walked straight to the bed without acknowledging Ted.

"What the hell!" Markus clapped a hand over the lower half of his face. Presently Ted heard him draw air in loudly through his nose.

"Shall I leave you alone with her, Markus?"

"How did it happen?"

"Have a seat." Ted indicated the armchair.

Markus said he'd stand, and the two men stood, on opposite sides of Karin.

"The message you got tells us she started for the cottage," said Ted. "But she must have come back for something. I don't know what. When she entered the house from the garage, a burglary was in progress. It looks as if, instead of running away, the intruder went to confront her. Some kind of struggle must have occurred in the back vestibule, the upshot being that she either fell down or was pushed down the cellar stairs." Ted didn't show Markus his photos or share his thoughts about Karin's hair.

"They catch the guy?"

"Not yet."

"Shit." Markus sniffed again loudly and wiped his nose. "Did you ever hear of my girl hurting anyone? Because I didn't, not ever—not once. Did you?"

"Markus—she was just in the wrong place at the wrong time."

The older man scowled. He plainly wanted the universe to make more sense than that.

"Yeah," he said eventually. "You'd better give me a few minutes with her, Ted. Thanks."

Chapter 4

Ted had first become aware of the Dark Arrows by accident. An accident with deep roots.

He'd grown up on the west island of Montreal. As a suburban kid, he'd depended on his bicycle both for transportation and for a sense of freedom. Independent and small for his age, he was the kid that didn't play hockey. He lived for the summer riding season and dreamed of engines more powerful than his short legs to let him bike faster and farther. He liked to listen to his Uncle Luc, who owned a country store in the Laurentians, talk about the Triumphs and Indians, the Hondas and Harleys he'd gassed up at his pumps. Then—as the years went by—more and more Harleys, and fewer of anything else.

Ted had been young during Canada's first experience of biker gangs. He'd been ten when the Hells Angels had patched over the Popeyes to establish in Montreal the first HA chapter in the country. He'd been seventeen when the Sorel Hells had purged the leadership of the Laval Hells, zipping their brothers' bodies into weighted sleeping bags and dumping them in the St. Lawrence River. He'd been eighteen when the first round of biker trials started. Biker gangs were the new face of organized crime, more murderous and reportedly more powerful than the Mafia. Far from being hedonistic users and losers, the Sorel crew were disciplined dealers—dependent not on substances they ingested but on pagers and spreadsheets. Here, for a keen and impressionable young

McGill University freshman, was a subject worth studying. Socially important, and spiced with a paradox: how had the motorized two-wheeler, so suggestive of the open road under an open sky, become the symbol of a paramilitary troop of conformist bullies?

It didn't escape Ted's notice that biker gangs were not the safest subject to research. So when he'd come to the University of Toronto in 1989 to do graduate work in criminology, he chose a thesis topic that would not necessitate contact with criminals. Instead, he surveyed and analyzed the public's attitude to sentences handed down by criminal courts. Much of his subsequent work had been on the youth criminal justice system, but organized crime remained a strong interest, and a subject on which he taught courses. And he never quite lost sight of the biker gangs. In 1995, during the war between the Hells Angels and the Rock Machine, a bomb in Montreal accidentally killed an uninvolved child only three years younger than Ted's younger brother Patrick. Again, in 2000, Ted's thoughts were drawn back to his hometown, when Dany Kane, a police informant against the Hells, was found dead in his garage and when—not long after—*Journal de Montréal* writer Michel Auger was shot six times in the back for writing about the gang.

Meanwhile, Ted had started riding motorcycles of his own, including the modest Yamaha that had carried him to the 1998 recital where he'd met Karin. He'd owned other bikes since, his most recent—bought in April of last year—a gently used Kawasaki Ninja.

That June, 2005, Karin had been on a western tour with her chamber orchestra, which left Ted many days for putting kilometres on his almost-new machine. On weekends, he would ride down back roads, practically at random. One spring Friday evening, he stopped at a bar between Wildfield and Snelgrove. His clutch cable was coming loose, and he found to his chagrin that he wasn't carrying the very basic tool that would tighten it. So when he noticed a row of polished bikes outside the Grey Mare Tavern, he pulled into the parking area. Near the front door, two large men in black leather were smoking weed and keeping an eye on the machines.

When Ted asked to borrow an adjustable wrench, the beefier of the two sentries retorted, "For that Jap crap? Let it die."

Ted ran his eye down the row of gleaming bikes, every one a Harley-Davidson. He concluded he was up against the vicarious U.S. chauvinism of a biker gang.

"I can't do that," he said pleasantly. "How'd I get home?"

The second biker walked to his machine and, taking a wrench from his tool kit, handed it wordlessly to Ted. The repairs made, Ted returned it.

"Much obliged," he said. "Can I buy you gentlemen a beer?"

"No thanks," said the second biker, speaking for the first time from under a heavy moustache.

"We don't drink with ricers," said his companion.

"Easy, Chuckles. The nice man is going to get on his little riceburner and take it where it won't offend your eyes."

Ted, who had been heading for the bar, took the hint and changed course. With one touch of the electric starter, his 250 c.c. engine came to life. Over its growl, a whisper to what would be the thunder of the big Harleys, he heard Chuckles retort—

"You're out of line, Scar. I don't go easy or uneasy on your say-so."

Ted sped away but was back the next day to make some enquiries at the bar. He was told a dozen men in black leather came to drink every Friday night, and a selection of them might turn up any other night of the week as well. They wore no club insignia on their vests or jackets, and they caused little trouble. In fact, their presence rather discouraged than encouraged drunken insults or brawls. End of story.

He wanted to know more. Nothing in what the bartender had told him made him think it would be hazardous to return, and if the Harley riders saw his Japanese bike as a provocation, so be it; he could leave it at home.

The following Friday, Ted came to the Grey Mare by taxi and spent the evening shooting pool. When the men in black arrived, several with female companions, he wasn't sure if he would once again be shown the door, but the previous week he hadn't removed his helmet in the bikers' presence, and it didn't appear at first that any of the gang recognized him. One of the leather crowd came over and challenged him to a match of nine-ball billiards. Ted had played regularly for pocket money two decades back as an undergraduate at McGill, but rarely in recent years and never for stakes. Tonight, he lost the first two games. Then he won four straight, dropped one more, and with a fifth win took the match and the fifty dollars riding on it. While his late opponent was placing the banknote in Ted's right hand, another biker was removing the cue from his left. It became evident that the gang members wanted a game among themselves, so Ted retired, paid his bill, called a taxi and went to wait for it outside.

"You come on that riceburner of yours?" asked a quiet voice behind him.

Ted wheeled around to see that Scar was once again on duty guarding the row of polished hogs.

"Naw, I sold it to the president of Hells Angels," he said.

"That's not so funny." Scar spat on the asphalt. "This your local bar? I never saw you before last week."

"Just moved into the neighbourhood," Ted improvised.

"One of the new subdivisions south of Mayfield Road."

A blue and white taxi made a left turn into the parking area.

"What's the address?" said Scar, making for the driver's window.

"I'll tell him myself, thanks." Ted lost no time climbing into the back seat of the cab, but was not quite fast enough to keep from hearing Scar's suggestion that next week he might consider coming to the bar another night, or better still going to another bar.

*　　*　　*

Ted was giving a graduate seminar on gangs that summer. He didn't return to the Grey Mare, but he made anecdotal use of his visits to an unspecified tavern north of Highway 7 in his teaching. By autumn, he had traded in his Kawasaki for a second-hand Toyota sedan. At the beginning of the new semester in September, a student Ted recognized from his summer course came to his office. Melody Clark had in fact got the top mark. Now she wanted to discuss with him a research project for her M.A. The squeak of her dingy sneakers on the linoleum announced her arrival. She was a heavy girl, with big glasses in purple plastic frames, a spotty complexion, and bleached hair in an unflattering pony tail.

"Professor Boudreau," she said, "I'd like to work with you on a study of that biker gang you discovered last spring."

"My impression is that they wouldn't make very good interview subjects," Ted objected, smiling to himself at the bookish girl's naïveté.

"Mine too." Melody cleared her throat. "That's why I took a job in August as a barmaid at the Grey Mare."

Ted sat up and studied the student's face for any sign that she was joking. There was none.

"You didn't mention the name of the bar," she added, "but my family lives in the area, and I put two and two together. Tell me I got it wrong."

Ted wouldn't have scrupled to tell her exactly that, except that he might thereby be leading her to underestimate the risk she was running. He thought of the servers he'd seen the time he'd been in the bar, their piercings and tattoos, their hard jaws and challenging eyes. It wasn't easy to imagine how Melody—today wearing a shapeless denim jumper over a fraying T-shirt—could join their ranks without arousing the bikers' suspicions.

"You're scaring me," he said.

"I can pass all right," she said quickly. "Contact lenses, tons of make-up, skimpy clothing. I even got a navel ring to go with it. I am a blonde, after all, as much of one as matters. And I watch my language. I say 'whatever' a lot, and I don't go near words like 'acculturation'. The thing is—I've only been there a couple of weeks, and I think I'm already onto something."

"Something of academic interest?" asked Ted. "Or something for the police? There are theoretical and practical reasons why a university criminology department shouldn't be doing the Biker Enforcement Unit's job for them."

"We're critical observers of the criminal justice system, not part of it. I understand all that. What I'm proposing is a descriptive study of a holdout motorcycle gang. My research proposal would go something like this—" Melody Clark quickly found a crumpled page of handwriting in her backpack, unfolded it and read aloud: "The big international outlaw biker federations like the Hells Angels and the Bandidos are battling for control of turf. In Ontario, one way in which they compete is by patching over smaller clubs; i.e., arranging for them to swap their coloured crests for those of the larger organization. Bikers that refuse either to merge or to disband may form holdout clubs. The long-term future of such holdouts is unclear. Quite possibly they will be liquidated as the giant federations continue to consolidate their power, but their short-term chances of survival are increased if they (a) make no public display of their colours and (b) do not engage in the lucrative drug trade that has become the big federations' *raison d'être.*"

"When speaking," said Ted, "it's customary to read the letters i.e. as 'that is.'" His pedantry did a poor job of disguising from Melody that she'd caught his interest.

"Whatever," she replied cockily. "Do you want to hear about my source?"

"Give that door a shove and keep your voice down."

Melody complied. "I hadn't been on the job many nights when I had to help a woman who'd collapsed in the washroom. Later she told me her name was Layla. This would have been a Saturday, and none of the bikers was around. They'd gone for a weekend stag run or something. Anyway, Layla had locked herself in one of the stalls and passed out. Drug overdose, I guess. I had to crawl under the partition, wake her up, and put her back together. Her jeans were down around her ankles. While I was pulling them up, I noticed a tattoo on her thigh. It looked like a black arrowhead with red on the tip, to suggest blood. By the time she was able to hold herself upright in a chair it was almost closing time, so I drove her home. I think she accepted because up to that time I hadn't asked her any questions. I did in the car, though. I asked about the tattoo, and she said it was the emblem of the Dark Arrows Motorcycle Club. She had been with one of the officers, a man named Scar. Now he didn't want to see her any more because he thought she was a junkie, but she believed if she hung around the club bar and showed Scar she was clean, he'd take her back as his ol' lady."

"That it?" Ted asked.

"That's it for now. But I'm continuing the friendship. I think this woman likes me and has a lot more to tell."

"Why are you doing this?"

"I think it's valid research," Melody shot back. "Your reference to bikers in the seminar led me to believe you thought so too."

"But do you have some personal connection to the scene?" If not, Ted hoped he might divert her energies into less dangerous projects.

"No, no. I've seen rides through my village, nothing more than that."

"Then what's going on?"

The student filled her cheeks with air and let it out slowly. "Okay," she said. "Back home in Pebbleton, Ontario, some girls were boy magnets. I was the mark magnet. There was no contest in high school, but university is something else. Here there are plenty of brains, plenty of readers. To stand out, I figure you have to be willing to do what other people won't."

"Quit that job," said Ted. "Interesting as the field of study may be from an ethnographical or sociological point of view, there's no safe way to pursue it. Your informant's a heroin addict. You can't trust her testimony, and you can't count on her discretion. If she's willing to betray Scar's secrets to you, what makes you think she won't betray yours to him?"

"I'm a risk-taker."

"Take your risks on the ski slopes, then. Or go whitewater canoeing."

"I didn't say I was athletic," retorted Melody.

"No, and you didn't say you were suicidal either. Undercover cops that mess with gangsters are at least fit and trained in self-defence. And quite apart from your own safety, think of the risk you're exposing us to. 'Student slain while doing research for Department of Criminology'. I don't ever want to read that headline, thank you very much."

"You want me to sign a waiver? Fine!"

"Cheer up, Melody. You're bright. You'll find another research project. And if not, I can always suggest one. Such as: the failure of strict discipline facilities for young offenders. Drop in any time, and I'll give you a reading list."

*   *   *

It wasn't that easy to get rid of Melody Clark. She did choose another research project, but she also slid sealed envelopes under Ted's door from time to time over the following academic year. One contained a purported list of members of the Dark Arrows, along with their occupations and club duties—including who was obliged to attend Thursday night meetings, who was excused, and the one member who was obliged to stay away so they'd have someone on the outside in the event of a raid. That one, the biker known as Chuckles, was most disturbingly alleged to work part-time as a Peel Region special constable. Another envelope held a description of the location, layout and fortifications of the DAs' Caledon Hills clubhouse, including the breed of guard dog used. Layla had told Melody she believed Scar preferred Dobermans to people.

All such documents Ted destroyed, but not before he had scanned, encrypted, and transferred their contents to a CD. There was a hiatus in the dispatches when the riding season ended in late December. Ted understood that the Dark Arrows still met, but without their precious Harleys, they frequented the Grey Mare less often. Melody's bulletins also informed him that Layla had cleaned herself up and been taken back by Scar. Her acceptance had made her far less communicative with Melody. Then in the spring, almost a year after Ted had first stumbled on the club, Melody returned to his office in a state of some excitement.

"They're dealing!" she exclaimed. "And they're manufacturing."

"I don't want to know," Ted protested.

He had to say this. He'd decided from the start that, while he couldn't keep Melody from putting herself in harm's way, he mustn't give her the least encouragement to spy on the Dark Arrows. He had not solicited her data. She'd forced it on him. True, he hadn't destroyed every trace of it either—his academic curiosity had prevented that—but he hadn't told Melody he was keeping it. His sense of obligation was no less under the new circumstances she was alleging. The danger was all the greater for anyone in the gang's vicinity.

"The significance is huge, Professor Boudreau. Remember I said that the Dark Arrows would be tolerated by the big biker federations only so long as they didn't show their colours and didn't involve themselves in the drug trade?" She didn't wait for an answer. The words tumbled out of her. "There's a DA nicknamed Walter Weed, the one that works in a doughnut factory. He was in the Grey Mare six weeks ago with a few of the guys—not a regular Friday gathering, just a mild spring night when a few of the gang felt like getting a jump on the riding season. Walter seems not to have a car, so he rides his hog earlier and later than most. They must have drunk a couple of pitchers of beer each. I'd brought them a bucket of peanuts, and some of them had bought bags of chips from the vending machine as well. After we closed, and the owner had finally got them out the door, I started to sweep the floor. Among the peanut shells and chip bags, there was a scrap of paper. It was a receipt for a pill press, $138.20. In the States, it's illegal for the ordinary joe to own one of those, because of the fear that it will be used to make drugs. Well, no kidding. And on the back of this receipt was scribbled a URL. I thought I'd just keep the paper and look up the Web address later, but then I heard one of the bikes coming back. I copied the address and reburied the receipt in the floor litter, just managing to hide the broom before someone started pounding on the locked door. I let Walter in. He's one of the smallest gang members, but—like the others—bulked up on steroids. His head looks like a pimple sitting on these wide shoulders. He shoved by me and went straight to the table where he'd been sitting. He found his precious scrap of paper, scrunched it into the pocket of his leather jacket, and made for the door. I've learned never to ask the bikers questions beyond, 'What are you drinking?' But Walter must have felt his behaviour was too weird to pass without comment. He looked at me on his way out and mumbled, 'Ol' lady's new phone number.'"

"Don't tell me the Web address led to a recipe for meth," said Ted. "That would be just too tidy."

"For ecstasy, actually—MDMA. And I can't help it if it sounds tidy. It's true. I have a cousin at McMaster University, someone really into the rave scene. She doesn't do Adam any more, but she knows one of the pusher boys that collects twenty-five to thirty dollars a pill from these kids—a rock star look-alike, she says, or used to be. Last week she saw him with several stitches closing a cut through his lip and his ear bandaged up. She wormed it out of him that he was warned to buy only from established wholesalers in future and to be 'afraid of the dark.'"

Ted let the dramatic pause extend between them. He noticed that a rash had broken out on the back of Melody's hands and that two of the spots on her forehead had been scratched raw and were bleeding. At the same time, her face glowed with pride.

"Look, Melody," he said, "I've had zero success up to now persuading you to stop pursuing this, but I don't want you to get hurt and, believe me, not just because it will make the university look bad. If I find you a detective that handles biker crime, will you please just leave the whole mess to him or her?"

"Personally, I think it would make a great article for *The Canadian Journal of Criminology and Criminal Justice.* But let's talk again when the dossier is complete, and I promise to take whatever advice you have to give. I just have to know first where the Dark Arrows' kitchen is. I heard a striker named Thorn ask Walter Weed why he's never around the clubhouse any more. Scar told Mr. Inquisitive to shut up, and from the glares that went around the table, I get the impression the Dark Arrows won't be voting him into the org anytime soon. Assuming Walter is the cook, his absences could mean he makes the pills somewhere else."

"Or in a part of the clubhouse a striker wouldn't have access to."

"Then I doubt if they'd let the striker into the clubhouse at all. Besides, I don't see room on the floor plan. My guess is there's a cabin somewhere in the woods."

"Somewhere in the woods?" Ted let his exasperation be heard in his voice and be seen in his wry face. He wasn't yelling, but he was pretty intense. "Now you want to go stalking bad guys through the undergrowth, like some commando. For Pete's sake, drop it."

"Okay," she said, clearly startled.

"Don't keep any of this 'dossier' on your computer. Don't keep any hard copy in your desk."

"Okay, I'll drop it. I won't try to find out where the cabin is. Just don't call the cops on me, okay?"

Ted waved her out the door, and to his relief she went meekly. Then he added a record of the meeting to his Dark Arrow disk. That night Ted slept poorly. When Karin asked what was wrong, he blamed a hot dog he had picked up on campus, but next day he dropped in on his colleague Graham Hart and partially unburdened himself. He told Graham he had acquired some information on a holdout biker gang, and he wasn't sure what to do with it. For one thing, he had no way of verifying its accuracy. For another, publication might lead to bloodshed. Although he had no intention of appropriating her work as his own, he took the precaution of not mentioning Melody, either by name or under the description "one of my students". Should he, Ted asked, hand the data over to the Biker Enforcement Unit? Should he sit on it until things cooled down? Or should he destroy the disk?

Although intrigued, Graham discreetly did not press Ted to reveal his source. He advised Ted to continue to collect what information he could and choose his moment to publish.

In the days following, Ted wondered if he shouldn't go to the police after all. While ecstasy was not in itself a lethal drug, it was an illegal substance with which deaths had been associated. Allowing the Dark Arrows to continue peddling MDMA could be dangerous. On the other hand, that risk had to be weighed against the risk that the police would not be able to protect Ted and Melody from biker gang reprisals. The two of them *and their families.* Ted shuddered to think of playing those unknown odds.

As long as he kept the data, which he was confident he could do securely, he retained the option of involving the cops later if circumstances changed. If, for example, the DAs' ecstasy started killing people or if all-out, bloody war erupted between the holdout gang and the Hells. In the end, Ted concluded that Graham's advice had been sound.

Chapter 5

When Markus came out of the room where they'd laid Karin's body, Ted was sitting in the hall opposite the police sentry. Ted thought it was a different constable than the one he had first found in the room, but he couldn't say he'd noticed when the substitution had been made. Time passed while he stared dazedly at his shoes, the brown loafers he'd buffed up with a Kleenex before chairing the discussion, many years ago. He'd slept a bit in the room before Markus's arrival and now could not even say whether he was tired. He was nothing.

A haggard Markus planted himself before Ted and looked down at him with bloodshot eyes. "Are we going back to your house?"

"Can't. It's off limits while they look for evidence."

"How long is that going to take?"

"They say they don't know. It's the long weekend."

Markus softened. "We'd better go to my place then," he said gently.

"You're exhausted. Let me drive."

It was proof of Markus's exceptionally low spirits that, instead of dismissing the suggestion with characteristic manly contempt, he wordlessly passed Ted the keys. From the two stalls it sprawled across in the hospital parking garage, Ted guided the battleship size, black SUV down Erin Mills Parkway and onto the eastbound ramp of the six-lane Queen Elizabeth Way. Markus lived in the near corner of Toronto, one where the north-south streets had numbers for names and the houses tended to be either twenty-first century and large or mid-twentieth and small. Markus's figured among the latter. It hadn't been Quirk's childhood home, a spacious suburban sidesplit Ted had seen only after it had been sold and only from the outside. Markus said that a two-bedroom brick bungalow was all a widowed empty nester needed. By the time Ted reached his father-in-law's drive, he was wishing he were back in the hospital room with Karin, but of course they'd have taken her body to the morgue by now. Maybe the pathologist was already sawing it open.

Markus mounted the porch steps slowly, just as the last tattered shreds of night were lifting, but he assured Ted he wouldn't be able to sleep yet. Instead, he suggested the two of them go into the living room and do some yoga-type relaxation exercises.

Dimly Ted recognized tools the professional counsellor would use to combat stress. They seemed miles from anything he could relate to or even politely decline. Should he say that tenseness wasn't what he was suffering from, thank you, or that he didn't want to relax? He lay on his back on the leather sofa while Markus sat cross-legged in the middle of the oriental carpet.

Ted didn't think he would sleep either, but presently he was dreaming about Karin. He was listening to her play Bach's first solo cello suite, the work celebrated in Toronto's Music Garden. He always found the Prelude sexy, and doubly so when she played it, grinning at him, knowing what he was thinking. After announcing itself, the cello bobbed along for about a minute and a quarter at a brisk, steady rhythm through a characteristic Bach series of non-repetitive repetitions. Then came a break. Just over half a minute of what Ted thought of as sweet noodling led at last into the insistent beat of the forty-second-long coda. Now Quirk's left hand slid down the neck of her instrument, drawing from it higher and higher notes, while her right bowed with a sense of unstoppable purpose towards the release. She was half a note from it when Markus's voice broke in—

"Right, Ted. How about a drink?"

It was light outside now, probably between six and seven. The only time Ted had ever had a drink at such an hour was when Karin had brought him bubbly and orange juice in bed on his last birthday. He followed Markus into the kitchen, and they sat on either side of the table with a bottle of Scotch and a pitcher of water between them. Markus got up again for glasses. He seemed, for the moment at least, to have found a fresh source of energy. His eyes showed clear grey in the dawn light. The deep laugh lines at their corners didn't look out of place under present circumstances, suggesting rather character behind his sorrow.

Markus poured two fingers of whisky into each glass. His fingers were thick. "Drink up," he said.

Ted took a sip, then added water. Markus waved the pitcher away.

"She was on the 400 headed north," said Markus. "What did she go back home for?"

"I don't think we'll ever know."

Markus's jaw seemed to tighten. He drank.

"Did you know she was dead when the ambulance took her away?"

"I thought there was still a chance," said Ted. "Medicine can do so much now—with strokes, with severed limbs—if you get attention soon enough."

"By the time they diagnosed Harriet's cancer, it was too late to treat. That didn't stop them trying, but they did their best to reduce expectations down to zero, so when their experiments failed, they could always say they told us so. Karin and I got our hopes up anyway."

Ted had, of course, heard before about the death of Karin's mother. He wondered if Markus were trying to bond with him as a widower.

"We were crazy about each other," the older man went on. Then he flashed a grin as he remembered something Ted had not heard. "And sometimes just plain crazy. Harriet was in the hospital for the last time over Hallowe'en. She had Karin bring her a gorilla mask. When I walked in the door of her room that day, the bedclothes were pulled right up to the rubber chin. She said something like—and you have to imagine this voice coming through a gash in the latex— something like, 'I think this chemo has a few side effects we weren't warned about.' She was dead by Remembrance Day."

Ten years ago, Ted believed. Could be a difficult anniversary coming up.

"I still grieve for her!" Markus declared, defensive perhaps on account of all his happy moments in the interval. "To lose the love of your life is terrible, Ted, and it will never be anything but terrible, so don't think I don't know where you're at. But—" Markus poured himself another drink, not so carefully measured. "But I'll tell you this: what you're going through, my friend, and what I went through and go through on account of the death of a spouse is nothing compared to the pain of losing a child. Take that from me and hope you never learn first hand. Death of parents—bad, but always to be expected. Death of a wife—bad, especially if she dies before her time, but one of you has got to go first. So the odds are no better than fifty-fifty. Death of a child— should never happen, and therefore insupportable. That's why I understand your pain, but you have no idea of mine."

Ted stared down at his drink, unresponsive, but he hoped Markus wouldn't ever read the autopsy report. Eventually, he stood up and went to the sink.

"I'm going to make some coffee," he said, managing to wash his face under cover of filling the carafe. "How did you get into a career in anger management, Markus?"

"Why are you asking?"

"I'd guess it's all just a matter of deep breathing, isn't it? In—out. In—out. Right?"

"To a point. Breathing, imaging, cognitive restructuring—if you want to get technical. But, as I always tell my clients, sometimes there's a place for anger."

"You mean after Denial?" said Ted. "Before Bargaining, Depression and Acceptance?"

"No, forget all that mechanical stages-of-grief thing. Anger can come at any stage. I see it as a sign that you haven't worked out how to respond to a situation. I knew a counsellor who got angry because her client wasn't experiencing the stages of grief in the 'right' order. What this colleague's anger was telling her was that she had to devise a more flexible paradigm. I see the management of anger as a matter of channelling your angry energy into action, whatever action absorbs it—whether that means going on a pilgrimage or playing a practical joke. Do you think we should hire a private detective?"

"No," said Ted—adding quietly, "Not yet, at least. Let's see how the police investigation goes."

While Markus and Ted were downing their second large cups of coffee, Detective Nelson phoned to ask if he and his partner could come over. Ted left voice mail with various members of his department to the effect that a family emergency would prevent him from attending the remainder of the "Punishing Homicide" conference.

*　　*　　*

The detectives didn't get over to the bungalow till after nine in the morning. They had a short private interview with Markus before asking Ted to accompany them to 11 Division, where he could give a proper videotaped witness statement.

The divisional headquarters stood at the intersection of two multi-lane suburban avenues in western Mississauga. Ted was driven in the back of an unmarked black sedan to the side entrance of a bunker-like concrete square with only one above-ground storey. The interior spaces received natural illumination only through skylights and a frieze of windows too high to afford views in or out. He was bundled off to an interview room furnished with one camera, one table, and some basic office chairs. Contrary to what he had seen on U.S. television, there was no one-way glass.

The session began with Ted relating once more under what circumstances he'd last seen Karin alive, what he had understood about her plans for the weekend, what time he had returned home Friday night, what he'd found when he got there, and which of the couple's possessions appeared to be missing from the house.

Then Nelson asked some new questions.

"Mr. Boudreau, do you have any idea who could have been responsible for what happened last night?"

"I have to admit I was responsible—"

"Hold it there, sir," Nelson interrupted. "Are you saying you weren't at that Faculty Club reception and you weren't on that 10:43 commuter train you told us about?"

Ted blinked. He hadn't been thinking in terms of establishing an alibi, but his criminological training kept him from being shocked. Women were most often killed by their husbands or boyfriends. It was simply the first hypothesis to eliminate. Well, he had witnesses if anyone cared to check: Lionel Kerr could put him at the club and Rose Cesario on the train.

"No," he said. "I was there—both places. But was my wife killed that early?"

"Preliminary estimates put the time of her death between nine forty-five and ten forty-five."

This news dropped into Ted's consciousness with a sick thump. So Quirk had already been dead for over half an hour by the time he had found her. He thought back to the deluded urgency of his 911 call. It bewildered him that he hadn't known.

"Mr. Boudreau," Rodriguez asked, "what did you mean by saying you were responsible?"

"I meant," he said, "responsible in part. I never had the alarm reconnected and the account switched into our names after we bought the house."

Detective Rodriguez scratched her scalp with a short, orange fingernail. "Who knew," she said, "that there was no working alarm?"

"Anyone either of us brought to an empty house would have noticed we didn't have to disarm the system on entering. Similarly, anyone present when we left the house empty might have noticed we weren't arming it. There aren't many people in either of those categories. It would take some thought, but I might be able to draw you up a list. Otherwise, I never told anyone."

"Might your wife have told anyone?" Rodriguez asked.

"She might."

"As I understand it, Mr. Boudreau," said Nelson, "you and your wife had originally planned to leave the city for your father-in-law's cottage before dark on Friday evening and not return till the holiday Monday. Is that right?"

"That was the plan," said Ted. "Then on Wednesday morning a colleague asked me to substitute for him at a conference this weekend. Karin was still supposed to leave for Muskoka before dark yesterday evening, and the house would have been empty till I got home after eleven."

"Did you tell anyone when the house would be empty?" asked Nelson.

"People in the criminology department knew."

"Neighbours?" asked Nelson.

"I didn't tell any of them."

Rodriguez repeated her earlier question.

"Might your wife have told anyone?"

"She might."

"Okay, Mr. Boudreau," said Nelson. "Who might your wife have spoken to about the alarm and about the house being empty?"

"I don't know. Neighbours, musical colleagues, people in shops."

"She was a chatty person?" suggested Rodriguez, as if she understood and rather liked chatty people herself.

Still the characterization nettled Ted. "No, I wouldn't say so. But it wouldn't occur to Karin not to tell a person she thought she knew. She wasn't so much talkative as open and trusting—until people proved unworthy of her trust."

"Would you like to take a break, Mr. Boudreau?" asked Rodriguez.

"No, I'd like to get on with finding this guy."

Find the criminals, Martha Kesler had said, barely thirteen hours ago. Find them so we can help them not to be criminals. Ted choked on the memory. Help them not to be, more like. Not since about age fourteen had he been visited by the desire to do personal violence. This morning, he believed it would be easy to slit a throat. He saw in the faces of the detectives that he was doing a poor job of hiding his feelings.

"Right," said Nelson, rummaging in his fanny pack. "Here's a package of Kleenex, never been opened. I'll make a couple of calls, and we'll pick this up again in five."

"Do you have a washroom?"

"Follow me."

When they had reassembled, Nelson had some news. "We've had uniformed officers trying to talk to the neighbours. So far they've had no luck on either side of you or across the street. Seems everyone's up in Muskoka. But there is an older gentleman two doors down who stayed home with his TV. Seems he glanced out his window last night in the break between his nine and ten o'clock programs and saw an unfamiliar black pickup parked in front of his house. He never did see the driver, and next time he looked, the truck was gone. He thinks it was a North American make, one of the big three. A shortbed with a regular cab, not the extended model. Know anyone with a truck like that?"

"I don't," said Ted. "What'll happen to the burglar if he's convicted?"

"That depends," said Nelson, "on how much part he had in your wife's death. Did she miss her footing and fall down those stairs by accident? Or did the intruder push or trip her?"

Once again, Ted offered the evidence of his cellphone. "This is how I found her," he said. "It looks like someone pulled her by the hair."

Nelson examined the displayed photo warily, Rodriguez looking over his shoulder.

"This was before you or the paramedics touched her?" she asked.

Ted nodded. "Yes, before."

"We'll have to see what the post-mortem says," Nelson cautioned. "Another question relevant to sentencing is whether— if the intruder did lay hands on her—he did so intending to kill her or intending only to push her out of his way."

"She wasn't in his way," Ted protested. "He could have left by the front door without her even seeing him."

"Breaking and entering in theory could get you life," Nelson continued, "but as you must know, it never comes to that. Especially on a first offence. Then we have theft, and the penalty there depends on the value of what was taken, whether it was over or under five thousand dollars. Speaking of which, the crime scene boys and girls are still hard at work, but they've given us the green light to walk you through so you can tell us what's missing or out of place. Okay by you if we go over there now?"

*　　*　　*

Another ride in the black sedan, only five minutes this time, over to Robin Hood Crescent. Number nineteen was still surrounded by police tape and police vehicles, but Nelson's badge got them past the gatekeepers. A man from Forensic Identification Services tagged along on their circuit of the house to tell them where they could walk and what they could touch.

The house, not Ted's house. Ted found it easier to think of it not as the matrimonial home into which he and Karin would have welcomed their child, but rather as the crime scene. The company of people not personally bereaved buffered him also. Ted expected much of the professionals. He was relieved to have a task to immerse himself in, a task initiated by others and one that—whatever its distressing associations—he believed necessary.

As before, he found nothing amiss in the master bedroom. The little Florentine chest where Quirk kept her few pieces of jewellery remained in place on her dresser.

Nelson used his ballpoint pen to raise the lid. Everything Ted believed should be inside—pearl necklace, silver brooch, gold cuff links, two pair of clip-on earrings—was there. Over the dresser hung a recent studio photo of Karin and Ted. Nelson asked to borrow it. Ted unhooked it for him.

The second bedroom was Quirk's studio. A chair and music stand occupied the middle of the room, and a writing table nestled under the window. One of the longer walls was decorated with a snapshot collection and a signed black and white photo of Yo-Yo Ma, the other with an oil landscape of Shield country—rock, waves and wind-sculpted pines under a dramatic sky. The FIS man used latex gloves to open the enclosed spaces. The closet contained a couple of black dresses Karin wore when performing, as well as overflow from the bedroom walk-in. A filing cabinet was stuffed with scores and miscellaneous personal files. Again, Ted noticed no absences: it was all here, everything but her. The guest room was easier to inventory, with nothing personal to trigger memories. Quirk had been meaning to repaint and redecorate but hadn't found time. Or motivation. Spare moments always got soaked up by a new piece of music, or—and he was right back in the personal now—a walk with Ted in some forested park.

For all their caution, the detectives were concluding there might be no need for fingerprinting on the second storey at all. There was no proof the house had been penetrated above the fourth step, where the wad of chewing gum still sat.

"Beth, has this Dubble Bubble been photographed?" their forensics escort called to a camera-toting associate headed towards the living room.

"From all the standard angles," came the prompt reply. "Want anything special?"

"No, that should do." The FIS man stooped and captured the gum in a plastic bag, which he sealed and labelled.

"Maybe this is as far as the burglars got when they heard Mr. Boudreau's wife enter," Rodriguez said to Nelson.

"Do you think there was more than one of them?" said Ted.

"I'm keeping an open mind," Rodriguez replied.

"Let's do the ground floor," said Nelson.

In the living, dining, and family rooms—by contrast to the upstairs—drawers and cupboards had been opened. Contents had been stirred about. Pictures had been pulled from the walls and the paper backings ripped off. Ted hadn't paid the mess any attention on his first quick search of the house but now concluded that the intruder had been looking for something he hadn't found. Computer disks, perhaps? He didn't think anything had been taken.

In the den that served Ted and, less often, Karin as a home office, not only a state-of-the-art computer but every disk that held personally stored information was missing. All the research and a third of a draft of an introductory criminology textbook Ted had been working on—gone. His armoury of quizzes and exam questions—gone. His lectures, speeches, financial documents, personal letters, e-mail archives—none of it remained. Anticlimactically, even the music CDs he played on the computer had been taken, popular stuff Karin didn't want in the bedroom. All that was left were plastic-wrapped and sealed blank disks, software backups and Quirk's Verdi DVDs.

"What do you think they were looking for?" asked Rodriguez.

"Three thousand dollars worth of hardware," Ted suggested, pointing to where the tower and monitor had been. "Wouldn't that be a pretty good night's haul?"

"It would," said Nelson, "but then why bother adding to the load a bucket of burned disks?"

"Beats me," said Ted, though he had a pretty good idea. Along with the downright sickening idea that if he hadn't had an interest in bikers, Quirk might still be alive. Leaving the alarm unconnected wasn't in the same league.

The larger part of him wanted to tell the detectives what he suspected, and yet he couldn't put it from his mind that they belonged to the same police service that employed Chuckles. Might the Dark Arrows' grapevine not have penetrated even farther through Peel Regional than Ted knew? To change the subject, he asked the FIS man if he could really tell that the gum was Dubble Bubble just by looking at it.

"Based on colour and consistency, that's what I think the lab work will show. But I wouldn't swear to it in court without doing the tests."

The forensics people wouldn't let Ted and the detectives into the basement where work was still being done on the wooden stairs, the concrete floor and the broken window. Ted was given assurances that they would board over the latter when the collection of evidence was finished. No promises could be made yet as to when that might be. They let him take some toiletries and a change of clothes from his bedroom before he left the house.

He walked out the front door with a sense of futility. His revisiting the crime scene had confirmed his impressions without adding to them. Then, as he was passing Quirk's sun-drenched roses, a straw presented itself for him to clutch. To leave behind gum with saliva traces—that suggested a thoughtless, cocksure kid rather than professional criminals. Might it just have been computer theft after all?

Nelson and Rodriguez drove Ted back to 11 Division to continue the taped interview. All three of them were tired, and the tone when they were sitting once more around the table was decidedly less cordial.

"Were you on good terms with your wife, Mr. Boudreau?" Nelson asked abruptly.

"Yes," said Ted, as if the matter should have been obvious.

"Was there any cause of friction between you?"

"None."

Nelson asked whether the couple had had any money worries, whether Karin's life had been insured, and whether either she or Ted had been seeing anyone else. Ted answered no, no and no. He was trying not to sound hurt. He knew that even if his alibi stood up, the detectives had to evaluate the possibility of a contract killer or a jealous mistress.

"Before you leave here today," said Nelson, "we'd like to get your fingerprints for comparison with what we've found in the house."

"Of course. How many people's prints have they found so far?"

"Mr. Boudreau," Rodriguez interjected, "it sounds like you're impatient to nail someone for this crime and, believe me, we can relate to that. But you've got to help us by telling us why you think those computer disks were stolen."

Ted let the silence lengthen.

"You've told us, sir, that you are a professor of criminology." Nelson mouthed the word with mild distaste. He was doubtless thinking that police and academics rarely saw eye-to-eye on questions of law and order. "Would any of your research have been of interest to criminals?"

"They might have thought so," Ted confessed. "You see, there was a rumour going around university circles that I was researching motorcycle gangs. It's not true, but someone in a gang might have believed it and come to see what I had."

"Ah!" said Nelson. "And were you keeping anything relating to biker gangs, either on your computer's hard drive or on any of the stolen disks?"

"No." A factual, if weaselly, answer.

"Trashed data can under some circumstances be recovered. Had you, Mr. Boudreau, erased or attempted to erase from those disks anything at all relating to biker gangs?"

"Not a thing." True also. Ted had scanned Melody's documents on his previous machine, which he had sent to the dump after scrupulously destroying its hard drive. It had been due for replacement anyway. The stolen computer, as luck would have it, was brand new.

"This rumour," said Rodriguez, "have you any idea who started it?"

"I don't know." Ted felt an imprudent urge to look at the camera, as if he would see there whether it had picked up the fact that he did indeed have an idea. He stared at an ink smear on the tabletop instead.

"Your wife?" coaxed Rodriguez.

"Definitely not. I think someone in my department misunderstood a question I asked him, and he may have spoken to someone else."

"Who did you ask this question of?" said Rodriguez.

Ted saw that the police could sleuth around the department and find this out whether he told them or not. Still he said nothing.

"Which gang," said Nelson, "did this rumour relate to?"

Ted didn't answer.

"Oh, come on, Mr. Boudreau," said Nelson. "Your loose lips have already cost you your computer, your disks and your wife. What on earth can you have to gain by clamming up now?"

Ted felt his face redden. After so much civilized and considerate treatment from the detectives, the rebuke was doubly stinging. He waited a moment to see if Rodriguez would dissociate herself from this attack, but she was nodding agreement.

This was crunch time. Only Graham and Melody knew that Ted had received information about the Dark Arrows, and only Graham knew he'd kept it.

Why then not give the detectives Graham?

Why not give them Melody? Let them surround her with bodyguards. Let them use her information to roll up the whole Dark Arrows crew and put in prison everyone behind Karin's death. Hey, he couldn't even be sure that Melody hadn't blabbed to someone else. Melody, not Graham.

Ted couldn't talk himself into it, though. The police might drop the ball, move too slowly. Let secrets out. He remembered the bikers' power in Montreal. People that had pried into gang affairs had died or come terrifyingly close. And numerous violent crimes had been punished lightly or not at all before any of the gangsters got serious jail time. Could the Peel Regional force—represented by the two detectives across the table—do any better at protecting the living and at acting for the dead when bikers were involved? One thing for sure: justice for Karin at another woman's expense would not be justice.

Cold-eyed and unsmiling, Nelson and Rodriguez were waiting. Ted felt he had to say something. He told them about his discovery of the Grey Mare tavern and its Friday-night patrons. No more than that.

Chapter 6

The rest of the weekend, after the detectives had dropped him back at Markus's house, Ted experienced as the beginning of a life sentence without Karin. The unreality attaching to the earliest hours of his widowerhood had faded—not to nothing but out of the foreground. There were still passages of numbness, but accompanied by too much lucidity to offer welcome relief. He saw ahead of him all the chairs she wouldn't be sitting in, the bedclothes she wouldn't lie between, the doors she wouldn't come through. He saw them as clearly through dry eyes as through tears. It seemed the new normal was to be unheralded hot storms of grief alternating with locked-in winters of depression. Opposites that came to the same thing. Karin was gone.

If anyone had told Ted, as he knew they would, that in a matter of years, if not months, he'd be smiling and laughing again, he would have found that prospect no consolation.

For lunch, Markus walked him the two blocks up to the Irish pub on Lake Shore Boulevard and all through the meal made soldiering-on conversation. Ted couldn't have said what about. He wondered why Markus found it necessary to be soldiering on. Why couldn't he let himself show more grief? Perhaps he felt he'd already betrayed vulnerability by letting Ted drive him home from the hospital. Now he had ground to make up. Having already declared his loss greater than Ted's, Markus must now demonstrate more stoic fibre in dealing with it.

When the check came, Markus grabbed it from Ted's hand. "You know what we should do?" he said. "There'll be no news from the police over the holiday weekend. We should go back up to the cottage to keep ourselves from brooding." Markus spoke of the tonic effect of sun, water, green trees, clean air—of opportunities for distracting activity.

"No thanks," said Ted. "I don't think—Markus, what's wrong?"

It had happened all of a sudden. Markus had his hand on his chest under his T-shirt. His eyes had lost focus and were moving nervously. His breath came in gasps.

"Your heart?"

Markus nodded. "Pounding as if it wanted to break out of my rib cage. My God, Ted, can you hear it?"

"Never mind. I'll bring the car around."

By the time Ted had driven Markus to the nearest ER—no messing with 911 this time—the pounding had subsided, and Markus was given a low priority by the triage nurse who took his particulars. The two men sat an hour together in the waiting area.

During that time, it came back to Ted what Markus had said at Ted and Karin's wedding, on the dock at Lake of Bays: "Am I losing a daughter or gaining a son? I'll tell you next fall after Ted and I go moose hunting." There had been no moose hunt. Now Markus had truly lost a daughter and Ted had acquired the responsibility of looking out for her father in her stead.

A wavy-haired man with a clipboard and a name tag reading *Dr. Alex Patel* eventually took Markus's pulse and told him he seemed to be suffering from a minor arrhythmia. Likely not too much to worry about, but at age—Dr. Patel consulted a form—age seventy-two, it made sense to be cautious. Markus was advised to remain in hospital a few hours for observation.

Ted meanwhile went back to the bungalow. He tried to draw up the list he had promised the police of all the people that might know about the alarm system. He tried straight Scotch. He tried to sleep. He tried to listen to *Saturday Afternoon at the Opera* on Markus's stereo. He couldn't stick with anything.

Eventually he sat down to the task of phoning Karin's friends and musical colleagues. The members of her chamber group, the gang she did Tai Chi with. Although it would be the hardest call, he had to start with the woman Karin had been closest to, Nancy Malik.

"Ted! Let me guess—you're calling to invite Raj and Rita and me up to that gorgeous cottage of your father-in-law's."

"No, I need to talk to you. Is this an okay time?"

The question hung a long moment between them.

"You sound awful," Nancy said at last. "What's happened?"

"Karin... Bad news. She's been hurt." This was not at all what Ted had meant to say. He tried again. "She's dead."

"I can't be hearing you right."

"Yes, last night."

Nancy's next words came in sobs. "I rehearsed with her yesterday afternoon. She was fine."

All the time Ted was telling her what had happened, he could hear her weeping. He started with the basics—a burglar surprised, a confrontation. While he was trying to add another sentence, his voice trailed off.

It sounded as if Nancy were blowing her nose. He followed suit.

"Look, Ted," she said, "I want to talk to you some more, but I need a time out first. What's the best way to get back to you in half an hour?"

He told her he was at Markus's, but gave her the number

of his cell rather than the land line.

When Nancy hung up, Ted went on with his phoning on Markus's line. Many of Quirk's friends were away for the holiday weekend, but the few he spoke to were magnificent—shocked, sensible of their own loss, sensible of his, and ready with offers of help. Karin had had a talent for friendship, he thought.

After forty-five minutes, he had an incoming call on his cell.

"Yes, Nancy," he said.

But it wasn't Nancy. Brian Neuberger of the CBC wanted to ask him about the break-in at his house. Ted said he wasn't up to giving interviews. He had to say it several more times as other news organizations phoned, from CTV to 680 News, from the big Toronto dailies down to the *Clarkson Echo.* It was uncanny how at more or less the same time they had all got his cell number from somewhere—whether a website, a friend, or a professional contact no one would say. As Nancy would have little chance of getting back to him through this swarm, Ted tried to call her, but got only her answering machine.

This was the point at which a taxi brought Markus home from the hospital with a diagnosis of atrial fibrillation, two prescription medicines, and a considerable amount of attitude.

"The little pharmacist asked me if I was related to the Karin Gustafson that was killed last night. Apparently it's been on the radio. I informed her that, including variants with double S and with V in place of F, Gustafson is probably the fifth commonest name in Sweden. Have you been blabbing, Ted?"

"Thanks for the vote of confidence," Ted retorted. "I've actually been fending off a media onslaught. There must have been a press release of some kind. Just be glad they haven't found your address yet."

The doorbell rang right on cue.

"There's the first," said Ted.

"I'll decorate the doorway with their entrails, and they'll be the last," snarled the cardiac patient.

Ted peeked out the living room window. "Hold your fire. It's Nancy."

Her arms were full of brown paper bags and Styrofoam containers that tumbled towards Ted when he opened the door.

"Ms. Meals on Wheels," observed Markus. "Haven't seen much of you this summer."

"Chinese food. I didn't know if you two liked Cantonese or Szechuan, so there's lots of both."

"We'll get through it all, won't we, Ted?"

"With Nancy's help," said Ted, more grateful than hungry. Under the kitchen lights, he saw that her eyes and nose were red. He thanked her for coming.

When the dinner had been deposited on the counter, Nancy turned to the men with freshly brimming eyes and gave them long, wet hugs.

"You better be well stocked with tissues, Markus. I cry buckets."

*　　*　　*

Markus's guest room was as blandly and cheerfully furnished as an IKEA showroom; notwithstanding, Saturday night brought Ted little rest.

In the talk over supper, Nancy—half a day newer to the tragedy—had expressed more shock than rage. She didn't stay long, however, as she had Raj and their daughter to pick up at the multiplex after the seven o'clock show. And, as soon as she left, Markus started sounding off about the prevalence of violent crime and the failure of the authorities to control it. However unscientific Ted adjudged such generalizations, the raw outrage behind them found its counterpart in him, releasing floods of sleep-killing adrenalin. Then too he kept listening for noises from the basement, in Markus's bungalow only one floor below his bed. Ted's most protracted doze ended at nine Sunday morning when he sat up with the realization he could no longer delay talking to his own parents.

Without mentioning the pregnancy, he told them that Karin had died in the course of a break-in. They were stunned. The crime hadn't made it onto the French television news, nor had either seen it written up in *La Presse*. Ted's father fumed at the injustice; his mother grieved the loss—both without tears, for which he was grateful. They each inquired supportively about funeral arrangements. He could tell they were relieved to hear nothing had yet been organized. They disliked travel, even as far as Toronto, and needed time to plan. Now it was health, now home repairs, now social engagements that kept them from coming to visit. In recent years, face-to-face contact had been limited to the times Ted and Karin could get to Montreal. Not above once or twice a year. Whenever he did see them, it struck Ted what a close, happy relationship they enjoyed. He'd always love them for having shown their children what lasting romance looks like.

Ted spoke also to his twenty-five-year-old brother Patrick, the only one of his siblings still living in the Montreal area. He was acting in summer theatre in the Laurentians before returning to graduate school. Free of their parents' travel hang-ups, he made a strong offer to come down to keep Ted company. Ted told him not to. Patrick had commitments enough finishing a run as Orestes in *Les Mouches* and preparing his directorial debut for the McGill Players. Besides, Ted truly could think of nothing for the kid to do in Mississauga.

The police told Ted he could go back to his house Monday afternoon. The news left him ambivalent. He asked Markus, almost hopefully, if he needed Ted's company. But Markus was itching to get back to his cottage and insisted he'd be fine on his own if Ted didn't want to come. His condition, he said, echoing Dr. Patel's reassurances, wasn't serious. He'd been given no special diet, warned against no physical activity. The only medical advice was to keep taking his pills and to arrange with his family physician for periodic blood tests— and he had a doctor in Muskoka he liked better than any he'd seen in Etobicoke. And, yes, he'd let Ted know if his heart started pounding again.

So, sixty-four hours after the time of death, Ted returned to Robin Hood Crescent to begin the cleanup. He vacuumed carpets, repacked and replaced drawers, arranged books on shelves, and stacked in the hall the pictures that would have to be reframed. None of it seemed to matter in the least. Monday night, he lay alone upstairs in the big bed and ached for Karin.

On Tuesday morning, as soon as his bank opened, he went to his safety deposit box to drop off the Family Photos disk he had been carrying around in his briefcase, just in case the Dark Arrows made another attempt to steal it. The fact that the intruders had not reached the second floor made him queasily afraid that they might think they had unfinished business in his house. From his safety box, he also retrieved his second set of backup disks. These had not been updated since the spring, so he was missing the most recent chapters of the textbook he was writing, but he still had his list of references. Together with some handwritten notes in the filing cabinet in his campus office, these should be enough to let him reconstruct what had been lost, when he was up to facing it. He took advantage of the lull between morning and afternoon rush hours to drive all the way downtown. Being distracted by traffic in any case seemed preferable just now to having to occupy himself on the train.

Ted laid out the materials on his desk and launched his word processing program as soon as he got in. It was no use. He found it impossible to concentrate. The sight of his office computer made him wonder why it hadn't been stolen as well. While burglarizing his office wouldn't have the same intimidation value as breaking into his home, the gang had to reckon with the possibility that the files they were looking for were here rather than there. In fact, Ted kept very little data on his basic and rather boring work machine, but how were the bikers to know? And yet nothing appeared to have been disturbed. Then he remembered the missing blank disk, the one he had been about to give Graham on Friday, but couldn't find in the desk drawer where he was positive he had left it.

Ted was not generally forgetful, though he had recently been joking with a student about keeping in his head all the meaningless passwords required for various research databases. Such half-serious gripes were apt to come up with Steve, who was writing a thesis on computer crime. Before Ted knew what was happening, Steve had Ted's keyboard plugged into a keystroke data logger, and this inconspicuously small cylindrical device plugged into Ted's keyboard port.

It was still there.

Ted opened the application. Now he had only one five-character password to remember. He typed it in—*vErDi.* The logger began listing for him everywhere the computer had been and everything it had done. There was even a time/date stamp.

Yes, a disk had been burned Thursday night between eleven fifteen and eleven twenty-one, at a time when Ted and Karin had been burning up the sheets at home. And yet he always locked his office on leaving it. He always found it locked when he came in—except for one time last June when the cleaners had accidentally left it open. Someone had clearly been on his computer Thursday evening.

The invasion of his workspace made him mistrustful and jumpy, not the best frame of mind in which to receive the colleagues who stopped by his open door to offer condolences and ask about the break and enter at his home. Most had by now heard something on radio or television, but he had repeatedly to go over details already available in the papers. Didn't any of them read? A minority, it seemed. The rest were too busy, or too cynical, or too fed up with sensational crime reporting.

In contrast to Karin's musical associates, these academics wanted to understand the situation thoroughly before they reacted emotionally to it, and of course there was no thorough understanding yet to be had. How many intruders were there? Who were they? How did Karin come to be there? How did she die? When Ted—despite his best efforts—failed to satisfy them, they went away shaking their heads. "Terrible," they muttered, "horrifying," and he had to take it on faith that they weren't just referring to the dearth of information.

On the question of how Karin had died, Ted hoped to have some light shed when Detective Nelson phoned in the middle of the afternoon.

"Can I drop in on you this evening?" said the detective.

"Do you have the autopsy results?" asked Ted. "Is that what this is about?"

"Would you be home by seven o'clock, sir?"

"I can't wait till then, detective. Could you please tell me now?"

"That's not the way it's done, Mr. Boudreau. Certain things are to be communicated face to face. Standard procedure."

"I understand. However, I can save you a drive. I read this kind of evidence all the time in the course of my work. I'm not going to go to pieces and then sue the police service."

Nelson took three long seconds to make up his mind. "Are you somewhere you won't be interrupted?"

"I'll just close my door. There. Now what does the pathologist say?"

"He doesn't think your wife died from falling, or being pushed, down those stairs."

"And I take it," said Ted, "you don't mean she had a stroke or something?"

"No, Mr. Boudreau, I most definitely do not. I mean that there turns out to be more than one blunt trauma to the posterior cranial region."

"Someone clubbed her? I need to hear it straight, detective."

"Ted, somebody lifted Karin's head up by her hair as you surmised and smashed it down onto that concrete floor repeatedly until she was dead."

Ted couldn't speak. Yes, he had surmised, but never—even in imagination—had he spelled it out so starkly.

"You still there?" Nelson asked.

"Repeatedly?" Ted got out. "How many times?"

"Four at least. I'm sorry, man."

"Thank you, detective. I'll talk to you later."

*　　*　　*

Ted's office door remained closed till opened by Graham

Hart late in the afternoon. Graham was fresh off the plane from Thunder Bay and still wearing his buckskin jacket.

"Well, that was worthwhile," he said, helping himself to a chair. "My only beef is that the guidelines for what cases can be handled by sentencing circles are too timid. It's time to extend the process to more serious crimes. When you've got, in Manitoba for example, aboriginal people representing eleven per cent of the adult population and sixty-eight per cent of the admissions to provincial custody, you know more people have to be diverted out of the system. I can see these circles working in non-aboriginal communities as well, as part of the whole move to restorative as opposed to punitive justice. Speaking of which, how was the conference? Hope the bloodthirsty rabble wasn't too much of a headache Friday night. Whenever you invite the public onto campus, you're liable to get—"

"Graham," Ted interrupted, "you haven't spoken to anyone in the department, have you?"

"No, I came to see you first. What's up? You don't look so hot. Has our budget been cut?"

"Karin's been murdered."

Graham's heavy eyebrows contracted into a continuous brown hedge. "I don't believe it."

"Kind of defies the odds, doesn't it?" said Ted.

A strangled sound came out of Graham's throat. "Ted," he stammered, "forgive me for rambling on there—I had no idea. You poor bastard. You two were the best—the best."

Ted didn't know if that were true, but it had certainly felt that way, and he thanked Graham for saying so.

Graham took a deep breath. "Look, let's get a drink, and you can tell me as much as you feel like telling. How did it happen? Is the killer's identity known?"

"Not yet."

"Hoo-boy, that must be one sick puppy."

Ted hoped so. He hoped the killer suffered from a chemical imbalance in the brain or had been an abused child, so that the social scientist in him would be able to see cause and effect, and he wouldn't be tempted into the unscientific attitude of blame.

They chose a bar in the Yorkville neighbourhood not likely to be frequented by faculty, and Ted told Graham as much of the story as was known to the detectives. Then he broached a delicate matter. "Graham, did you tell anyone I was researching biker gangs, or any particular biker gang?"

"I might have said something to that dweeb at Simon Fraser when he was looking for someone to peer review an article on organized crime. This would have been a month ago or so. I don't remember your swearing me to secrecy or anything."

"No, of course. I'm not blaming you for anything. And until I heard the post-mortem results, I was hoping to keep your name out of the investigation. But I can't do that now that I know Karin's murderer is out there walking free. I have to give the detectives what I have."

"Including your source on the holdout gang?"

Ted pushed his half-finished beer aside. "I told the cops I gathered the data myself by hanging around the bikers' bar. As far as you know, that's the truth."

"No problem," said Graham. He hesitated sympathetically before going further. "I can see you're in a bind. If you have a source, that source has to be protected, from the law and the bikers. On the other hand, the police must be pressing you to tell all, and you have to wonder if telling all isn't the only way to resolve the case. Do you have enough dirt on these jokers to identify a likely suspect?"

"I have practically nothing, Graham. When I raised this

with you, I was talking big, but there's nothing backing it up, really."

"If you say so."

*   *   *

If the Dark Arrows were behind Friday's crimes, Ted believed the key role had to have been Scar's. It wasn't clear how the rumour that Ted Boudreau had a dossier on the gang might have got from the Simon Fraser academic back to the biker. But once it had, a Google search for Ted's name on the Internet would have led to his publisher's website, where Scar would have found a photo of the Kawasaki rider he'd lent a wrench to at the Grey Mare. Perusing the regional phone books would have yielded the Robin Hood Crescent address. According to Layla, Scar was the brother assigned to watch everyone's back and to deal with nosy outsiders. The counter-intelligence officer, in effect. This didn't mean Scar had done the dirty work personally, but he might well have been the one to assign the job to some expendable foot soldier, possibly not even a patch holder but a wannabe—a striker, a hangaround, a friend of the club trying to earn favour and a shot at membership.

When he got home, Ted called Nelson to tell him about Graham and Scar. The detective had by now had a long day, but didn't grumble that Ted could have spoken up sooner.

"I'm going off duty now," Nelson said, "but come to Police Headquarters at 7750 Hurontario Street. Tracy will meet you there and take your description of this biker. Even if we can't find him in any police rogues' gallery, we'll get a sketch we can show around. And while I've got you on the line, I'll give you a number your funeral parlour can call to arrange for the pickup of Karin's remains..."

Funeral arrangements, thought Ted, suddenly nauseous. He couldn't stomach the prospect of speaking to undertakers. Wouldn't dealing with the grief trade workers be a good job for his father-in-law? Ted and Karin hadn't been churchgoers, but if Markus wanted to involve the pastor who'd presided over Harriet's send-off, it wasn't going to add to Ted's distress. It might even help take Markus's mind off the horrifying results of the post-mortem. When Ted called, however, the only point to which Markus attached any importance was that Karin should be buried, not cremated, in case subsequent developments made further examination of the body desirable. That she had been murdered, Markus claimed never to have doubted.

"She was as nimble with her feet as with her fingers," he said. "Catch her falling down stairs? In a pig's ear."

Peel Regional Police Headquarters was another fortress-like building—a three-storey L with the entrance at the inside corner. At the front counter, a uniformed woman established Ted's identity and errand. Detective Rodriguez was said to be on her way down from her office on Derry Road. A quarter of an hour later, having entered by a back way, she appeared at a door you needed a security card to open.

"James says you've thought of a suspect," she said, beckoning Ted in. "Let's get your description on tape in an interview room. I've asked someone from FIS to sit in and see what she can make of it with EFIT."

"Is that like Identi-Kit?" Ted asked.

"Yeah, sorry. Electronic Facial Identification Technique is the program we use, but the name is misleading. It gives us pictures of bodies and clothes as well as faces."

"I don't know that Scar executed the break-in and murder," said Ted, "but he might have planned it."

"Enough to make him a person of interest." The detective held open the door of an interview room furnished like the one at 11 Division. "Scar sounds like a gang handle. Do you have a last name for our boy?"

Ted thought back to Melody's list, blanking for a moment. "Hollis," he said. "No, Hollister."

"Too bad."

Before he could ask why, they were interrupted by the arrival of a fortyish woman in a nubbly orange sweater and jeans. She carried a laptop, which she plugged into an outlet under the table. She wasn't introduced and sat where Ted couldn't see her screen. He volunteered to move, but Rodriguez suggested he describe Scar first and make any necessary corrections after.

The description he gave was of a man just under six feet tall and in his early thirties. Muscular, but leaner than his brother bikers with their steroid-bloated arms and torsos. The easiest things for Ted to describe about the face were also the easiest to change. On the other hand, membership in a motorcycle gang was all about image and bravado, Ted thought, and no biker would sacrifice his trademark look lightly, especially if the reason for doing so was disguise. So he told Rodriguez about the heavy black hair, parted on the right and falling over the forehead to obscure the left eyebrow. And about the full, wide black moustache, which hid the mouth, except for the middle of a narrow lower lip. For the rest, the jaw was long and tapered, the nose short, the eyes narrow slits. Ted wasn't sure about eye colour, but the upper lids, already low, fell even further towards the outside corners.

When he walked around the table to look over the sketch artist's shoulder at the image her software had constructed from his words, he suggested the chin should be even longer, made a few other corrections of proportion, and eventually concluded it was not a bad likeness in a cartoonish sort of way.

"So where is it?" said Rodriguez.

"Where's what?" Ted asked her.

"The scar."

"Never saw one. Maybe under his leathers." Or maybe, Ted quietly thought, he's called Scar because he leaves scars on others. "Why did you say, 'Too bad', when I mentioned the name Hollister?"

"Because," said Rodriguez, "it's almost certain to be an alias. Hollister, California, was the site of a big biker riot in 1947, what really got the outlaw biker movement going."

"I remember now," said Ted. "Is this picture going to be in the papers?"

"We'll see what Nelson says. My guess is we won't want to let Scar know we're looking for him, at least till we've exhausted the alternatives."

"Can you let me have a copy?"

"What for? So you can make your own inquiries? We ask you not to do that, Mr. Boudreau. There are a lot of rules these days about the ways in which evidence can be collected, and it's hard enough for us professionals to keep them straight. What you can do is make me a list of people and businesses in your neighbourhood you think we should show this to."

After Ted had done so, Rodriguez got him to describe as fully as possible any other members of the Dark Arrows he might have seen. She said she'd be checking for matches with the OPP's Biker Enforcement Unit in Orillia.

*　　*　　*

That night, Tuesday, September 5, was Ted's worst since the

break-in for getting to sleep. On Saturday, Sunday and Monday, the exhaustion of grief had eventually let Ted drift off, but on Tuesday, the faces of the Dark Arrows he had described to Detective Rodriguez loomed up at him when he closed his eyes. Each image was like a pot of strong coffee. As much as the menace, what racked and prodded him was the uncertainty. Which of them had killed Karin? And if they had delegated the dirty work, as was biker custom, what other face should he imagine?

He could hear the engine noises of a truck passing the house. What would it be doing on the crescent at this hour? Leaves rustled in the wind. He wondered if he heard a noise from inside the house as well. Except to reinforce the plywood the police had nailed over the broken window, he had avoided going down to the basement since Friday night. The image of Karin, dressed for the cottage, lying lifeless on the concrete took vivid hold of his imagination. He knocked over the bedside lamp in his haste to turn it on.

He got up and looked for something to read in a pile of old periodicals, settling in the end on some Amnesty International reports. He'd long been convinced that the risk of judicial error constitutes a conclusive argument against executions, so had never stopped to think much about the phrase *legal murder* that abolitionists love to trot out. He found it again in a 1992 speech by a future Attorney General of Trinidad and Tobago: "Putting the prisoners to work so they can contribute financially to the victim's families would be more constructive than resorting to legal murder. The Government is committing murder under the guise of law." By this logic, it occurred to Ted for the first time, imprisonment was legal kidnapping; imposing a fine, legal theft; putting prisoners to work, legal slavery.

Chapter 7

Two weeks earlier, back on Tuesday, August 22, summer had still been sweet for Shawn. His parents were dropping hints again about his enrolling for a course, but he knew he could hold off serious nagging until after the Labour Day weekend. He had been feeling downright cocky for the ten days since August 12, when the five-year disclosability period had expired for the last break and enter he had committed under the Youth Criminal Justice Act. That was for a stereo he'd boosted from an Audi when he was seventeen. It seemed unfair that when he became an adult at eighteen and for four years afterward that offence could still have been dredged up and added to his adult record if he got caught again. Not that he was planning to get caught again.

His mother had asked him to turn off the hip hop when there were customers or potential customers in her gas bar/convenience store, but today Shawn just turned the sound system down instead. He didn't turn it down much. The customer was Arnold Somers, a Lincoln Navigator driver, but with nothing in the way of strut or swagger. Fifty years old going on seventy. He wouldn't be complaining to dear old Meryl about the music.

"Taking holidays this summer?" asked Somers. His arms were full of hundred-watt bulbs, which he attempted to set down gently on the counter. Shawn thought he must have a big house to buy all those at once, but maybe he just had a big closet. Eight packages of four, not a sixty or a forty in the bunch. It might be worthwhile to see where he lived.

"Too busy here, Mr. Somers. My brother's taking his courses, and my dad's got his rig on the road all the time. I can't leave Mom alone."

"Quite so. Do you have any whipping cream? In cartons, I mean."

Quite so? thought Shawn. He couldn't believe what a loser this guy was.

"The cream in the cans is just as good," he said.

Somers laughed. "That hasn't been my experience."

"I take your point," said Shawn, smiling back sympathetically. "But actually, this is a premium brand, one we've never carried before. It's a totally new process. I've read where they did blind taste tests, and the experts couldn't tell it from the kind you whip yourself. If you don't like it, just bring it back. How many cans would you like?"

Somers submissively went back to the dairy cooler and picked up a can of the same old dairy whip that had been stocked exclusively since Meryl had bought the franchise. It helped that the colours on the can had recently changed.

"That'll be nineteen sixty-nine," said Shawn, packing the light bulbs into two bags. Christ, they weren't even on sale! "Year of your birth, right, Mr. Somers?"

"Flattering thought." Somers handed over his gold card.

"What about you, sir? Will you and Mrs. Somers be taking your Navigator into some rugged back country next weekend?"

"No, we'll be in town. We're entered in a mixed doubles tennis tournament."

"Give them heck." And don't have his-and-hers heart attacks, Shawn mentally added.

He gave Somers time to pull out of the parking lot before he locked the store and followed on his chop shop rat bike. Of course, leaving the Handy Buy unattended was against franchise rules, every one of which was holy writ to Meryl, but Shawn wasn't about to hurry on that account. He mustn't catch up too soon if he was to see this mansion that needed all the light bulbs. He timed it perfectly so that he pulled up beside the big SUV as it was stopping in the driveway.

"Sorry about this, Mr. Somers." Shawn made his voice breathless, as if he had been running or pedalling hard. "I just realized I overcharged you fifty cents for that whipping cream. I guess I got too absorbed in the conversation. Here you are, and have a nice evening."

Somers looked at the coins. "You could have waited till next time, but it was good of you all the same. It's a pleasure to meet an honest man."

The house was no bigger than its neighbours, but had a nicely tended garden and a satellite dish. The other car parked in the driveway was a vintage T-Bird. All good, but not so good was the German shepherd lying on the front step. If it was on a rope, the rope wasn't visible. Shawn didn't like dogs.

When he got back to the shop, the red-headed woman from two streets down and around the corner was waiting outside the locked door. The chick that drove the gas-electric hybrid. Older but very desirable. Because she never paid by credit card, he'd had to ask her name. What was it now?

"Hey, Shawn," she said, following him inside, "when does Dwayne get his mechanic's papers? Soon, I hope. Then your mom can add a service bay to this place."

"Afraid the terms of the franchise agreement don't allow for that. He'd do an oil change for you, though, if I asked him. I guess your Insight still needs oil. Say, Karin—" There, he had it. "I've seen your car or one just like it outside 19 Robin Hood. Is that your house?"

Karin had filled her arms with snacks—potato chips, Toblerone, salted cashews and a tin of black olives. Everything she needed to get through a five-hour rehearsal: the Tuesday evening one was always a brute. She nodded absently as she piled her purchases on the counter.

"The reason I ask," said Shawn, "is I was wondering what your experience has been with Alarm Protection Service. From what people tell me, they're very slow to respond to any sort of emergency."

"Oh, we're not subscribers. The sign's just left over from the previous owners." Karin watched the numbers Shawn punched in and handed him exact change when the total came up.

Next time, thought Shawn, I'll find out if she has a dog.

"Have a good evening," he said, and filled the store again with the kick-ass rants of Ice T. Shawn liked the album title— *Freedom of Speech... Just Watch What You Say*.

* * *

"Did you check the washroom?" his mother asked when she returned after seven p.m.

"I was just about to." Shawn didn't look up from the copy of *Outlaw Rider* he was thumbing. He couldn't see himself as one of those steroid-pumped oafs, so heavy they had to change the break pads on their hogs every three months. Cooler was the Peter Fonda type from the sixties. Biker rags still ran his picture. Peter wore the sunglasses well—you had to give him that—but what appealed to Shawn about bikers was the easy money rather than the easy riding. Managing strippers, call girls. Dealing dope. Maybe there was a way of getting in on the action without submitting to all the regimentation of a gang.

"Shawn!"

Meryl was leaning across the counter on her elbows. She was trying to sound perky rather than nagging, trying not to look her fifty years, trying not to show the tiredness she felt. There had been a horrendous lineup at the bank, and the discount hair salon where she'd gone was breaking in another new girl from some part of the world where English was no more than a boring subject in school.

All the subjects had bored Shawn. Not Dwayne, Meryl thought. Dwayne had genuinely struggled to get adequate marks, but Shawn was bright. He'd dropped out because he couldn't be bothered. Meryl thought that once he found out what he wanted, Shawn would apply himself. He'd take a community college course like Dwayne. And then, watch out, he'd have the world by the tail.

"Yes, miss. What can I do for you?" He flashed her the smile he knew she couldn't resist—although seeing her in that pukey gold Handy Buy convenience store golf shirt made him want to do anything but. "Do you have to fly the company flag when you're not in the store?" he asked, switching in a heartbeat from flirtatious to reproving. "You wear that yellow rag in the mall; then you complain about slow service. People see you in uniform, and they think you should be serving them."

Meryl's face dropped. Her best T-shirt needed ironing, her best blouse needed a button, and her other blouse was in the laundry basket.

"What I'd like you to do for me, Shawn," she said wearily, "is check the washroom. It's company policy that we look in every hour to make sure the facilities are clean and that the supplies aren't running out. That's once an hour. I've been gone four hours. How many checks have you done?"

"I told you, Meryl, I was just about to." Shawn stood up and glared down at his mother. He had been holding his gum in his cheek, as she'd asked him to when customers were in the store, but now he chewed it at her with open mouth.

A woman interrupted their standoff by coming in to pay for her gas.

"Never mind," said Meryl. Cheery face, cheery voice. "I'll see to it while you look after Mrs. Howse."

"How are you, Mrs. Howse?" Shawn's face and voice were just as cheery. "Are you going to get up to the cottage this weekend?"

That was one thing about Shawn, thought Meryl, as she scrubbed the toilet bowl. He was a wizard at friendly chat with the clientele.

*   *   *

Meryl's big task for the evening involved shuffling papers at her cramped desk in a broom closet. Inventory, Goods and Services Tax, water, electricity, blah, blah. Or maybe it was all done now on the cheapo company-supplied computer. Shawn really had no idea. Meryl had suggested he learn about all this in case he wanted to run a business of his own one day, but he had a strategy for putting her off. He'd had Dwayne bring him a Humber College course catalogue, which he'd pretend to study. Once he'd found the career that was right for him, he liked to say, all that detail stuff would come easier.

Four washroom checks later, when Meryl finished work in her rat hole, had swept the floor and Windexed the glass in the doors (the full windows only got done twice a week), she put on her grubby pink rubber gloves and went out to pick up trash from the parking lot. Her hair kept falling from behind her ears into her line of sight as she bent over the nachos and cigarette butts, and she'd have to push it back with her wrists. *Why do I even bother going to the hairdresser?* she thought. She always ended up re-cutting it herself, hacking away because they'd left it too long.

By now, she was getting on Shawn's nerves big time. He had told her weeks ago to throw those gloves out and help herself to a new pair off the rack. What point was there in having a store if you couldn't do that? But she said that she kept them odour-free with baking soda and that they'd do the job as long as they didn't have holes in them.

"Why don't you go home, Mom? You look bushed."

"You must be tired too, son." She peeled off her gloves before giving Shawn's arm a squeeze. "It's only two more hours till Dwayne comes on at one. I can manage. And then, if you get a good night's sleep, you'll be fresher to give your dad a hand fixing the porch steps in the morning."

"Cliff's never up till noon on days after he gets in from Winnipeg. I was just going to have a coffee anyway. I'd rather do that than sleep."

"Okay, honey." Meryl tidied away the trash, washed her gloves and hands, and got her purse from the back. "Here's a dollar fifty for the coffee."

Shawn didn't know whether to laugh or chew her out. "Did I tell you your hair looks nice?" he said.

Without having suspected it, it was what she had most wanted to hear. Meryl walked out the door blind with love.

*   *   *

Shawn didn't want coffee. Pocketing the dollar fifty, he went out into the parking lot to smoke a joint. He didn't know why he was restless. He thought of the magazine photos of the biker girls with their thongs and tattoos, but more than sex it was adventure he wanted. And money. Living at home, he had cheap room and board and was paid for every hour he worked at the store. Then there were the twenties and fifties he could part his parents and Dwayne from. He'd worked out just how many before the heavy sermonizing set in. But none of it was enough to trade in his rusty old scooter for something newer that would really turn heads.

Something like that, for example. Though on more careful inspection, the machine pulling up to the pump wasn't new at all. You could tell from the dinky little bullet of a gas tank that didn't contour into the frame and from the shape of the rocker covers, which—according to the magazines—Harley-Davidson hadn't made that way for over forty years. Not new, but pampered. Not a trace of rust on the paintwork. Shawn liked the fact that there was no pillion pad. This was strictly a one-man machine.

He shifted his attention to the rider, a dude maybe ten years older than himself. Black hair, black leather trousers and vest, black T. He turned when he heard Shawn approach. His eyes were narrow, his chin long, and he wore a heavy black moustache.

"Righteous chopper, mister," Shawn said. "I have an older Harley myself, only I haven't had time to work on it yet."

The customer nodded. He was holding a ten dollar bill in Shawn's direction.

"I'll get you change from the store." Shawn didn't move, though, mesmerized by the gleaming chrome.

"Air's sweet around here," the customer said quietly. "If you can let me have a smoke, we're square."

Shawn grinned. This guy is cool, he thought. Bet he'd be

worth knowing—if only I don't scare him off by looking overeager. Nonchalantly, he passed over a joint and his lighter. When the man had let out his first lungful of smoke, he cocked his right eyebrow approvingly. The left was hidden by his hair.

"Mind if I have a look?" he asked, nodding towards Shawn's machine.

"Hell no." They walked over together, and Shawn wheeled his bike away from the store wall out under the lights of the pump island.

The customer—Shawn was starting to think of him now as the biker—squatted and ran his index finger over a couple of places where serial numbers had been filed away. He looked up at Shawn.

"Yep," said Shawn, "it's just as it was when it left the shop. Pawnbroker's actually."

The biker dragged his finger over the fender and looked at what had been deposited there. "Dusty shop," he said.

"I should polish it," Shawn admitted, "but it's nothing special, not like yours."

"It's a Harley," said the biker. "Something can always be made of that. Know where Robin Hood Crescent is?"

"Sure. Turn right out of the lot here. Two streets down, hang a right."

The biker finished his joint, flattened it with his boot, and dropped it in the trash before returning to his own machine. "If you ever want anything stronger," he said, "I'll be back this way."

"Sure thing," Shawn lamely replied. He would have agreed to anything at this point, anything the man suggested.

"And just so you know—customized panheads like this one? They're bobbers, not choppers."

Shawn stood staring out at the street for a long moment

after the "Potato-potato" rumble from the bobber's over-and-under shotgun exhaust pipes had faded out down the block, then, surprisingly soon, the same rumble faded in again, and the biker swept by, heading back the way he'd come. Whatever his business was on Robin Hood Crescent, it hadn't taken long.

Chapter 8

In the end, it was Karin's friend Nancy who insisted there be some sort of memorial service, even if secular, and the date settled on was September 12. Ted told his parents but discouraged them from attending. Reluctant travellers though they were, they'd been fond of Karin and put up a fight—his mother particularly. Ted reconciled her with a promise to visit Montreal a month later, over the Thanksgiving long weekend. By then, he thought, he'd be better able to handle the emotions.

Meanwhile, Ted left Nancy to manage just about everything to do with this non-funeral, starting with the music. There were many performers besides herself who wanted to give their sister a send-off in the language she'd loved best.

One of the offerings would be an excerpt from Beethoven's A Minor String Quartet, opus 132, the otherworldly third movement, said to be in the Lydian mode. Of the Lydian mode, Ted knew only that in Beethoven's hands, it had the power to reach in through his ears down to his toes and pull him inside out. Quirk had believed there was a necessary element of aggression in artists, a ruthless determination to affect people and to do it more strongly than anyone else. Aggression for good, to be sure, but something much more muscular than might be suggested by the composer's title, "Holy Song of Thanks from a Convalescent." And muscularly was the way Quirk had practised in her home studio, over and over, no compromises—whatever the piece. Often the fight had left her trembling and dissatisfied. Occasionally, she could be heard to exclaim through clenched teeth, "Nailed it!"

Ted found he didn't want to share this, or any of his memories of Karin. After struggling with two abortive drafts of his own, he asked if Nancy would also give the eulogy. She was a big, sturdy woman, a violist accustomed to bearing heavy burdens. Her chestnut hair was shoulder-length, curly and dramatic. She had stage presence in spades.

Among the things Ted would later remember hearing her say—

"Earlier this month, my dearest friend was murdered. Since I heard the news, I've thought a lot about Karin Gustafson's death and wondered who was cruel enough to intentionally cause it. I think at this point it is a blessing that we don't know. For if we did, if we could put a face to that killer, I'm afraid I'd have some pretty cruel intentions myself.

"I can't say anything that will help you reconcile with Karin's death. For that you'll have to consult with your pastor, if you have one. Or with an expert in anger management like Karin's father, Markus. Or with an expert on crime and its causes like Karin's husband, Ted. All I can tell you is why I am grateful for Karin's life.

"In rehearsal, our colleague Karin Gustafson was more adaptable than a well-oiled contortionist. Last minute changes of tempi, or even of repertoire? No problem. Key shifts? She'd do them fast, accurately, and without a murmur of protest. But if a publishing house changed the size of their paperbacks partway through a series or if the Second Cup discontinued her favourite coffee bean—batten down the hatches.

"In a world of self-absorbed geniuses, Karin Gustafson was the exception. She was interested in other people, genuinely, and not as a matter of public relations. I think she believed great music could be made on no other basis. Her deskmate in the opera orchestra tells me that when Karin played she most often sang along in Italian or German under her breath, involving herself in the human drama unfolding on the unseen stage above her. For her friends, this interest meant she remembered your birthday. And your kids' birthdays. And what your kids wanted for their birthday. I once phoned her, in confusion and embarrassment, to ask whether my daughter's favourite flavour of ice cream was maple walnut or pecan crunch. And she knew.

"And yet, in spite of all Karin's good qualities, I hated her. Couldn't stand having her around, especially in summer. She just looked too darn good in a bathing suit."

No one expected Ted to hold himself together during this speech, and he didn't. The funeral parlour had provided him with his own box of tissues. He must have used a third of it as he sat listening in the chapel pew. However positive Nancy tried to be, just beyond the margin of every sentence hovered the outrage of goodness destroyed. The vision of Karin alone with her killer, life pounded from her blow by blow. The unimaginable sound of her skull being broken beyond repair. It was easier afterwards in one of the funeral parlour's reception rooms, handing out coffee and listening to people's cliché condolences and vague generalities about his wife. Markus seemed to be bearing up well, serious but with a sweet sparkle in his eyes. Father and husband were both doing their best to follow Nancy's cue and keep the occasion celebratory.

Not that Ted had forgotten the investigation. He'd asked Nelson if the police wanted to have anyone at the funeral. Rodriguez had come in the not implausible guise of a neighbour. She wore a white lacy blouse, dark pantsuit and patent leather shoes. Ted wondered if her pistol was concealed under the jacket. When the other attendees drifted off, she took him to her car to brief him on the latest developments.

"Your basement window first," she said. "It was pretty thoroughly bashed in, leaving few sharp edges, but our Forensic Identification Services have found a couple of threads of very dark grey sweatshirt-type fabric snagged on one of the few remaining peaks of glass. Know anyone with a garment like that?"

Ted was at a loss. "I'll let you know if anything comes to me," he said.

"Just a shade lighter than black. Now for the other grey, the Grey Mare Tavern. Ownership has changed in the past month, and none of the staff are the same. None of the present crew admit to having seen any bikers, including our boy Scar, and the new management have no intention of letting the premises be used as a bikers' bar. In fact, they're changing the name to Little Burgundy and bringing in jazz musicians on the weekends. Nelson's had a good laugh over that. He's sure the motorcycle clubs will avoid the place like the plague because—and I quote—'those outlaw riders love every last thing to be black except skin.'"

"What about here in the neighbourhood?" Ted asked.

"None of the residents on your block recognized Scar, and we struck out at the Bouquet Bistro too. But he may have been spotted at your local gas bar—what's it called?—the Handy Buy."

"Tell me more."

"Since it's a round-the-clock operation, we asked at different times of the day. And night. The elder son, Dwayne Whittaker, is usually on from one to seven a.m. He told Nelson he thought he'd seen the subject of our sketch a week before your wife's death, but not in biker gear. He was wearing a short-sleeved dress shirt and driving a small car of some sort. Scar, or his double, bought some cigarettes and asked when 'the other guy' would be on duty. Dwayne thought he must mean his brother Shawn. Dwayne told him that was hard to predict and asked what it was about. The customer replied that it was nothing special, that he'd had a further thought about a topic they'd been discussing, and was wondering when he might have the opportunity to pursue the conversation."

Ted remembered Dwayne as a quiet young man in his mid-twenties, courteous but not one for small talk. Ted rarely saw him, since Dwayne had gone on night shifts. If Ted bought gas or anything from the store, it was usually Meryl or her younger son Shawn who took his money. Shawn always gave the impression that he didn't really work at the Handy Buy: he was just filling in as a family favour while waiting for his true calling to call.

"Did Dwayne ask the subject of this conversation?" Ted wanted to know.

"Uh-uh. It didn't seem important to him and he says that, when he can, he stays out of other people's business. I did go round later that morning and talk to Meryl Whittaker, the boys' mother. The sketch meant nothing to her. She'd heard from Dwayne about our inquiries, and she wanted to know if Shawn was in trouble. Not with me, I said. I just wanted a word with him. Would he be at the store that afternoon? She told me Shawn was taking a few days off. He'd packed some things in his saddle bags and ridden off on his motorcycle. He didn't say exactly when he'd be back, but she didn't think it would be more than a week at most. He's registered for a night course starting September 11."

"Yesterday," said Ted. "Did he attend the first class?"

"He did not."

"So now you're looking for Shawn Whittaker."

"You got it. At least, now we have photographs and a real name to work with. But he is our only lead. Nothing has turned up on any of the Dark Arrows. And, as suspected, Scar has no criminal record under the name Hollister."

*　　*　　*

Ted had—in a vague, uneasy way—expected the funeral to be a milestone. Wasn't it supposed to be the saying goodbye that made it possible to move on? He shuddered at the thought. Herein likely lay much of the reason he had resisted and delayed the ceremony, and in the end kept his family away. He had no inclination to say goodbye.

Afterwards, however, as early as the morning of the following day, he found that the funeral had changed nothing. Karin had not been "sent off". She was as present to him as at any time since her death—turns of phrase she used, the taste of her earlobe, the sweetly kinky feel of the string-player's calluses when she brushed his cheek with the fingertips of her left hand. As for moving on, the only progress he felt possible or desirable was in the area of bringing her murderer to justice. Otherwise, the most he could aspire to was to move *back*. Back into the routines that had been suspended during the earliest days of his bereavement.

Accordingly, Ted found himself in his office once again looking over the materials for the textbook he was writing. He had left aside for the moment as too demanding the task of reassembling from his scattered notes the parts that had been stolen and was rereading sections he had thought complete.

"After studying 588 criminal homicides," he had written, "Marvin Wolfgang found that twenty-five per cent of the victims precipitated their own murder."

Ted felt his blood pressure rise, his hands form into fists. He couldn't immediately say why he was so angry. What he had written was true. And as far as he knew, Wolfgang had reported his findings honestly. What Ted hated at that moment was people's fondness for statistics like this. They love to blame the victim. It must make them feel safe.

"Quirk did not kill herself," he muttered.

Bill Nikolic's white head appeared around the frame of the office door.

"Is this a good moment for a word?"

"Of course, Bill. Come on in. Thanks for your help yesterday."

The chairman of the Department of Criminology had been at the funeral and had surprisingly taken it on himself to pass plates of cookies during the reception afterwards. Maybe not so surprisingly at that. Long before being voted chair, he'd been responsible for bringing Ted and Karin together.

"Does your son Dan still play piano, by the way?" Ted asked.

"Only at parties. He works in a bank." The older man settled into a chair and crossed his legs. "I'm surprised to see you here so soon, Ted."

"I need something to keep me from brooding, and there's the new year starting."

"Is it three grad students you're supervising at present?"

"Just two, but I could take on a third. My course load isn't particularly heavy this semester."

"Nor mine. Ted, I'd like you to let me take on your seminar on organized crime. I've got a teaching assistant who'll give the lectures for the fall portion of your introductory course."

"Come again?"

"It's early days yet. The Dean and I think you'd benefit from some time off."

Ted hadn't seen this coming, and yet recent experience—as Bill had likely been able to hear for himself—showed him he couldn't totally depend on his moods. By insisting that he shoulder his full teaching load, he wouldn't necessarily be benefiting his students.

"I'd like to keep my two doctoral candidates. Steve Nishimura is just about ready to submit his thesis on computer crime: it'd be a shame to bail out on him now. And Colin Young's fresh off the plane from B.C. No heavy lifting there yet."

"Okay, let's try with the two for a while. Just let us know if you want to go on a round-the-world cruise."

"That's not likely as long as the police are investigating. So don't hesitate to get in touch if you need any help with that seminar."

"Will do. One other thing: I'd like you to consider getting some counselling."

"Good grief!"

"Yes, Ted, up to a point."

"Sorry, Bill. I was just being sarcastic—no pun intended."

"The pun is apposite. But you've got more than grief to deal with. There's sudden loss of a wife through malevolence. That's traumatic stress and mighty hard to handle on your own. I'm not talking about anything that'll 'get you over' what happened to Karin in one year or fifty. Just some tools for your emotional workbench."

"You're a sweet man, Bill," said Ted.

"I'm a buttinski. Are you sleeping well?"

"Not particularly."

"See your family doctor about that. And if he can't recommend someone for the other, I can."

*   *   *

That evening, behind a club in Niagara Falls, Ontario, a twenty-two-year-old man, who looked much younger, tried to exchange three ecstasy tablets for sex with a twenty-six-year-old woman, who looked very much younger, and not at all like the police officer she was. She was wearing a pink Hello Kitty tank top and turquoise braces on her teeth. When she brought him in, personnel at the Morrison Street station joked about babies arresting babies. The kid refused to identify himself until it was explained to him that this was one piece of information not covered by an arrested person's right to remain silent. By then, it was little more than a formality anyway, because they had already searched him and were copying information from his driver's licence. The name Shawn Whittaker prompted the most alert of the sergeants to go back and look at a photo that had recently come attached to a bulletin from Peel Regional. Soon after, the sergeant put in a call to James Nelson.

"I had to drive down after midnight," Nelson explained when he phoned Ted the next morning. "Niagara has charges of soliciting and trafficking to hold him on overnight, and I just wanted to talk, so I couldn't expect them to send him up. What a night! If Shawn's tight with the Dark Arrows, they've really drilled into him the wisdom of zipping his lip. So far he hasn't said where he got the Adam. He hasn't told me anything about his friend Scar. And he hasn't admitted to ever being in your house. What he couldn't stop himself from doing is smoking the cigarettes the police so very thoughtfully supplied and leaving the butts in a police ashtray, so we have a DNA sample that we're going to compare to what's on that chewing gum you found on your stairs."

Shawn? Ted wanted the killer identified, of course, but he didn't want it to be Shawn. Someone they had conducted countless small transactions with since their arrival in the neighbourhood. Their neighbourhood seemed indeed to be defined as the households that depended upon this store. Gas, newspapers, that odd litre of orange juice or milk when they ran short, half a dozen eggs. Ice cream on a stick, when late on a sultry August night Karin and Ted had gone for a walk with the Handy Buy as their unplanned but fortuitous destination. Every time, for seven years now, they had been grateful that Meryl, Dwayne or Shawn was there to keep the lights on, take their money, wish them a pleasant evening.

Handy Buy was a convenience store, and Shawn was convenient. He didn't have to be a hero, but—someone that might bash your wife's skull in?

There was more. There were Cliff and Meryl Whittaker, working like fiends to get their boys on their feet. Ted thought of Meryl in particular, keeping the Handy Buy open 24/7. He imagined her getting a call in the middle of the night telling her that her younger son would be going before a Justice of the Peace in the morning nearly a hundred kilometres away and warning her that if she wanted him to come home with her, she might have to stand surety for him.

Ted hoped the DNA would not be a match.

*   *   *

Bill Nikolic didn't wait for Ted to ask for the names of therapists. Almost immediately after their conversation, there appeared in his e-mail a short list. The name at its head was Martha Kesler.

Ted didn't feel the need of counselling. At the same time, he had never been the sort of person whose back went up at any suggestion he look for outside help, or who thought the less of people that do. If he had been, his recent experience with assisted fertility would have cured him. What billions of men and women throughout history had done unthinkingly, even unwillingly—namely, conceive a child together—had taken Karin and Ted more than three taxing years of medical procedures. Attempts at artificial insemination first, with all the attendant drugs and ultrasounds. Then, when conception did not occur, four cycles of in vitro fertilization. More hormones for Karin by mouth and by injection into her stomach, legs or buttock. Four cycles of aspirating eggs from her ovaries, introducing them to Ted's sperm carefully separated from his semen, incubating embryos, and inserting said embryos into Karin's uterus with a catheter. And daily hospital tests from the moment she started taking hormones. Karin had been magnificently plucky. But scarcely less magnificent had been the family doctor who had held their hand through every disappointment and supported them every step of the way, Rebecca Ornstein.

Ted thought that the advice he would most respect would be hers. He made an appointment for noon on September 18.

Dr. Ornstein's office was in the same strip mall as a Thai restaurant. Her young receptionist Sally Lee had a container of noodles open on her desk when Ted entered the waiting room. On seeing him, she put down her chopsticks and wiped her mouth quickly.

"Mr. Boudreau, we're so sorry about Karin." She left a space in case Ted wanted to say anything to that, and—when she saw he didn't—hurried on, "As soon as Dr. Ornstein is off the phone, I'll let her know you're here."

Ted sat in a brightly upholstered chair and found himself facing the corner of the room filled with trucks, stuffed animals and building blocks. Much of his grieving up till now had been for the lover and wife he knew rather than for their future daughter or son, but all these reminders of childhood touched a nerve. If he'd had to lose Karin, he thought, why couldn't he have kept a part of her—the human embodiment of their love and their hopes?

The top magazine in the stack on the table beside him was the children's monthly *Owl*. He picked up a newspaper, flipping past front page stories of the most recent Canadian fatalities in Afghanistan to the technology feature. Usually he enjoyed descriptions of new gadgets or of gadgets' new tricks. As fate would have it, today's article was on the launch by Telus of a GPS tracking feature called Kid Find. On the comic page, Tom Fisher and his wife Alison had a new baby. Nice for them, but not many laughs. Eventually, he settled into a soothingly routine discussion of waste disposal. The sound of his name interrupted a deep consideration of incineration versus landfill.

"Ted, come in." Dr. Ornstein had the look of an old-style grandmother. Her body underneath her dark dress and fresh lab coat was thick and shapeless, her hair silver-grey. Her deeply-lined face gave the impression of having seen a lot. She had been widowed young, Ted recalled, and had never remarried. It was a sad face in repose, so she usually tried to smile with patients. Today she didn't make the effort. "How are you bearing up?" she asked.

"Pretty well."

"That's the social answer out of the way." She beckoned him into her office, waved him into a chair, and closed the door before settling herself behind her desk. "Now if your doctor asked you the same question...?"

"Nights are worst. I have trouble getting to sleep. Every noise startles me. Lying there in the dark, I see Karin stretched out on the basement floor, just as I found her."

"Finding her must have been dreadful. Is sleeplessness interfering with your work?"

"My department chairman has relieved me of most of my work this semester. I really only came to see you as a courtesy to him. When I think about what happened to Karin, my difficulty sleeping is nothing."

"Do you think you don't deserve to sleep?" Dr. Ornstein asked.

"I wouldn't put it that way."

"Good, and I hope you don't act that way either. Your suffering can't help Karin, or what would have been your child. I know it's the last thing she'd want. Honour her by looking after yourself."

"We were supposed to go up to the cottage together that evening. There was a conference at the university, but I wasn't involved. Then a colleague was called away. I agreed to substitute for him. I let Karin drive up to Muskoka on her own."

"None of those things are wrong, Ted."

"She got partway up and turned back. We'll never know why. The upshot was she entered the house alone when the burglar was there, and he killed her." Ted paused for breath. The pain of missing Karin, which he had thought at its maximum, ratcheted up two more notches. "It's hard," he said, "not to think, 'If only...'"

"If one thing had been different, many things might have been different. You can't hear that right now, but think it over later, when you're better rested. And to that end, I'd like you to consider moving out of the house for a while. Your home is where Karin was attacked. All its sounds and smells and sights can't help but remind you. A week with family or friends or even in a hotel might buy you—not hour after hour of sound sleep—but enough extra rest to give you back your edge and keep other health problems from developing. If a change of beds doesn't do that, I am willing to prescribe you a ten-day course of benzodiazepine, though I find it constipating myself."

"Wouldn't it be unhealthy to run away from the house? I already find I'm avoiding the basement."

"I'm not telling you to avoid the house." Now Dr. Ornstein did permit herself a smile. "Just don't sleep there. Ted, go easy on yourself. This is going to be a long road. I'm not speaking only as a doctor now, but as a survivor. I'd like you to call me in a couple of weeks. Come and see me in six months at the latest. You'll be due for a checkup then anyway. Will you do that?"

"Sure."

"Good. Have charges been laid yet in Karin's death?"

"Not that I've heard," said Ted.

"The best we can hope is that the monster is killed by police while resisting arrest. We've no sentences in law that wouldn't be too good for him."

*   *   *

Ted decided to move in with Markus for a week. His father-in-law had invited him repeatedly since returning from Muskoka for the funeral, and had been politely put off. Now Ted thought that, while giving himself a break from the house on Robin Hood Crescent, he might as well work at keeping Karin's dad company.

The evening Ted drove around with his suitcase, they ate again at the Irish pub. Markus still appeared to be medicating his grief with Scotch and showed surprise that Ted had no interest in doing the same. Notwithstanding, the old Viking was affable company through all three courses, salad, steak and lava cake. He wanted to reminisce about his various careers as a jazz drummer on the Prairies, construction worker in B.C., and social worker in Ontario before he really found his niche. Ted wanted to know about the workshop where he'd met James Nelson.

"Ah, yes, I had these stressed-out detectives from the Major Crime Unit, people that were doing just fine, but were afraid that at the pace they were going, something was bound to snap. They were sure they were about to snarl at family members, harangue other drivers, belittle witnesses. I said, 'Don't get angry. Get mad.' I tried to get them to see the power of creative insanity—not true insanity, but crazy jokes. I don't even know if it made any sense, but Nelson loved it. He sent me an e-mail about how the very next week he'd put my idea into practice. Seems someone always parked his VW Beetle in front of a fire hydrant on Nelson's street. Nelson and his buddies finally picked the little buggy up and turned it 180 degrees. Then on the windshield they left a note purporting to be from the Fire Department. The note said they were sorry but that they'd had to move his vehicle to get water to put out a fire, and they hoped they'd put the car back right and that everything still worked. Let's have coffee at the house, shall we?"

Only when they got back to Markus's living room and the whisky was wearing off did Markus become argumentative.

"What did that woman Nancy mean by saying Karin looked too good in a bathing suit?" he asked from his place in the centre of the couch.

"She meant she was jealous. It was supposed to be a compliment, a light note to end on."

"Karin didn't wear a bathing suit."

"Maybe not at your cottage after dark," Ted replied.

"Never."

"Come on, Markus. You remember the scarab green one-piece with the white straps?" Inane conversation, thought Ted. That bathing suit had looked as if it had been custom made. *Quirk has a sweet butt.* Dammit, now he was going to cry. "I'd better call the police to let them know where I am," he said, jumping up from his chair and turning his face from the light.

"Here, relax. They have your cell number, don't they?"

In the kitchen, Ted helped himself to a paper towel and dried his cheeks while waiting for Nelson to answer. Eventually, he did. "Ted, I've been meaning to have a word. The head of my unit is not pleased about the conversation you and I had regarding the pathologist's report. So far I don't think he knows about the call I made to you after Shawn's arrest in the Falls, so I'm asking you to keep that one under your hat."

"I have so far," said Ted, watching his words in case Markus could hear. "And will do in future. Does Shawn's DNA match what's on the gum?"

"I am not authorized to tell you anything about that. Here's the question I'd like you to ponder: if Shawn stole your computer, where will we find it? Let's talk soon."

Just as Ted was hanging up, Markus ambled in from the living room. "Do you think Nancy is a lesbian?" he said.

Chapter 9

Relieved of teaching duties, Ted found he had time on his hands. He could have got on with writing and research, but ideas and beliefs that had seemed rock solid before Karin's death now looked problematic and out of touch. This shift made it difficult for him to spend time at his office, surrounded by colleagues for whom the old verities still held.

When, for instance, Parliament began its fall session, a backbench MP resurrected the familiar idea of a fetal homicide bill. His idea was to make it a separate criminal offence to harm an unborn child in cases where the expectant mother was attacked or killed. Graham Hart went on CBC Radio, his voice dripping with disdain, declaring this bill a sneaky way to establish the personhood of a fetus, despite previous rulings by the Supreme Court.

"It's nothing less than an attack on a woman's right to choose," he said. "All the supporters want is to make abortion difficult or impossible."

"What would you say," asked the interviewer, "to those people we have heard from, many of them pro-choice, that want this bill because they have been touched personally by the death of a pregnant loved one?"

"I'd say nothing at all if they are in the first throes of grief, because they won't be capable of hearing anything. To those that've had a little more time to reflect, I'd say, 'Be careful not to become dupes of the anti-abortion lobby. This bill won't give you what you want in any case, because sentences for separate crimes are commonly served concurrently in Canada.'"

When Graham next appeared at the Department of Criminology, he was greeted with the academic equivalent of high fives. Asked over coffee in the lounge what he thought, Ted replied that the question of concurrent versus consecutive sentences needed to be better explained to the public, and might in some cases bear re-examination by the lawmakers. Eyebrows went up. People remembered suddenly they had a class to teach.

Ted didn't blame them for not knowing how closely the private member's bill touched Karin's circumstances. He had confided in no one regarding her pregnancy, let alone the hard-won victory over infertility it represented. Yet he now saw the criminologists from the outside, saw them not as the loose collection of enquiring minds and free spirits he had thought he belonged to, but as a narrow sect with a rigid orthodoxy. It was as if the boundaries were invisible from the inside, but once you'd been out in the world where real crimes happened, you would never again be able to forget those boundaries were there.

The office felt stuffy these early days of fall. And besides, Ted could see his presence made his colleagues uncomfortable. From their perspective, he was a wounded animal. The herd had to move on for its own survival. So he thought about ways to be elsewhere.

His persistent suspicion that his Dark Arrows dossier had been the object of the fatal break-in made it hard for him to take a hands-off attitude to the police investigation. He remembered the elderly neighbour who had seen the black pickup on the night of the murder. Mentally, he reviewed Nelson's account. Yes, this was someone he and Karin had noticed taking regular walks around the subdivision. In accordance with suburban tradition, few adults did so unless they had a dog to air. Since Karin and Ted were walkers too, they had got in the habit of greeting each other. Karin had somehow discovered that their neighbour's name was George Panopoulos. He wore cardigans for half the year and a blanket coat for the other. Ted thought he must often be too hot or too cold. He appeared to live with a married son or daughter.

To secure an opportunity of speaking to him alone, Ted intercepted him as he was setting out on his afternoon stroll.

"Hello, Mr. Panopoulos. I'm Ted Boudreau."

"Your wife died." Panopoulos touched his white moustache, as if thinking how to soften this abrupt beginning. "I'm sorry."

"Thank you. Do you mind if I walk with you?"

"Please."

Ted fell into step beside Panopoulos. He was a heavy man with a rolling gait. There were no sidewalks, but the two were facing the traffic, which drove around them.

"The police tell me you saw an unfamiliar truck that night."

"Yes. Through the window. I didn't go out."

Ted had the man confirm all the details he had got from Nelson as to colour, make and model. Then he asked, "Was anyone with you at the time? Did anyone else see it?"

"No. Everyone was away that weekend. Camping." Panopoulos gave a little shiver, as if to signify that camping was not to his taste. "They all asked me to go. I said, 'You go. I can camp here in the house.'"

Ted smiled. "Was there anything about that truck that would make it easy to find again?" he asked. "Any scratches or dents you could see? Special hubcaps? Missing hubcaps? An extra big radio antenna perhaps, or a hood ornament?"

When he got no answer right away, Ted wondered if he had gone too fast, asked too many questions at once.

"Everything was standard," Panopoulos said at last. "This is the truck of the man that killed your wife?"

"The truck he was driving, at least. We think so, yes."

"Maybe you'd better talk to the man with the sausage dog."

"Which man?"

"He was going by when I looked out the window. He takes his dog out after dinner. I never meet him on my walks."

"A sausage dog?" Ted searched his memories. "I don't think I've seen him. Does he live on this street?"

"I don't know. Young guy—thirty-five, forty. Fat." Panopoulos laughed and patted his stomach. "Fat like me."

"Did you tell the police about him?"

"I didn't think of him. He was just passing by, nothing to do with the truck. I don't like to tell the police about people that aren't doing anything wrong. But you—you're a neighbour." Panopoulos stopped in his tracks and patted Ted's shoulder. "Somebody killed your wife."

Ted wasn't sleeping at the house, but he paid it a visit after parting with George Panopoulos. He forced himself to go down to the basement, to make sure the wood was holding over the broken window. He made a mental note to call a glazier. Then he drove back to Etobicoke to cook supper for Markus and himself, using commercially prepared pasta sauce, plastic-wrapped linguini, and a Caesar salad kit. He got none of these from the Handy Buy. He had no idea what he could say to Meryl, or Dwayne for that matter.

Returning to Robin Hood Crescent after the evening meal, he started his search by knocking on neighbours' doors to see if any of them owned a dachshund or knew anyone that did. No luck there. Some thought they had seen the man and dog, but not often, which suggested the route of the walk varied from night to night. One thing Ted believed to be in his favour was that a dachshund's legs are short, and he was unlikely to have to scour an area larger than a few blocks. He chose four streets including his own to drive up and down for the hour between nine thirty and ten thirty.

Ten thirty came and went. He decided to extend his patrol by one more full circuit. If that failed, he'd try again next day. Then he saw them on William Tell Boulevard. A heavyset but brisk man encouraging, not to say dragging, a long, low-slung dog. Ted parked well ahead of them and stood waiting as unthreateningly as he knew how on the edge of the road.

"Hi there," he said. "Could I have a word?"

"Lost?" The dog walker had floppy brown hair and a loose, friendly smile.

"No. The fact is I live in this neighbourhood, and my house was broken into sometime before ten p.m. on the Friday of the Labour Day weekend. Were you in town?"

"Yep. Working all weekend, worse luck. Are you on this street? Merkel and I were out walking off our dinners at that time, and we didn't notice anything like a break-in."

The dachshund started to bark at the sound of her name. Ted raised his voice. "I'm on Robin Hood Crescent, the next left there. Were you over that way at all?"

"Quiet, girl. We sometimes go that way, but again there was nothing—"

"Might you have seen a fairly ordinary black pickup truck, North American make?"

Merkel had fallen silent. She was taking the weight off her back legs and looking thoughtful.

"Yes, I do remember that," said her owner. "Because of the licence plate."

"You remember the licence number?" Ted couldn't believe his luck.

"Not all of it. But Merkel was taking one of many rest breaks, and, while I was waiting, my eyes lit on the back of this Ford pickup with a plate AVHD something something something. A three-digit number."

"An Ontario plate?"

"Yep. And incredibly dirty. Maybe someone had smeared mud on it so it wouldn't be readable by the cameras on the toll highway. From where I stood, though, it was perfectly legible—AVHD. I remember the letters because as soon as I saw them, I thought, *A Very Heavy Dachshund*. This dog is twenty-two pounds, so any three-digit number would be very heavy indeed."

"That's tremendously helpful," said Ted. "Might the first digit have been a one, as in 122?"

"I can't see the numbers at all, I'm afraid. It's the same when I read a history book. My eyes slide right over the dates. No, I don't think the first digit was one, just because that's so narrow. But it could have been any of the wide numbers from two to nine. Not zero. I can't do better than that."

Ted nursed his disappointment, at the same time giving Merkel's owner time for a further thought. But when the dog walker spoke again, it was not about the licence plate.

"Was this the truck the burglar carted your stuff away in?" he said.

"Possibly," Ted replied. "You're sure it was a Ford?"

"The brand was right on the tailgate. Letters, not numbers. You can trust me on that."

"Model year?"

"You flatter me. Let's see: it wasn't an antique, though, and not brand new either. Dusty but not rusty."

"Maybe five years old?" Ted prompted.

"Or less. I mean, how much does pickup truck design change?"

"Did you notice a dealer's name? Maybe on the plate holder. Or a plaque or decal attached to the tailgate."

"I'm pretty sure there was no sign of the dealer. Lose much?"

It was the obvious question. "A new computer and quite a lot of data," Ted got out at last.

"Bummer."

Ted wondered briefly whether a fuller answer from him might sharpen the man's memory for numbers, but decided that dubious experiment was better left to a more accommodating time and setting. He handed over one of his cards with his cell number circled. "Could you get in touch if anything else occurs to you?"

"Sure. I don't have any cards with me, but I live in the second house from the end there. My name is Henry McGregor, and I'm in the book."

*   *   *

Maybe Dr. Ornstein had a point. On this visit to Markus, Ted was sleeping better, although his waking hours remained dominated by loneliness and longing. Even a homesickness—not for the marital house, but for the Land of Karin, her geography, her air. In his exile, however, he was also finding new energy for plans of action. Three weeks to the day after the murder, Ted broke the news to the police about Henry McGregor and the Ford pickup. He chose Rodriguez to contact in case Nelson felt Ted was trying to show him up.

"We don't encourage private sleuthing," she said after listening to his news, "but when it bears fruit, we're certainly not going to ignore it. I'll take what you have to the Ministry of Transportation's Vehicle Registration Database. There may be a few similar vehicles with plates beginning AVHD, but not too many to check."

Ted decided it was time to speak to Melody Clark. He hadn't seen her around the department this fall and didn't want anyone there to know he was looking for her. From an acquaintance at the university records office in Simcoe Hall, he learned that she had switched faculties and was taking first year law. He was welcome to leave a number where she could reach him if she chose. He said that wouldn't be necessary. After consulting a law timetable, he intercepted her on her way out of a lecture and took her for coffee at the Bora Laskin library. She looked not only healthier, with her skin ailment in retreat, but very slightly more stylish too. Her hair was shorter, bouncier and dyed a softer blonde than before. Steel-rimmed glasses hid less of her face.

She was clearly surprised at Ted's seeking her out. He could tell by the way she looked at him that he had changed from what she remembered. He ran his hand over his face to make sure he had shaved—he had—and looked to see if he had a food stain on his white shirt, or if his socks were mismatched—no and no.

"Professor Boudreau," she said dutifully as soon as they'd found armchairs in the lounge, "I was very sad to read what happened to your wife. That's dreadful."

"Thank you." Ted took several sips of coffee before going on. "I need to ask you—have you been in communication with anyone about the organization we were discussing?"

"Not at all."

"Tell me, did anything happen to scare you out of criminology?"

"Scare me? No, I switched faculties because I found I needed to be doing something active and not just academic.

When I had to drop my fieldwork, the thrill was gone."

"You haven't had the feeling you were being followed, spied on?"

She started to smile, but cooled it when she saw Ted wasn't joking. "Uh-uh."

"You haven't kept any notes that could have been seen by the wrong people?"

"No way. What's this about?"

"Be careful," Ted urged. "It's possible they suspect I've been collecting data about them. I don't think they know I received any of it from you, but take no chances."

Melody's eyebrows went up. She leaned forward. "You know this how?"

"I'd rather not get into that now—but I have to ask you whether any of the gang owned or had access to a black Ford pickup."

"Oh God, you think the criminal events at your house were a result of my fieldwork."

"They were crimes," Ted retorted, "not criminal events." She might as well drop the social science bafflegab if she wanted to be a lawyer. "The criminal is the one responsible," he added, "not you, not anyone else. Now about that black pickup?"

"There was one parked outside the Grey Mare some nights," said Melody, still stunned but game. "Winter nights, when the bikes were off the road. It belonged to Thorn, the striker. Big, fair-haired oaf with a big curly beard. Keen on motorcycles and physically imposing, but you had the feeling he flapped his jaw too much for that crowd. He was going to have a hard time proving to them he was worth having as a full-patch member."

"Any more to his name than that?"

"Thorn is all I ever heard."

"I remember," said Ted. "He was in your notes. Works in Hamilton."

"Lives out by Drumbo. I only know because he offered to drive me home one night when my car was acting up, and he told me where he went."

"Any other details?"

"He and his mother live on a farm, but don't work it. Stelco pays him better. They rent out a couple of fields. The rest are going back to forest. As I say, he hasn't got the silent thing down." Melody sat forward in her chair. "Look, I didn't want to talk to the police before, while all this was a research project, but with the turn things have taken, don't you think I should?"

"No," Ted insisted. "Leave it to me."

"I no longer have *any* intention of publishing an article."

"Word might get back to the gang, and I don't want anything to draw you to Scar's attention." As her professor, Ted had occupied a position of trust. She had trusted him in ways he'd never asked for and now regretted, but that regret left his obligation undiminished. "If your information is ever used against the Dark Arrows," he told her, "they have to think it came from someone else."

"Okay. Who?"

"You wouldn't have Thorn's actual address?"

"Squarefield Road, I think. I never heard a house number."

"You've given me more than I expected. Thanks."

"Glad to help, but..."

"Yes?" said Ted.

"I hope Thorn didn't kill your wife. It's hard to think of someone you know in that light."

"No question about it."

Ted couldn't get the black truck out of his head. If it had been used in the commission of a crime, a crime more serious than the break and enter that had originally been contemplated, perhaps Thorn would have taken it off the road for a while. It might even be sitting somewhere on Thorn's farm. After leaving Melody, Ted considered how to find the address. He didn't want to show up asking questions at businesses in the village of Drumbo. There Thorn might indeed be known, but inquiries about him were almost certain to get reported back to him the next time he came in.

On his office computer, Ted got a list of Ford dealerships in Thorn's neighbourhood. Then he took the list to a public phone, which he used to call them one by one. He asked each if they had any more pickups like the one they'd sold a man out on Squarefield Road. When was this? Oh, a couple of years back. The name of the purchaser? Ted said he knew him only as Thorn; they'd met in a pub. When asked if he was satisfied with his truck, Thorn had been very complimentary. If the person Ted reached at the dealership were nonplussed, Ted would ask to speak to a senior sales rep. He drew blanks with the first four calls and was prepared for another with the fifth. Then a salesman at Mannheim Ford up towards Kitchener surprised him.

"Oh, yeah. I know who you mean. Big blond guy with a set of Santa Claus whiskers. What model was it he bought now? I'll have it in my card index here if you can hang on."

Ted said he could. He could hear some free-form whistling while the cards were thumbed through.

"Yep, Thornton Laverty, a second-hand black 2003 pickup. On the lot right now, we have a red 2004. I think you'll like it just as well—or does it have to be black?"

Ted said he was afraid so and told the man that he guessed he'd phone around some more.

Next he searched WhitePages.com for the Lavertys' street and phone numbers. With both noted down, he was ready for the drive down to Drumbo. That was an hour west on the 401, which he left at exit 250. He followed Oxford Road four kilometres east to the village crossroads, then turned right and right again off blacktop onto gravel. The potholes were frequent at first, but small and possible to straddle if you didn't mind driving down the middle of the road.

He pulled over and, taking care to block call display, phoned the house while he was still some distance from it. The ringing went on and on unanswered. Ted was encouraged. He preferred not to meet anyone, and it seemed to him a ringing phone is less likely to be ignored when there's no answering machine ready to kick in.

Ted eased the Corolla forward again. On the south side, a mailbox marked Laverty presently loomed up. He parked on the road and continued on foot. A long drive beside a field of dry cornstalks led up a gentle rise to a Victorian red brick farm house with paint peeling from the window trim and a sag in the roof of the front porch. To the left and back, an aluminum two-car garage stood with its overhead door open. There were no four-wheeled vehicles parked, inside it or out. Only a motorcycle under a fitted black slip cover.

The porch deck creaked under Ted's shoes. He reasoned he had to make one more effort to find out whether anyone were home. If someone came to the door, he was prepared to ask how to get back on the freeway and leave. A break in Squarefield Road just beyond the Laverty property would make his confusion plausible. After driving out this far, to miss his chance to look around would be disappointing, but better than being caught snooping with no excuse.

The doorbell was the pre-electric type that rang faintly so long as you were turning the key. He twisted it a few revolutions, then tried knocking. Eventually, he went round to the kitchen door and knocked there. The result in all cases was the same—silence from inside the house. He walked all the way round, scrutinizing the upper windows for any sign of an occupant that didn't want to answer the door. The twitch of a closed curtain, for example. There was no such sign. The curtains were open.

Time for a closer look at the garage. There were recent grease spots on both sides of the pale concrete floor, suggesting the building housed a car or truck in addition to the pickup and Thorn's Harley. Thorn and his mother might have driven to their respective jobs in separate vehicles.

But Ted also found himself wondering if there were anywhere else on the property the black pickup might be parked. Somewhere less conspicuous.

He walked around the house again, this time looking out. Up here he had a good view in the late afternoon sun of the recently harvested fields sloping down and away to the road in front and to the property lines on the east and south sides. No truck lurking anywhere there. To the west, however, lay the scrub forest Melody had mentioned. There seemed to be no track into it from the house.

Ted got back in his Corolla and drove west along Squarefield Road until he found what he was looking for—a track, wide enough for a half-ton, winding in among the trees. There was a metal gate, but no chain or lock. Ted parked on the shoulder facing back the way he'd come and got out of the car to take a closer look. Beside the track, in a clump of dried grass, lay a plasticized NO TRESPASSING sign that appeared to have been ripped off the gate. Thorn had let the defence of his perimeter slide. Ted was emboldened to leave the public road and step inside, even though an encounter with the brawny biker could still be awkward.

The track twisted to the left and back to the right, a low but steep ridge adding to the difficulty of seeing what lay ahead. Less than half the leaves had fallen, but enough to cover any recent tire tracks. A crisp carpet of browns and yellows crackled with the passage of man or squirrel, the only sound apart from the ill-tempered cry of an unseen blue jay overhead. In the low spots, Ted's leather-soled loafers slipped on mud beneath the leaves. The trees and bushes were thick enough to make it impossible to see up to the sky or around the next bend. Shade kept the air cool.

He zipped up his windbreaker and stuck his hands in its pockets for warmth. After two more twists, he saw the anticipated black tailgate, the mud-smeared licence plate, and something unanticipated that gave him a jolt. What looked like the hose from a vacuum cleaner had been attached to the Ford's tailpipe and run up to the driver's side window. Through the rear cab window could be seen the outline of a broad-shouldered man with his head slumped forward. A chill gripped Ted's heart. If his teeth weren't chattering as he warily approached, it was only because he was clenching his jaw.

The truck's engine was not running, presumably because the tank had run dry.

To delay the moment when he would look inside the cab, Ted stared at the licence plate, which was attached with screws rusted tight. Through the grime could be read the raised blue letters AVHD followed by three digits.

Ted's eyes dropped to the grey hose, held over the exhaust

with a twisted wire coat hanger. He cautiously followed the plastic tube around the left tail light assembly and up the left side of the truck. He discovered that its front end had been wedged between the window and the upper frame of the driver's door. A blanket had been stuffed into that portion of the opening not filled by the hose so that the carbon monoxide would not escape before doing its deadly work.

Was there any chance it hadn't?—any slim possibility that the man behind the wheel was still alive? Because then Ted could not just retreat to his car and drive off. Suppose Thorn, if that's who it was, had intended to kill himself, but his nerve had failed him before he lost consciousness, and he had managed to turn off the ignition.

Ted pulled the sleeve of his windbreaker down over his right hand. He tried the truck door an found it unlocked. As it opened, Thorn's stiff, lifeless body fell into his arms. The weight was considerable. The face that struck Ted's shoulder was open-mouthed and cherry red. Ted pushed at the dead man, trying to get a firmer footing on the loose leaves. He feared he might succumb to fumes escaping from the cab, but they must have leaked away, for he managed to shove Thorn back inside. It looked as if the corpse might balance in a more or less upright position, but then Thorn toppled over onto his right side, his head in the passenger seat.

At this point, Ted saw the note, a single sheet of white printer paper with bold black lettering. He needed to know if this was a confession to Quirk's murder. He hurried around the truck and, with hands bare, pulled open the passenger door—by now thoroughly reckless as to the fingerprints he was leaving. He had to tug the paper out from under the dead man's curly blond beard so he could read it.

"I played SM games with a brother's ol' lady," said the

note. "I am too ashamed to live. Thorn."

The signature—like the rest of the note—was printed, not handwritten. There was no date.

Time to get out. The flight reflex obliterated any horror or queasiness. Ted left the note on the seat, slammed the cab door, and made for his own car. What started as a fast walk ended in a run. He wasted no time driving back to the 401 and heading east. Only at the service centre between Cambridge and Guelph did he stop to deliberate over coffee what he had better do. When he sat down to relax at last, his hands started shaking. The coffee was tepid by the time he was able to raise the cup to his lips. He found as well that his stomach didn't want it.

He needed the evening to collect himself—not to spend answering the repetitive questions of various levels of a whole new suspicious police force, whether the Oxford County constabulary or the OPP. Nor did he want to have to justify his meddling to the detectives of Peel Regional. So he was tempted to tell no one. On the other hand, it nauseated Ted to think of leaving a human body quietly to rot. Thorn's mother might be quite used to her son's taking off for a few days with biker friends, and some time could elapse before she thought to visit the wooded corner of her property where the pickup was stashed. How would Thorn look and smell by then?

On his cellphone, Ted placed an anonymous call to the Crime Stoppers tips line. He told the operator where the body of a suicide might be found—though his years of researching gangs made him doubt it was a suicide. Even without knowing Thorn, he thought the note far-fetched in content and far too easy to forge. It seemed to be saying to the authorities:

We'll give you a convenient explanation. Take it if you want an easy life. Take it if you think a dead biker is always good news, and you see no point in inquiring further.

But be aware also that we run our own parallel justice system, and that we always collect on our debts and settle our accounts.

The we in this case, Ted thought, must be the Dark Arrows, the gang that never flew its colours in public. Thorn had not been killed in what the media had taken to calling "execution style," with a bullet to the back of the head. That style was more typical of the big international biker federations that didn't feel threatened by a little publicity.

Melody had suggested Thorn was indiscreet. Perhaps the Dark Arrows had killed him for sexual shenanigans, or perhaps because he talked too much to the wrong people about gang affairs. But the fact that his truck had been on Ted's street the night of September 1 prompted another line of speculation. If Thorn had been assigned to steal Ted's computer and disks, perhaps he had been punished for not having secured the information he had been sent for. Or for having attracted too much heat by killing someone.

While staring at his full cardboard coffee cup in his booth by the window, Ted entertained the possibility that he had held in his arms the lifeless body of Karin's murderer, and that more justice had been done her—albeit by a criminal gang—than Ted could have looked for from the courts. Tempting thought! All the more tempting in that Thorn and his family were strangers.

Yes, but had the right party been punished? Tight-lipped as Nelson had been about the gum left on the stairs, Ted suspected it was Shawn's. Besides, Ted couldn't see a man Thorn's size climbing in through that basement window, whereas for a kid like Shawn it would have been no surprising feat. Scar could have put Shawn up to the burglary and have had Thorn lend his truck. Risky that, though perhaps the gang had felt there were risks also in stealing a vehicle. Possibly

Shawn had been instructed to remove the licence plates from the Ford, but because of the rusty bolts, he had tried none too successfully to obscure the numbers with mud instead.

Beyond the plate glass windows of the service centre McDonald's, dusk had drawn in. Ted told Markus's voice mail he'd be eating dinner out, though at present he no more wanted food than company. He had an unpleasant moment when he wondered if, as a result of his encounter with Thorn, the flashbacks to finding Karin were going to start up again. A walk around the darkening parking lot in the cool air returned him to the present, and he climbed into his car feeling less at the mercy of his thoughts, though still uncertain as to what he should do or expect.

*   *   *

He got to sleep late Friday night and would have slept in late Saturday morning but for a prolonged barrage of door knocking at eight a.m. When the knocking went unanswered, he concluded Markus must have gone for his morning run. Pulling on a dressing gown, Ted got up to answer the door himself. He opened it to find Detective James Nelson on the verandah.

Ted hadn't seen the detective since the Labour Day weekend and was surprised at how unwell he looked. Nelson was suffering from the sneezes and sniffles of a head cold. His eyes moved restlessly, as if he were afraid he was missing something. When he started speaking, it was plain he was out of sorts. "Man, you must think we are cretins!"

"Won't you come in and sit down?" said Ted.

In two strides, Nelson was across Markus's living room and in the compact kitchen. He took a place at the table there without pausing for breath. "Yesterday morning you gave

Detective Rodriguez a vehicle description and the letter portion of a licence plate. Are you pretending you aren't the person that discovered that very vehicle yesterday afternoon in Oxford County?"

"No," said Ted, "I'm not."

"You have two detectives, Ted—Rodriguez and myself—prepared to take your calls at any hour and use what you've got to nail the dirtball that killed your wife. We are on your side, as you ought to know by now." Nelson whipped a tissue from his jeans pocket and blew his nose. "So why the juvenile call to Crime Stoppers?"

"Because I messed up the scene. I touched the door handles. I moved the body. I handled the note. I thought if I called you, you'd be just as unhappy with me as you are now."

"I'm due for a decongestant tablet. Could I have a glass of water?"

By the time Ted brought it, Nelson's blood pressure—or at least his decibel level—had dropped appreciably. "Truth is," he said, "if that gentleman with the big yellow beard took his own life, there is no crime, and no scene as such."

"Think he did?" asked Ted.

"Other forces will make that determination. Here's what matters to my investigation. First, if it was murder, not suicide, our boy Shawn Whittaker didn't do it. He has convincing alibis for any time the pathologist thinks it's possible for death to have occurred. Second, despite your pawing around, we did find Shawn's prints in that truck."

"None were found in my house," said Ted. "I thought you'd concluded he wore gloves."

"I did, and he probably wore them while driving too. But it's not so easy to take a CD out of its jewel case and load it with gloves on."

"The truck had a CD player?" Ted was becoming aware of his caffeine deficit. "I didn't notice."

"That's why we were able to read *his* prints."

"So do you have enough to charge him?"

"I'd like more. And that's where you come in. If—instead of Crime Stoppers—you'd called me, I'd have had the prints from that truck hours earlier and wouldn't have had to work literally in the dark. Now you're going to give me everything you have. And from now on, you're going to tell me everything you learn as soon as you learn it. Because if you hold out on me again, Ted, I'll see that this case goes into the freezer. You hear me?"

"Yes, sure."

But Ted still wasn't ready to give him Melody. Letting her be turned into the Crown's key witness against the bikers would be like painting a bull's eye on her back.

"So what is your next move?" asked Nelson.

"Beats me. Offering you a coffee?"

"If you let me make it."

Nelson was making it when the front door banged open. Markus's post-exertion pants and gasps could be heard even before he appeared in the kitchen wearing a blue-and-yellow exercise outfit and a sheen of sweat. He buried his face in a tea towel. When his eyes had been wiped, they surveyed the detective balefully.

"Are you preparing something we can drink," he inquired, "or mixing concrete?"

Nelson sniffed. "I like it strong, Markus with a K. Add water if you like."

"Thank you. Have we laid a charge yet?"

"Getting closer."

Markus took the third and last seat at his kitchen table,

the tea towel hung around his neck. "I was thinking," he said, "that if you found Ted's computer, it might be useful evidence."

"We've executed search warrants at Shawn Whittaker's home and at his mother's store, not to mention all the pawn shops and known fences we've checked out. Nada. Ted thinks the computer was stolen for a biker gang, but neither my force nor the OPP have caught up with them yet. What do you suggest?"

"It sounds to me as if these bikers didn't want a computer. They wanted to know what Ted had on his computer about *them*. When they discovered there wasn't anything in the computer, I'm wondering if they mightn't have let Shawn keep it, on the understanding that if he was caught with it, he was on his own, and he'd better not bring them into it."

"So where did Shawn hide it?" said Nelson. "Did he dig a hole and bury it?"

"Karin told me—I forget in what context—that one of the boys at the gas bar volunteered in a—can we pour that now?"

"Volunteered in a what?" asked Ted. This was all news to him.

Markus made them wait while the coffee was thinned.

"Volunteered," said Markus when he was good and ready, "in a thrift shop. His mother's notion of the type of community service best suited to his talents, or some such thing. I've seen computers for sale in such places, but I'd never think of buying one, nor would most of the customers. No hook-up instructions. No guarantees. You'd have to be a geek to give them a second look."

"You're suggesting one of the Whittakers donated my computer to a thrift shop?" said Ted.

"Nothing so philanthropic. But maybe he's storing it there

till the heat dies down."

"And if some geek bought it in the meantime...?" asked Nelson.

"It was just a thought," said Markus. "Anyone want eggs?"

While he was cooking them, Nelson worked his cellphone.

"Meryl Whittaker," he presently announced, "says her son Shawn volunteers at the Fair Share Shop in Meadowvale Town Centre. Who's coming?"

*   *   *

After breakfast, Ted dressed and climbed into the front passenger seat of Nelson's unmarked Impala.

The Fair Share occupied a hangar-like space at one corner of a vast shopping plaza. The shop had the smell of all second-hand clothes, no matter how many times washed. Ted and the detective made their way down aisles of blouses and bed linens, sneakers and slacks. Then there were the kitchen appliances—toasters with fraying cords, microwave ovens with cracked glass in the doors. The computers were balanced on shelves along the back walls. Ted recognized a Compaq Armada laptop from the mid-to-late nineties and even a Mac Plus desktop from the eighties. He saw nothing, however, that looked like his Dell XPS 700 and told Nelson so. This was enough to send the detective looking for the senior person on shift. She proved to be a middle-aged blondish woman with a butch haircut. On her denim vest she wore a name tag that identified her as Lu and a large round orange and blue button that read, SHOW CARING THRU SHARING. Nelson showed his badge and asked to see the backroom.

"Sure thing," said Lu. There was a smoker's rasp to her voice. "Just watch your step."

The clothes in the backroom had, from their smell, not all been washed. A couple of old top-loading machines were working on it, but the size of the piles on the floor promised a long campaign. In this room too, there were shelves of dated and suspect hardware. Ted started working his way along them.

"Looking for anything in particular?" Lu asked.

"Do you have a volunteer here named Shawn Whittaker?" said Nelson.

"Uh-huh. He's not in right now."

"Did he bring in a computer sometime this month?"

"As a matter of fact, yes. It should be on that shelf, waiting to be priced. Keep looking. Some of the machines are behind others."

Ted kept looking.

"Where did he get this computer?" asked Nelson.

"Beats me. We've got enough to worry about—sorting and selling—without finding out where all the stuff comes from. A lot of it is just dropped off in a box at the door, and there's no one to ask anyway."

"Here it is," said Ted, wondering how he could be so sure. The equipment was too new to be distinguished by any scratches, coffee stains or sticky keys. And yet he believed he was going on something more than the unlikelihood of any other computer like his finding its way here. It gave him no joy that from now on it was going to be much harder to hope for Shawn's innocence. "In behind," he added, "as you said. And it has a SOLD sticker on it."

"Now that's something I do object to," Lu grumbled. "I've told the staff it's strictly cash and carry. We're not a storage depot. You buy it—you take it with you."

Nelson came over to look at the computer. He matched the serial number against the one he had written in his notebook, the one Ted had given him the night of the break-in.

"How could it have been bought," said Ted, "if it hadn't even been priced?"

"Whoever put the sticker on will have to answer that one. Until I talk to the staff, I've no idea who that was."

Nelson got Lu to give him her last name and the names of the store employees and volunteers.

"And what kind of person is Shawn Whittaker, Ms. Moscovitch? How do you find him?"

"Smooth. Most of the people here are well-meaning but rough-edged. Shawn's easy to deal with because he's never out of sorts. He doesn't have good work habits, but that's par for the course around here. I usually have to ask four to six times if I want something done. In that respect, he's pretty average."

Chapter 10

Shawn Whittaker felt important as never before, and scared. Things weren't going well. It looked like they wouldn't for a long time. Between the Peel cops' interrogations, he had lots of time to think of how it could all have gone better.

The night Scar had motored into Shawn's life on his panhead bobber had promised so much glamour. Scar inspired confidence. Whenever they talked at the Handy Buy, Shawn felt himself capable of more. Not that he was in awe of Scar. Shawn thought he was just as cool as the biker. It was just that if you were a superior person, you wanted others of your kind around you. You thrived in their company. The rest of the human race, whether they were strangers or your family, just dragged you down.

The job Scar had proposed had sounded easy. The house was already one Shawn had his eye on. He knew the security company sign was a leftover from the previous owner, and he knew when the couple would be away. Why did that freaky woman have to go changing her plans without telling him? Yeah, that would have saved her and him some grief. Just a simple phone call: *Shawn, I've changed my mind. I'm not going to the cottage Friday night after all. I'll be sleeping in the city.* As if.

Killing her hadn't been in the program. Scar had thought it pretty uncool; that was a minor point, though, as Scar hadn't been there. A bigger point was that Shawn liked the woman. She was friendly, not boring. And she was hot in an older sort of way. Shawn was definitely going to miss her. The

154

need to kill her was a drag.

The killing, on the other hand, once he'd really accepted the idea—the power to do that... Yeah, that had been great. Looming up before her in that tiny vestibule. The startled look on her freckled face. Something told Shawn she was afraid of those cellar stairs. The panic in her eyes pointed to them, drew them to his attention, so of course he had to push her down them. It seemed natural, easy, what the situation called for.

Damned thing was she wouldn't fall. She kept her balance, however closely he crowded her, however hard he pushed. She always managed to get a steadying hand on the rail. Not until the very bottom did he manage to trip her, get her pinned to the basement floor. Now she looked like a proper victim, though she still hadn't cried out at all. She gave up her chance for last words, and Shawn did what the fall had been supposed to do—crack her skull like a nut.

He still had nightmares about it, but when he was awake and had his head together, he felt extra mature. Had Scar ever broken open anyone's cranium? Shawn had. He was in the major leagues.

Scar didn't like that there'd been a murder, and he didn't like it that neither the computer nor the disks had what Scar wanted. Still he'd let Shawn have both the computer and X tabs with a street value of six hundred dollars or more. Enough to get him started in a new career. When he had enough for a condo of his own, he'd go back to the Fair Share and pick up his computer to put in it. Shawn counted himself a natural for the rave scene. He was young. He'd be accepted much more easily by the teenaged ravettes than a whiskery old guy like Scar would be.

And XTC was a safe drug. Except that it was supposed to make you love everyone, which was the last thing Shawn wanted. But safe in the sense that users rarely died, and only if they were stupid enough to let their bodies overheat or if they drank too much water. Shawn didn't want to push drugs that killed people. That would attract too much attention from the police.

Bad break about the undercover babe in the Falls. He'd seen the lines around her eyes but just thought she partied too hard. As soon as he was nabbed, he decided he wasn't going to talk. He liked to talk, so it was going to be difficult and no fun either.

He did ask "to retain and instruct counsel"—by now having the caution down pat. He considered applying for legal aid but was afraid they'd ask him to sell his Harley. He had no inclination to do that and couldn't legally in any case on account of the missing serial numbers. So he ended up phoning the well-meaning old dork who'd represented him in youth court.

Shawn remembered Fred Fanning as a tired-looking baldie in his sixties, who had been easing himself out of criminal work. His ambition, Shawn had heard him say, was to move into something quieter like wills. He wore shapeless suits and white shirts that always looked as if they were struggling to make it through their second day. Maybe a more aggressive partner wore them on day one.

Fred Fanning thought that Shawn would find it hard to beat the trafficking charge: seventeen tabs were found on him and he'd nothing to bargain with if he persisted in refusing to say where the ecstasy had come from. On the other hand, bail shouldn't be a problem. This was Shawn's first offence as an adult, and as a young offender he'd always shown up for his court dates and kept his nose clean before them.

Fanning hoped Shawn didn't expect him to drive down to

the Falls that night. Shawn said not to rush. It would be soon enough if he made it to the bail hearing in the morning. In the meantime, Shawn planned to drink the police coffee and smoke their cigarettes while telling them nothing.

He pretty well thought they'd given up trying to pump him by the time the black dude named Nelson arrived. Shawn sort of thought he must be a policeman, or what would he have been doing there? But he didn't ask to see a badge. Nelson, who wore a silver chain Shawn coveted at first sight, looked in turn with interest at Shawn's hoodie. Maybe he'd never before seen the colour, which was called asphalt—and which, to Shawn's mind, was even less visible than black at night.

"This rocks," said Nelson, rubbing the cloth between his thumb and finger. "Buy this here in the Falls?"

Shawn couldn't help preening a little. "Here? There's nothing but tourist junk here. I bought it at Sherway Gardens last spring."

"And I bet you don't lend it to anyone, do you?"

Weird that this cool guy would want to borrow Shawn's hoodie, but that seemed to be the case. "Afraid not." Shawn put some regret in his voice, just to keep life pleasant.

"Right." Nelson briskly removed the ashtray containing Shawn's butts. "I understand, Mr. Whittaker, that you were informed of and that you exercised your right to phone a lawyer before interrogation on the soliciting and trafficking charges. And, from what I hear, you've been handling yourself well. I just have to ask if you wish to instruct counsel further now that the charge you're to be interrogated on is break and enter."

Choke on it, Bling Boy! Shawn managed not to say.

*   *   *

157

Fred Fanning and Meryl were at the boxy, modern St. Catharines courthouse in the morning when Shawn went before the Justice of the Peace in Courtroom 3. The lady in the black gown and green sash huffed and puffed a little before releasing Shawn on his own undertaking without surety or deposit and with only three conditions: he was to neither use nor possess non-prescription drugs; he was to continue to be employed in his mother's store; and he was to continue to live at home.

Meryl was sick at heart: she had truly thought that now that Shawn was in his twenties he was through with courts and crimes. Nevertheless, her first reaction upon stepping out with her son and his lawyer into the fresh air was relief.

"Well," she said, "nothing too harsh in those conditions. Are you going to ride your motorcycle home?"

"How else is it going to get there?" Shawn teased. He knew he'd be seeing Detective James Nelson again in Mississauga, and wasn't feeling nearly so jaunty as he pretended.

"I just wondered. It's looking like rain. Now Fred, how about I stand the three of us some lunch before I drive Shawn to the police station to pick up his bike? I see a Tim's sign up there on the corner."

Fred Fanning looked glum and said he'd better hit the road back to Toronto. He already had his car keys in his hand. Shawn spotted the lawyer's ancient, mustard-coloured Mercedes in the lot across the street—a relic, Shawn guessed, of his long-ago prosperous years.

"A coffee then, Fred. It'll be a chance for Shawn and me to say a proper thank you."

"If it's going to rain," said Shawn, "I'd rather get going. Just one question, Fred. Excuse us a moment, will you, Mom?"

Meryl thought, since she was paying Fred's bills, she had a right to be part of this conversation, but she did want Shawn to feel mature. She said she'd wait in her car, parked by the curb in front of City Hall. Five minutes max!

"Can they lock me up again on this B and E thing?" Shawn asked when she was out of hearing.

"What thing?"

"I called you about it last night," Shawn replied patiently, even though he believed vagueness this vague had to be an act.

"You mean when you woke me the second time. Your freedom of movement is already constrained by these bail conditions this morning. If they think they have enough evidence to charge you with breaking and entering, they might just give you a court date without ever arresting you."

* * *

Back home in Mississauga, Nelson and his Latina partner kept coming by the store or the house and pestering Shawn with questions about events at 19 Robin Hood Crescent on the Friday of the Labour Day weekend. The soliciting and trafficking charges were back burner stuff now. They even got him to go before the video camera at the cop shop. Much good it did them.

What did Shawn know about the Dark Arrows? He said he knew nothing. Well, what about the biker named Scar, who had come to the Handy Buy asking for him? Shawn said he didn't know anything about that either.

Nelson shook his head. There were awkward circumstances that needed clearing up. How, for example, did Shawn explain the presence of threads from his asphalt-grey hoodie on glass in Ted Boudreau's basement window? How did he explain the presence of gum he had chewed on Ted Boudreau's stair runner? Shawn shrugged. Someone was trying to frame him. He didn't know who.

Later Nelson asked how Shawn explained the presence of his fingerprints in the late Thornton Laverty's truck. How did he explain the presence of his fingerprints on the jewel case of a CD stolen from Ted Boudreau's house and found in said truck? How on earth did he explain taking Ted Boudreau's computer to the Fair Share?

It was after the discovery of the computer that Shawn was charged with first degree murder, and a Justice of the Peace sent him to the Maplehurst Correctional Complex in Milton.

These developments triggered a certain amount of media attention and a change in his legal representation. On September 25, a thirtyish barrister named Natasha Cullen approached Shawn's mother and volunteered her services. She had, she said, already spoken to Fred Fanning, and he was agreeable to the idea of handing Shawn's case over to her. She was willing to take it on for less than Fanning was charging. A heartbroken Meryl told Natasha Cullen that she'd speak to Fred and to her son.

The three-way meeting took place at the jail, some forty klicks from the Handy Buy. Morning visiting hours were from nine thirty to eleven fifteen, but—owing to some unexplained "situation"—the guards didn't let Fred and Meryl in till ten. There were four sets of locked doors to pass through before they reached a room resembling a high school cafeteria with a glassed-in guard station in one corner. Under the artificial light, they were confronted by rows of rectangular tables, at each of which four hard, backless stools were bolted to the floor. There was no way not to be overheard by people at neighbouring tables.

When the prisoners were at length allowed to enter the room through a door on the opposite side, Shawn affected to look as if none of the institutional hardness bothered him.

Meryl was in two minds about this. She didn't want his spirit broken, of course, but she wanted him to have a proper realization that he was confined among adult offenders for the first time in his life and that he should never allow himself to feel that he belonged here. When Shawn made no move to embrace her before swinging himself onto the stool opposite, she thought physical contact must be forbidden. Then she saw other prisoners hugging sweethearts or parents. Mastering a pang, she turned briskly to Fred Fanning and urged him to tell her son about this Cullen woman, who had shown such confidence she could get him out.

"She's a publicity seeker," said Fred. "But that doesn't mean she isn't good. She belongs to a firm that's always trying to outdo itself in involvement in headline-catching cases. Three-parent families, mercy killing, people detained on security certificates, mortgage fraud, whatever's in the news. Her thinking is that the reputation she establishes will attract enough business in future to offset lower fees now. At the same time, she does her homework and, considering the tough cases she takes on, her success rate is remarkable."

"Is she a babe?" said Shawn.

Meryl gave him a dirty look. Her dirty looks had never had much effect on him. This one was the dirtiest yet, but he didn't care. He was all grown up.

"Why don't you check her out?" said Fred, plainly anxious to pass on a client who had grown too hot for him to handle.

"You're not going to be checking her out, honey," said Meryl. Her voice sounded hard to her. "We know this murder charge is a crock. You have to decide whether you think Ms. Cullen has what it's going to take to clear it all up. Now I'm counting on you, Shawn."

At Shawn's invitation, Natasha Cullen came to Maplehurst

the next day. She had a thin, acne-scarred face and a chest flatter than a fit man's. She wore no make-up. Her grey-blue suit looked like an airforce uniform that had spent three years behind the wire of a prison camp. Shawn's first thought was that this is what the policewoman in Niagara Falls should have looked like. Then he'd never have made the mistake he had. Still, it was his habit to be pleasant with someone he was meeting for the first time, and he looked for something flattering to say.

"I like your hair, Natasha." He did like it. It was sandy-coloured and shorter in the back than in the front, where it fell in a curve over her forehead.

She combed it back with her fingers. "I'll give you my stylist's name later," she said. "First things first. If I represent you, I don't have to believe you're innocent. My job is to compel the Crown to make its case. If they don't make it, you're not guilty. I understand there are a pack of things you don't want to talk about. Fine. But I do need to know everything about that Friday night that the prosecution knows or has a good chance of finding out before we go into court. Clear enough?"

"Crystal clear." Shawn liked this dumpy chick's torque.

"Let's go through some of the Crown's evidence," said Natasha Cullen. "When you said you never lend your hoodie to anyone, was that before or after the police told you they were interested in the break-in?"

"Before, I think."

"Good. And—I take it—before you were advised of your right to retain and instruct counsel with respect to the break-in charge?"

"Uh-huh."

"Good. And, subsequent to being so advised, did you admit that the hoodie was not out of your possession or control on the Friday of the Labour Day weekend?"

"It was late. I don't remember." Let's see how uptight this makes her, Shawn thought.

Natasha Cullen ran a set of crooked upper teeth over her lower lip.

"Whatever statement the police took from you will have to be disclosed to the defence. We'll see what they think they've got then. You say it was late. Would you say you were deprived of sleep?"

"Maybe. I didn't ask to lie down."

"With all those police around, you were too intimidated to ask. Your DNA was collected from cigarette butts. Was that DNA taken with your consent?"

"No. I left the butts in an ash tray, and the police took them to the lab."

"Were anyone else's butts in that ash tray?"

"I don't know."

"Did you see anyone else smoking in that police station?"

"No, I didn't."

"Not surprising considering that smoking is illegal in all workplaces in Ontario, including government offices. Are you a regular smoker of tobacco?"

"I smoke Mary Jane when I have a choice," said Shawn with a wink.

"And I take it you usually do have the choice, when you're not in a police station—is that a nod? Yes? Then let's not complicate the question. Let's just say no, you're not a regular smoker of tobacco. Perhaps this drug you are not used to, namely nicotine, influenced you to say things in your statement you would not normally have said."

Shawn laughed. "Pretty cool. What are we going to do about my prints in the truck?"

"There's always something we can do." Natasha Cullen shut

her notebook and pushed back her hair. "But before we go further, are you retaining me? Your mother says it's up to you."

*   *   *

Cliff Whittaker knew Shawn was in trouble again. The drug trafficking charge pained him, but he didn't really know what ecstasy was, so the crime couldn't help but seem a bit abstract. He understood the pills were related to amphetamines, which were common enough among truckers trying to squeeze a few more hours into a day. Cliff had more respect for his body than that but wasn't inclined to be judgemental. And then these X tabs were supposed to be hallucinogenic as well, which no one thought made driving easier. Maybe in a club setting they were safe enough. As for talking to a prostitute, that was something that as a single man he'd done himself, not that he was about to admit it to Meryl.

Cliff had signed his family up for a long distance rate plan. He believed he stayed in touch pretty well while he was on the road. Still, separated by two thousand kilometres or more, with Meryl's voice his only sensory link to home, he found it hard to come to grips with the doings of his younger son.

How difficult Cliff found it Meryl well knew. Her husband was in northern Manitoba when the more serious charges were laid on September 23, so Meryl made a point of asking the Peel Regional policewoman who broke the news to her whether the force could postpone releasing Shawn's name to the media until the young man's father returned home. Detective Rodriguez replied that she was not in a position to make any promises of this kind, but that she would be certain to relay Meryl's request up the chain of command. So it was that on his way south from The Pas, Cliff heard on the news that charges had now been laid in the case of the Labour Day weekend break-in and murder in Mississauga, without ever guessing that Shawn could be involved. Nor did Meryl speak to him at three a.m. on September 28, when he at last brought his cab's wheels to rest in his own drive.

On waking up at eleven thirty, Cliff found by his pillow a note in her hand asking him to come to the Handy Buy as soon as he'd had his breakfast and by no means to turn on the radio. This was odd to his way of thinking. But he couldn't ask Dwayne, who was at his classes. When he phoned the shop, Meryl said she was with a customer and that she'd speak to him when he came down.

Cliff opened the fridge and looked at the pot of active-culture yogourt Meryl had left for him. She thought he ate too much grease when he was on the road and tried on the rare occasions when he was home to clean him up. He'd never got used to the taste of yogourt, though, especially Meryl's healthy unsweetened kind, and he needed a proper breakfast if he was to handle a heavy conversation. He reached for the eggs, boiled one for four minutes, and broke it over a piece of whole wheat toast. Not much grease there. When he'd finished that, he felt he could use another piece of toast at least, but his trousers were already tight in the waist, and he didn't want to have to replace all the forty-twos in his closet with forty-fours. He wolfed down a banana in three bites before he could think whether the potassium—good—outweighed the calories—unnecessary. Coffee he didn't bother making. He could get that at the Handy Buy. It would be bad coffee, but no worse than he drank every day on the road, and there was no point in spoiling himself for the two days he was home.

Meryl had a lineup at the till when Cliff arrived, so he slid into the washroom and did the one o'clock inspection for her. Where did the toilet paper go? Someone must be collecting for a Hallowe'en costume as a mummy. The tiles and porcelain were exemplary, though. The trucker's eye had lots of basis for comparison. His Meryl kept her place so clean, he believed, that she inspired the customers to wipe the basin and mirror after themselves.

During the next quiet interval, Cliff sat to Meryl's left behind the counter on a stool matching hers. The compressor on one of the freezer cabinets was growling a bit. He wondered if he shouldn't have a look at it after their talk. The only other sound was the dry swish of passing traffic. The sky had been darkening when he drove down from the house, but he could hear without looking out that the clouds had not yet burst. Wet tires had a song of their own.

Beside him, Meryl seemed to be gathering her courage. She opened her mouth, shut it again, then straightened her shoulders and, facing her husband, came out with what she had to say.

"Cliff, Shawn has been charged with breaking into a customer's home and murdering her."

"Hold on!" Cliff wrestled with his shock. When he studied Meryl's face, she must have seen that he doubted his hearing, for she was nodding grimly. He couldn't think what to ask first. "Which customer are you talking about?"

"Her name is Karin. I don't know if you know her." Meryl sounded knocked flat, but pushed on anyway. The way she always did. "Regular for gas, sometimes treats. Early thirties, I'd guess. Summer evenings, she'd come in for ice cream with her husband."

"Oh, yeah—redhead, right? I just didn't connect her with the Karin they've been jawing about on the radio. I heard there'd been an arrest."

"Shawn."

"I don't believe it."

"He's in jail."

"They must have made a mistake."

"Cliff—Cliff, you're never here."

She exaggerates when she's upset, Cliff told himself. "I know my boys," he soothed.

"Remember, Shawn did break into cars."

"Youthful pranks, Mer. He's grown up since then."

"What sitcom did you get *that* from?"

Cliff felt the sting. It meant Meryl was more than upset. She was angry, something that didn't happen more than twice a year. Experience told him that when it did, his best course was not to pour fuel on the fire. They said nothing more to each other until after the next two customers had been served and left the store. Then the sky opened. The start of the rain, sheets of it drumming the tin roof above them and pounding the asphalt apron in front of the store, practically guaranteed the couple an undisturbed interval. When they sat down again, Meryl's hand slipped into Cliff's.

"I'm sorry, baby," she said. "I'd love to share that old-time view you have of boys that soap people's windows and tip over their outhouses and then grow up to be responsible homeowners and truckers. But what if Shawn?—what if?— oh, Jesus, Cliff—maybe Shawn turned out..."

"What?"

"Different."

Cliff was momentarily shaken. "You think so?" he asked.

"I don't know what to think. He won't talk to me about what happened that night. I mean—" She looked down at her hand tucked into his. "Even if he did it, he's still our son—but I'll never be able to feel the same about him."

"Mer..." Cliff breathed again. She hadn't made her mind

up yet. He could still hope. "Why couldn't it be a mistake?" he asked. "Like the one the police made with that Arar guy you hear about on every second newscast. Fred Fanning will straighten this out."

"Not Fred. Fred's lost his stomach for our son and his trouble. There's someone else, a woman, that wants to defend him."

"Does Shawn like her?"

"He says she makes him laugh. I tried to tell him that's not the point."

Meryl's shoulders were drooping now, and there was a quiver in her lower lip. If Cliff let himself, he could get angry too. Guilty or innocent, how could Shawn put his family through this? Someone had to stay calm, though, and it had better be Cliff, even at the risk of being thought slow.

"I know this is rough," he said. "Look, I'll mind the store while you go home and get a good rest. When you get up, everything will look better."

"We have to arrange bail for him. It won't be like when he was a juvenile and they released him on just his undertaking that he'd show up for his trial. Or even like this Niagara business. It's murder he's charged with! They may not let him come home at all. And if they do, they're going to want to know how much we can afford."

"We're in good shape, Mer. The truck's almost paid off. Go home as soon as the rain stops. Get some rest. Then we'll talk about it."

*　　*　　*

Ted's week with Markus had stretched into two. Both men felt the need of a well-ordered existence just now, and Ted found routine easier to maintain when compelled to share someone else's living space. Markus continued to counsel his angry clients, and indeed was kept busy by the judges, who often made anger management part of a conditional sentence. Meanwhile, in the lulls of the criminal investigation, Ted worked as best he could on his academic writing.

Then two days before Shawn's bail hearing—on Monday, October 2—Markus came home with a story of a woman whose husband would tell her stories of injustices he'd suffered at work and let her get indignant for him. She was doubly angry because he seemed so indifferent himself. Markus had had to explain to her that she should let her husband do his own reacting, not feel she had to shoulder that responsibility herself.

"The situation reminded me of us two," said Markus, spooning pickled herring onto two plates. "I get furious at you for staying so cool."

"Cool?" Ted put down the glass of mineral water he was raising to his lips. "No cooler than you, Markus."

"I'm seething inside."

"Inside—exactly." Ted helped himself to pickles and salad. "Although right now I'm more sorrowful than angry, I think."

"Sorry for yourself?"

"How could I not be? But sorry for Karin too, about everything she's missing. The autumn colours she went nuts over. The new opera house she never got to play in. The painfully corny movies she won't get to see." In his mind Ted added, the child she'll never watch grow up healthy, take music lessons, make the swimming team, graduate, fall in love, give her grandchildren. Or do none of the above and still fill her heart to bursting with fierce joy. The crisp bread cracked in Ted's hand. "Maybe angry too," he added, "underneath. The rotten unfairness of it."

Markus looked pleased to have got him going. "So what are they going to do to Shawn Whittaker?"

"First degree murder carries a mandatory life sentence without eligibility for parole for twenty-five years."

"Guess I'll have to keep eating my veggies," said Markus, with a chuckle, "so I can be there with my gopher gun to meet him at the prison gates when he gets out."

The joke stank; still, Ted bit. It occurred to him that some time down the road Shawn might try to convince a judge that he was a changed man and that a jury should be given the chance to revisit the conditions of his parole eligibility.

"If you're really lucky," he replied, "he'll get out under the faint hope clause after fifteen years. Think of it: a whole decade less to wait."

"And you, Ted? What would you like to do to him?"

"Nothing. I never want to see him again. Remember, Markus—I know him. He's counted change out for me. We've traded banalities about the weather. I'm hoping there was someone else that broke into the house with him and did the murder, because I hate to think that a young man I could practically draw you a picture of smashed the life out of Karin on our basement floor. He's in custody now. If he is guilty, let him die in custody. Quietly, in his sleep." Then Ted found himself voicing an opinion that repeated on campus would be a career-ender. "A state that declines to hang murderers should keep them until they're dead."

When they had eaten, Markus cleared the dishes and made coffee.

"Retribution is in bad odour," he said later, punching on the CD player. "If you want to punish someone for a crime, it means you're vengeful. How terrible! What's wrong with vengeance, I'd like to know? Think how Karin loved Verdi.

There's revenge in just about all his stuff."

Ted was not a lifelong Verdi fan like Markus, but had gone when Karin had been in the orchestra. "In the operas I've seen," he said, "vengeance goes hideously wrong—*Rigoletto, A Masked Ball...*"

"But not in *Macbeth*." Markus gestured towards the stereo speakers, which were keening out an ominous prelude. "Not in either Verdi or Shakespeare. Are you with Macduff the avenger or are you against him?"

"Drama is different from life."

Markus smiled grimly.

"Also," said Ted, "if I remember right, an army comes to topple Macbeth from the throne, an army Macduff is part of. It's not as if he goes careening around on his own."

"If there'd been no army available, I've a feeling he would have, though. We should go to the bail hearing on Wednesday."

"Why?" Ted was startled. Hadn't he just told Markus he had no desire to see Shawn this side of hell?

"Watch the circus. If they let him out, I won't have to eat my veggies after all. And you know the kicker, Ted? I'm now taking beta blockers to slow down my heart. That stuff is so good for your aim that it's banned in competitive shooting."

Give it a rest, thought Ted.

His own rest that night was interrupted around three twenty, when he heard Markus banging about the living room. There was a sound of glass breaking. Then the front door slammed. The engine of a large vehicle, presumably Markus's SUV, roared to life and moved off rapidly. When Ted went to look, he found the television screen lying in shards on the carpet and the heavy leather chesterfield opposite it overturned.

He rubbed his eyes. No, it wasn't a dream. To dysfunctional

social workers, crazy shrinks, divorced marriage counsellors, and sick doctors, add enraged anger managers. Ted was on the point of warning the police to be on the lookout for an erratic GMC Yukon with a berserker behind the wheel when the vehicle returned, screeching to a halt out front. Its owner stormed into his house and slammed the door.

"You can stop making noise now," Ted called from the kitchen table. "I'm up."

"That's exactly what Karin would have said." Markus, all contrition, dropped into the chair opposite. The face behind the yellow-grey beard had fallen and looked older than Ted had ever seen it. "How long were you two together?"

"Eight years this past August." Ted spoke gently, though his father-in-law should have known this.

"You must have been close," said Markus.

"As flesh to blood."

"Did I ever tell you, Ted, how excruciatingly painful it is to lose your only child?"

Ted let the silence stretch out between them. Next day he went back to his own house.

Chapter 11

The October 4 bail hearing in Brampton turned out to be a much bigger deal than the one twenty days earlier in St. Catharines, or than either of the two Shawn had faced in the youth criminal justice system. He'd expected arguments to be made when he went before the Justice of the Peace hours after being charged with Karin Gustafson's murder. In view of the gravity of the crime, however, all the JP could do was send Shawn to jail. If he wanted interim release, he would have to apply for it, then wait in Maplehurst until a Superior Court justice was available to hear his application. Natasha Cullen told him that it would be up to her to show why he should be released, not up to the Crown to show why he should stay behind bars, but that his situation was far from hopeless.

Inspired by television, Shawn advised her to jump up with objections while the other side was making its case. "Shout, 'That's hearsay, Your Honour!'" he urged. "Stuff like that shows them you mean business."

Natasha curtly informed him that it was common practice in bail hearings to let a police officer lay out the case against the accused without other witnesses being called. For her to object on hearsay grounds would show the other side nothing but that her client was represented by a buffoon.

When the hearing date rolled around, the lawyer wanted as many members of Shawn's family as possible in attendance. Dwayne took a day off from community college to escort Meryl. Cliff, meanwhile, was turning down a run out west to man the Handy Buy and to break in a new employee.

Shawn rode down from Maplehurst in a vehicle something like a Brinks truck, only less comfortable. Then he had to wait in a holding room until a prisoner escort officer hustled him into a cattle pen on the side of the courtroom. He had a good look at the judge to see what made him different from a JP. Not much, it seemed. Just a red sash over his black gown instead of a green one. And the lawyers had to grovel a bit more. His face didn't look mean or anything. In fact, he reminded Shawn of Arnold Somers, the ineffectual Lincoln Navigator driver. Turning his attention to the public area at the back of the room, he picked out his mother and brother. He also recognized, some seats away, the black detective and—sitting on the other side of an older man with a trimmed beard—Karin's husband. *What's Ted doing here?* thought Shawn. *Just stirring himself up for something that isn't even a trial.*

Right off the bat, Natasha Cullen asked for and was granted a publication ban. She had previously explained to Shawn and his family that she didn't want potential jurors' minds to be tainted by any discussion of the evidence. The judge agreed that his decision could be reported, but none of the testimony that it was based on.

Black gowns were worn by Natasha Cullen and her Crown counterpart—an older, taller, and more fashionable woman. The judge called her Ms. Haughton. She got to make her case first.

The only witness she called was Detective Nelson, who testified as to the multiple traumas to Karin Gustafson's skull that had caused her death, as to the evidence against Shawn, as to the circumstances of his arrest in Niagara Falls, and as to his criminal record. Shawn had thought all that was no longer disclosable, but Natasha Cullen didn't object.

Shawn was afraid she wasn't going to cross-examine, but she did have one or two matters to get off her flat chest. She got Nelson to admit he had no witness who had seen Shawn kill Karin and that he had no idea whether, when arrested in Niagara Falls, Shawn had been carrying any passport or papers such as would permit him entry to the United States.

When it was her turn to make the case for Shawn's release, Natasha called as witnesses his mother and Shawn himself. Meryl was every inch the good soldier Shawn expected. She'd dressed up in a satin blouse and new high heels that made her look any woman's equal. Her face showed strain, but no sign she might blow her cool or anything. Yes, Shawn had a criminal record as a juvenile, she admitted, but he'd complied to the letter with all conditions both times he had been granted interim release. Through his work at the Handy Buy and his volunteering at the Fair Share, Shawn was well integrated in his community. Meryl professed herself willing to act as surety for him and had every confidence that he'd appear for his court date. After Natasha sat down, Ms. Haughton stood and asked Meryl if Shawn listened to her and did what she told him to, at which she bristled becomingly. "He's a grown man, and I don't expect him to ask 'How high?' whenever his mother says jump. But my son and I are very close. I know that in the big things, he won't let me down."

Next up at the hearing was Shawn. Natasha had warned him that she would not be asking him whether he had killed Karin Gustafson and that he must say nothing about any of the offences he was charged with. If he did, he would be giving the prosecutor permission to question him about those offences. What Natasha wanted him to testify about was whether, when apprehended in Niagara Falls, he had any intention of fleeing, either within Canada or to foreign parts. No, he said. He was simply taking a holiday. Natasha also had him deny that he was addicted to any drugs.

When the lawyers were finished, the judge looked at his watch and stroked his jaw with a tinge of regret. "We are running well past the time when we'd normally break for lunch," he said. "But I don't want to hold you all here over the noon hour, so I'll give you my decision now. Murder in the first degree is a reverse onus offence, and it was therefore up to the defence to show why the accused should benefit from judicial interim release. Having regard to the nature of the evidence against Mr. Whittaker, to his record of compliance with past orders, and to the degree of his integration into the community, I am satisfied that the defence has discharged its burden, and I am ordering Shawn Whittaker's release with his mother Meryl Whittaker as surety on a recognizance of $10,000."

In long-winded legalese, the judge went on to enumerate three conditions, which Shawn interpreted to mean (1) that he had to report to the police station nearest his home once a week between now and the date of his trial, (2) that he couldn't possess any explosives or weapons, and (3) that he couldn't come within a hundred metres of 19 Robin Hood Crescent. Was that it? Not quite—

"I remind the defendant that all of the very sensible conditions of the release order made on September 14 of this year in St. Catharines are still in force and must be observed. Shawn Whittaker, your mother will now proceed to the court office. Once the paperwork relative to your release is complete, you will be able to return home with her. Court will resume sitting at two thirty."

The prisoner escort officer fitted handcuffs on Shawn and opened the cattle pen. Before she could quite get him out the door in the side wall of the courtroom, Shawn managed to lift his manacled hands and flash a double thumbs up at Natasha. When he met his mother in the office as directed, his arms were free to hold her till she stopped shaking.

"It's okay, Mer," he soothed. "We did it."

"Shawn—Shawn, I'm glad you're out of that place," she murmured into the front of his shirt.

"Yeah. Don't cry now. What's the envelope you're crushing in your hands?"

Meryl handed it to him. Inside he found a business card and a two-line note from his lawyer. "Let your hair grow out for another six weeks," it said. "Then get Emilio at this salon to give you a conservative cut with a part on the left."

*　　*　　*

Dwayne's fellow students heard on the news that Shawn had been charged with murder. When they asked him about it, Dwayne had nothing to say.

He thought he remembered his mother's pregnancy and Shawn's birth, but Dwayne had only been three at the time, so maybe he was imagining things. He had loved Shawn, had been proud when his parents had let him babysit his little brother. Shawn was cute: everyone saw that. Had they spoiled him? Dwayne didn't think so—though now, looking back, he believed Shawn should have been pushed harder in school. Dwayne didn't get good marks, so Shawn thought it was all right not to do well either, even though Shawn was smarter.

Laziness, wanting things you hadn't worked for, Dwayne understood how that could lead to stealing. But he didn't know what to make of the murder charge. Did taking things lead to taking life? Maybe, as the boys' father thought, it was all a mistake. But their mother wasn't saying anything one way or another.

When they all got home after the bail hearing, Dwayne asked him point blank: "Did you do it, Shawn?"

"Hey, big guy! Think the Leafs are going all the way this year?"

"Let's watch a few games together and see."

"Yeah, whatever."

"I was just wondering," Dwayne persisted, "whether this is the last fall we'll be able to do that for a while."

"Depends how good a job my pit bull Natasha does."

"But you're innocent, right?"

Shawn cocked an eyebrow.

"Tell me you didn't kill her, Shawn."

"Dwayne, don't you have a car to grease?"

*   *   *

A couple of nights later, Shawn was just finishing a stint at the Handy Buy when two Harleys pulled into the lot. Dwayne was doing a washroom check and would not have been visible to the bikers through the front windows. Leaving his machine running, Scar came to the door and beckoned Shawn outside. Shawn went out to warn the bikers that he wasn't alone. The second man in black leather immediately inserted himself between Shawn and the shop door. He was clean-shaven and wore his black hair closely cropped. Thick-limbed and stiff in the joints, he gave the impression of being bloated and enraged with steroids.

"C'mere," said Scar, squatting beside his bobber.

"My brother—"

The second man clapped Shawn on the back, propelling him forward.

"Shh," said Scar. "Get down here. I want to show you something."

Shawn squatted next to Scar and dropped his voice. "My brother's in the shop."

"Don't say anything. Just put your hand, better be your left hand, on this rear cylinder."

"What?"

The second man, who had so far said nothing, was whistling under his breath. Meanwhile, he squatted to Shawn's left with his right arm around Shawn's back and his right hand immobilizing Shawn's right arm. Scar grabbed Shawn's left wrist and forced his left hand onto the hot cylinder.

"The louder you squeal, the worse you get burned," Scar hissed into Shawn's ear.

Shawn wasn't squealing. He was trying his damnedest to suck up the pain and the humiliation. Scar pulled his hand away from the scorching metal.

Pain. Injustice. This was the worst thing that had ever happened to Shawn, and he hadn't squealed. Now he wanted credit for having passed the test, acknowledgement that he was one of the tough guys.

"I—" Sensation crowded thought from his head. It felt as if the burn was moving through his blood vessels up his arm. He expected he'd be feverish soon.

"No need to say anything," Scar whispered.

The other man pulled Shawn to his feet, still whistling the old Police song "Every Breath You Take".

"And remember," said Scar, "we have friends at court. C'mon, Chuckles."

As the growl of the two motorcycles faded, Shawn burst into the shop and made for the dairy cooler. On returning from the washroom, Dwayne had glanced out the window, puzzled—but not worried—by the sight of the three crouching men. Now he sprinted out from behind the counter, catching up with his brother just in time to see him rip open a pound of butter and hold it to his left palm.

"A burn?" he said. "Run cold water over it."

The customer washroom's one tap produced only a lukewarm blend, so Shawn headed for the staff sink. Dwayne brought him a bag of ice.

"What happened?" he asked.

No need to say anything, thought Shawn, but the words were already spilling out of his mouth. "He wanted to show me something on his bike. I touched something I shouldn't."

Ice was starting to numb the pain. Shawn pushed more of his arm under water.

"Is that the guy Scar the police were here asking about?" Dwayne wanted to know.

"You didn't come out while they were here."

Shawn's voice was still so distorted by stress that Dwayne couldn't tell if this was a reproach or not. "No," he admitted.

"Good. You didn't think it was any of your business, right?"

"Yeah."

"Well, it still isn't."

Dwayne wondered if he'd done wrong. If he'd thought his brother was getting hurt, of course he'd have been out there with him. From the counter, though, the situation hadn't looked dangerous.

*   *   *

Ted had attended Shawn's bail hearing more at Nelson's urging than at Markus's.

"You've been pretty involved in this investigation," said the detective in a phone call Tuesday night. "You're going to want to know what's going on, and you're not going to be reading any blow by blow in the papers."

"I'd rather not have to look at him," said Ted.

"Yeah, well chances are you'll soon be seeing him around the neighbourhood. Everyone gets bail these days. Come on, Ted. You'll be a witness at his trial, so you'd better get used to Shawn Whittaker, murder suspect. And—who knows?—maybe the sight of him will trigger the memory of something more the prosecution can use."

This last remark made Ted uneasy, as did the bail hearing judge's suggestion that the nature of the evidence against Shawn told in favour of his release. They had—on the witness stand, Nelson had confirmed this at last—Shawn's DNA on the chewing gum. They had Ted's computer, a thread from Shawn's hoodie on the window glass, Shawn's fingerprints in the truck and on one of the CDs stolen from Ted's house. What more did they want? Karin's hair under Shawn's fingernails?

Ted struggled to keep an open mind. Taking a deep breath, he rehearsed the names of innocent men convicted of murder and only long years later exonerated. Donald Marshall, David Milgaard, Guy Paul Morin, Stephen Truscott. It was hard to imagine Shawn Whittaker in their company—hard but not yet quite impossible.

The next hurdle was the preliminary hearing, which Nelson thought would be scheduled sometime before the end of the year. Meanwhile, there were to be long weeks when Ted heard nothing from the detective.

At Thanksgiving, he drove to Montreal as promised, staying with his parents for the long weekend and a few days more. His younger brother Patrick was directing his first play, a student production of *Rosencrantz and Guildenstern Are*

Dead, and Wednesday, October 11 was opening night. Patrick, who'd been only seven when Ted had moved to Toronto, was himself of two minds as to whether Ted should attend. He wondered if the subject might be upsetting. But Ted found much of the play merely absurd and, at the same time, took naïve pleasure in Stoppard's reframing of the Hamlet story so as to cut the young prince's interminable dithering.

Ted stayed for the party following the performance and slept in Thursday, starting back down the highway to Mississauga well into the afternoon. Arriving home after ten, he realized he had no milk for next morning's breakfast cereal. That's when he considered going back to the Handy Buy. He knew he might meet Shawn there. Could he handle that? The prospect made him gag: he remembered all too vividly the young man's triumphal raised thumbs on being granted bail. But then again, nothing had yet been proven against the accused. Why should Shawn's liberty deprive Ted of the right to shop in his own neighbourhood? Ted would act as if there were no issues between them. He would leave all that to the state. He wouldn't chat, but would thank Shawn for his change and leave at a normal pace without looking back.

Shawn, however, was not around. Dwayne was in sole possession of the store.

Dwayne was not only older than Shawn by a couple of years, but taller with a longer face. He wore yellow-tinted glasses in brown plastic frames. Ted and Karin had once characterized the difference in the boys' personality like this. If something they were liable to buy were on sale—soda water, for example—Shawn would be practically yelling the savings to them across the parking lot. Whereas the first Dwayne would know about the twenty per cent discount would be when he read on the receipt what amount the till was subtracting from the regular price. At the same time, if Karin wanted three cases of the soda, Dwayne would be the one who'd volunteer to carry it out to her car.

Ted lingered at the counter after he had paid for his carton of milk and had the bag in his hand. "This is hard on both our families," he said.

"It is," Dwayne agreed.

"I'm grateful to you for telling the police about the time Scar came to the store."

"I didn't," said Dwayne. His face flushed in confusion under the fluorescent lights.

Ted felt no less confused. "I understood a guy with a long jaw and a big moustache drove in here in a compact car of some sort and bought cigarettes from you a week before the end of August."

"Oh—yeah."

"You thought I meant the second time," Ted guessed.

"How'd you know about that?"

Patiently, monosyllable by monosyllable, Ted got the story out of Dwayne—a story to make a brother anxious—of how two bikers had ridden into the lot two days after the bail hearing and of how, when they left, Shawn's hand was badly enough burned that it still wasn't right nearly three weeks later.

"Has Shawn said anything about it?"

"Only that it was an accident. He's not a squealer, say what you like about him." Dwayne sounded reluctant to speak, but impelled to set the record straight. "That's what they don't understand about him. He didn't need to be warned."

He's proud of his brother, Ted realized with a shiver. Dwayne must have forgotten who he was talking to. Best leave it there. But Karin's husband turned in the door of the Handy Buy. "Dwayne, I think I have to let the detectives know about this."

"If you want to make more trouble for us. But nothing I've told you proves Shawn did the things they say."

*　　*　　*

"Is that Mr. Ted Boudreau?" The voice on the phone next day was male and distantly familiar. "Eliot Szabo here. I was on a panel you moderated, the Friday of the Labour Day weekend."

Day of hated memory.

"Yes," said Ted. "How are you?"

"Okay—but this is a little spooky. I'm the Crown that's been assigned to prosecute the man charged with your wife's murder that night."

"Oh."

"Exactly. I know I said some things that, if I were in your situation right now, I might find pretty hurtful. So I'm wondering if you'd like me to withdraw from the case and, hopefully, leave the field to some real blood-and-thunder prosecutor. Officially, crime victims don't get to shop around for Crowns the way the accused get to shop around for lawyers. But I'm willing to plead conflict of interest on the basis of our close and long-standing friendship—never mind that we've only met once."

As Eliot Szabo spoke, Ted visualized the lawyer with loosened tie patting his high forehead and diffusing the tension between Lionel Kerr and Rose Cesario. Ted remembered Szabo saying his sympathies were with the accused, but that he'd switched from defending them to prosecuting them for the money. Words spoken in jest, but possibly true.

"Are you telling me you wouldn't give this case your best shot?"

"I'd give it my best shot, and my best might even be better

than that of a colleague only six years out of law school. For example, I know the defence bar's delaying tactics and know how to show them up. I put guys in jail. Shoplifters, no—what's the point? Murderers, yes. Since I changed sides of the courtroom, I've never had a jury verdict go against me. Hell, Ted, I don't even know what your penal philosophy is. As moderator, you didn't get a chance to lay it out for us at the panel. All I'm saying is that, if part of the horror of that night is the memory of my lame attempts at humour on a subject that was about to become more than academic for you, you don't have to have anything more to do with me. No hard feelings."

Ted could have asked for time to think the offer over. But the fact that the offer was being made showed a level of consideration he couldn't count on receiving from any other Crown counsel. Ms. Haughton hadn't even wanted to talk to him.

"Thanks, Eliot," he said. "I'll stick with you."

"Reckless words. Now the police will be sending you a Victim Impact Statement form. It's four pages long. Fill it out and return it to one of the detectives. This won't be used in court until sentencing. Still, the sooner we get started on it the better. Our boy isn't pleading guilty at the moment, but he could do so at any time. We have to get a copy to Natasha Cullen, and it'll help give me an idea of where you're coming from."

*　　*　　*

The third Saturday in October, Ted had dinner at Raj and Nancy's. They had invited another couple and a single woman named Ingrid. Nancy very sensibly got inquiries about the court case out of the way at the beginning of the evening. No one wanted to pretend the murder hadn't happened. No one wanted to linger on it, at least in public.

Ted participated in the subsequent conversation about federal politics, global diplomacy, the direction the economy was headed—the other man was a colleague of Raj's at the Rotman School of Management—without having a lot to contribute. He hadn't been reading the papers very carefully or listening to as many newscasts as he once did. It wasn't that he felt unable to concentrate so much as that what happened in the world mattered less to him.

He hadn't yet opened the envelope from the police. He kept thinking that the victim was not he but Karin. She should have been filling in the Victim Impact Statement. Reaching from the grave with fiery pen or sawing out with her bow a savage song of indictment.

When the six diners moved back from the table to the living room for more coffee and brandy, Ted found himself sharing a two-seater sofa with Ingrid. She'd been so quiet all evening that he'd scarcely noticed her. She wore a sleeveless black dress that made her arms look fat and a lot of black make-up around the eyes. Ted understood that she was a musical friend of Nancy's. He thought the dramatically slanted cut of her straight, black hair was intended to make an impression on the concert stage.

Nancy brought the cream pitcher to their corner. "Did I tell you, Ted, that Ingrid's a cellist?" she said.

"I don't believe so," he replied. He looked again at Ingrid. "I don't recall seeing you at any of the opera orchestra parties, Ingrid. Where do you play?"

"She's with the Kitchener-Waterloo Symphony," Nancy answered for her before serving the rest of the party.

Ted and Ingrid chatted about the acoustics of the hall, the farmers' markets in the K-W area, the universities, and other amenities until the other couple took their leave. Ted was about to follow when Nancy asked him to sit and stay a moment longer.

"You know, Ted, a cello really should be played. Now this idea is mine, not Ingrid's, but would you mind if she borrowed Karin's Commendulli, just while you're sorting out what you want to do with it? Not for her orchestra work, perhaps, but for recitals."

"I'd like to think that over."

"Have a brandy and think it over now," Nancy urged.

"Ingrid," said Ted, "can I let you know in a few days?"

"Of course." Ingrid's hand dived into her chic little purse and quickly surfaced with a business card for Ted. "My cell number's there. I can see this suggestion is coming rather suddenly. There's no rush, really."

That should have been the end of it, but Ted couldn't stand up: his hostess was still planted squarely in front of him.

"Ingrid has a van. She could follow you home and pick it up tonight. It's sad to think of that extraordinary instrument just sitting there."

Cry me a river, thought Ted.

"Nancy," Raj called from across the room, "have you seen the Anna Netrebko CD?"

"Coming," she called back. "Really, he's infatuated with that woman. Before that it was Renée Fleming. And before that..."

As she drifted away, Ted excused himself to Ingrid and retrieved his coat.

In bed that night, not having Karin in his arms was torment. The strange thing was that while she was alive, many women looked attractive. Karin would agree—this actress yes, that one no. Now no woman was touched with any beauty. Ted had sexual feelings all right, but no object. Self-pitying? Damn right! He reminded himself to think of it from

Quirk's side of the grave. He'd lost so much in losing her, but she'd lost everything.

Nancy phoned next afternoon. "Forgive me, Ted," she said. "I was tipsy and behaved badly. I'm sorry."

"It's okay." She's grieving too, he reminded himself. "You've been a tower of strength," he said. "I don't know how I'd have got through these early days without you."

"Thanks for not chewing me out. Raj accused me of trying to set you up with Ingrid, and I wanted to make sure you didn't feel that's what I was doing. I know it's barely been seven weeks. I'd hate you to think I'd be that tacky."

"You're a class act in my books," said Ted. "Bona fide."

"It really was about the cello. I thought it was what Karin would want."

"Tell me," said Ted, "do you think Karin would want me to fill out a Victim Impact Statement?"

"What's that?"

"It's a form in which I tell the court what the effects of the murder were—are."

"Lord Almighty, Ted, doesn't the judge know?"

"Seems not."

"Well, Karin was a great believer in education."

*　　*　　*

When Ted did open the envelope, it bothered him that, even though the form could only be used after a finding of guilt, the convicted criminal was still referred to as the accused. There were three sections. Ted imagined what Karin might write under each heading: Emotional Loss—total; Physical Injury—dead; Financial Impact—need for cash much reduced.

The enclosed guidelines said that not all parts of the form

had to be filled out and that indeed a Victim Impact Statement could be filed without using the form at all. Those needing more direction could attempt to answer a series of questions for each of the three headings. The first question pertaining to Emotional Loss was, "Has the crime affected your lifestyle?" Ted doubted whether anyone who could think in such terms would need to fill out the forms at all. Lifestyle was for the un-impacted.

The package also included repeated warnings about what not to say. Describe the impact of the crime on your life, but don't describe the crime. Make no criticisms of the accused. Make no recommendations as regards sentencing. Ted drew up an experimental draft in his head.

The murderer (a purely descriptive term), whom I'll refrain from calling a brutal scumbag, deprived me of a loyal and passionate lover, a promising musician, a woman blessed with all the beauty of good health, the mother of my child, and an inexhaustibly fascinating friend. The cause of death, which I won't mention, makes me sick every time I think of it and I can't help thinking about it every day. The cracker of my dear wife's skull (sorry, it just slipped out) is, so far as I'm concerned, not deserving of any particular punishment. That call should be made by a judge who never heard of Karin Gustafson and couldn't care less.

Tuesday morning Ted set aside for serious work on the VIS. While he was making himself a pot of coffee, it came back to him that Graham Hart had written an essay on the subject for a journal special issue or bound anthology a year or so ago. Ted's library was well enough organized that he soon had the piece open in front of him on the kitchen table.

Never one to pull his punches, Graham had let it go to press under the title "Just Desserts or Just Nonsense? How

Victims' Rights Victimize Offenders." He took the position that a criminal trial is a proceeding that pits the prosecution, acting in the name of the state, against an accused. Adding an ill-informed third party, the private victim, creates distortions. Sentences handed down after a consideration of impact statements are apt to be mutually inconsistent and harsher overall. Vengeful and punitive crime victims push the system away from the worthwhile public policy goal of reducing incarceration rates. Prisons are expensive and should be saved for the most dangerous offenders, not for those with the most articulate or impassioned victims. Is it really worse to kill a well-loved society woman than a friendless bag lady? Graham also pointed out that some victims recover more quickly than others. How can a housebreaker know in choosing his target whether he is stealing from someone that will move on right after the burglary or from someone that will go to pieces? Giving victims the right of allocution in a sentencing hearing invites intemperate outbursts and inappropriate criticisms of the justice system. Graham denounced sympathy for crime victims as generating—in the words of criminologist Ezzat A. Fattah—"a backlash against criminal offenders." In the revolution of rising expectations, crime victims will next be clamouring for participation in plea bargaining. What a disaster that would be! A more hopeful direction for victims' rights, Graham concluded, is taking them out of the criminal trial process and creating programs to promote victim-offender reconciliation.

Ted turned to another essay in the volume. This one—called "Are the Judges Listening?"—took a different line against Victim Impact Statements and, though less dismissive in tone, depressed Ted a good deal more.

After a thorough study of the literature, a researcher from

the University of Ottawa concluded that fewer than fifteen per cent of prosecutors believe that judges consider harm to victims in their sentencing decisions. Further, the author could discover no evidence that the filing of impact statements by victims resulted in harsher sentences, or indeed had any effect at all on sentences handed down. With one exception. When—despite expectations—the victim recommended lenient treatment for an offender, the judge was more apt to be influenced by the submission.

Ted's brooding was cut short. A glance at his watch told him he had to get downtown and meet with one of his doctoral students. Before coming back to university, Steve Nishimura had been a computer engineer, code writer and security expert. That background gave Ted the glimmer of an idea.

Chapter 12

Steve Nishimura was anxious at the start of their October 24 meeting. It was their first since the murder, and he plainly didn't know how much to say. Ted surprised him by cutting short his stammering condolences with a question. Could Steve hack into a smartphone or personal digital assistant in such a way as to make it seem in every way to be off when it was on? Steve confessed that he'd never thought about it. What would be the point? Ted told him the point was to mess up the biker gang behind his wife's murder. That caught Steve's interest, and the next day the two of them went shopping for a likely device. Ted had set money aside to take Karin to the Caribbean between Christmas and New Year's, intending to buy the tickets in late August. The cash—unspent at Karin's death—was now available for a grimmer indulgence.

Over the following week, while Steve got started on the technological problem, Ted made it his business to locate Walter Weed's home: Melody had listed only the biker's gang moniker and workplace. To make enquiries at Spinners Doughnuts where he worked would attract too much attention. On October 25 and 26, Ted did manage to survey the employees' parking lot at Spinners, but there was no Harley parked there either day. Melody had said Walter had no car. If that were still true, he likely took the bus to work and back. Still, to try shadowing the drug cook home from the plant gates, even if Ted managed to identify him from Melody's description, would be to risk detection or worse.

There had to be another way.

Ted racked his brains in the course of a five-kilometre walk by the Credit River and afterwards sat stewing at his kitchen table late into the night, before his eye lighted on the phone directory. In the end, the solution was ridiculously simple. The man known in gang circles as Walter Weed, Ted hypothesized, might have a related last name. Alliterating, synonymous, or—simplest of all—rhyming. Because of the familiar speech impediment that substitutes W for R, he started with Reed and Reid and checked first the address most convenient to public transit.

On Friday, October 27, Ted watched Walter Reid come home and, after changing into his leathers, take his hog from the garage. For six more days, Ted studied Walter's movements. Not the safest occupation for a surveillance amateur, though at least he had the protection of his car. In the two months since the break-in, moreover, the Dark Arrows had made no further attempt against Ted or his property. He dared hope that they had by now discounted whatever rumour they had originally heard about him and no longer believed they were objects of his study.

*   *   *

Walter had many grievances, starting with the handle Weed. What did the brothers expect? The steroids made him so irritable that toking was the only thing that seemed to settle him down. He'd experimented with H, but the leadership were dead against it. Scar had just about throttled Layla when he'd found her rig. Vigilance was the Dark Arrows' watchword, and "a vigilant junkie is a contradiction in terms." Yeah, yeah, Walter knew. As for unwinding with sex, forget it. With the doses of stanozolol he was injecting, he simply couldn't get it up. When he hung out with girls, it was just for show. He plied them with treats for playing along, and with threats of what would happen if they ratted him out. Relaxing it wasn't. Still, without the 'roids, he'd have shrunk back into the skinny runt of his pre-biker years. Then he'd have been called Weed for a different reason.

If keeping up appearances in the gang was tiring, work was exhausting. At the end of September, the cops had raided a Hells Angels' lab and scooped up, among other goodies, fifty thousand tabs of ecstasy. Worth as much as one and a half million dollars retail. Ever since, Walter had been scrambling seven days a week to fill the gap between the diminished supply and the rave scene's demands. Quality had suffered. Short of sassafras oil, he'd had to use more than the usual amount of adulterants. Appearance also had been compromised. He liked to turn out nice clean-looking pink tabs with a heart stamped on them. Girls thought they were cute, which sold them to boys too. But Walter hadn't had time to replenish his preferred shade of food colour and had been producing pukey-looking olive drab lumps. Depressingly, they sold just as well.

The worst of it was that in addition to the hours at the lab, he was working five full shifts a week at Spinners Doughnuts. During the summer riding season, he'd used up all the vacation time and unpaid leave they were willing to give him. Chuckles, who called Walter's day job zero-making, advised him to quit. But Walter felt the need of a cushion of savings, however thin, and of a straight job to fall back on. These boom times for the lab were all fine and good. At the same time, if the Hells could get busted—well, who could ever say they had enough muscle?

The Hells bust had set Scar on edge too. His nagging

insistence on security made one more hefty contribution to Walter's stress levels. Yes, he insisted, he varied his route to the lab every day. No, he had told no one where it was. Jesus Christ, he didn't want to go to prison. Freedom to ride was what Walter lived for.

When he got out of Spinners at four, he'd take the Dundas bus home to the Applewood Heights neighbourhood of Mississauga. The unsupervised factory parking lot was no place for his customized hog, which had a parking stall of honour in the garage of the semi-detached house where he rented a room. There's more than one way to modify a Harley. Walter had no interest in the low-slung chopper that risked bottoming out on any obstacle higher than a speed bump. All the changes he made were in the direction of cross-country ruggedness. So when he changed each day from his factory jeans to his leathers and wheeled his machine into the drive, he was able to take advantage of an escape artist's bagful of shortcuts—of sidewalks, hydro corridors, parks, forest footpaths and railroad rights of way. From time to time, a chain link fence would be installed or repaired across his chosen path, but for such occasions he carried twelve-inch bolt cutters. No cage driver could follow him on routes like these. Any tail would have to show his face and travel on two wheels, not four. He might meet a jogger, walker or mountain bike rider, but most stood aside without comment, and those that yelled about no motorized vehicles being permitted were soon eating his dust. Only once had a foolish old codger tried to block his way. Walter had grabbed the man's coat collar and given him the scare of his life by dragging him ten metres on his heels before letting him drop in a convenient mud puddle.

By late October, the pressure on the Dark Arrows' ecstasy cook had eased. Other suppliers had moved in with product.

The Hells themselves were likely manufacturing at another location. Meanwhile, the DAs had done well, and Walter—though he still rode out to the kitchen every day—felt entitled to a little reward. Something beyond beer and marijuana.

Such was the mood in which he found the cellphone on the evening of November 2. It lay where it must have fallen, not far from his home. The route he always took cut across a vacant lot, a parcel of real estate with a long history as the future site of some sort of distinctive collection of fabulous dwellings. He hadn't read the sign too carefully. Walter was as usual enjoying the way his Dunlops spit up the loose gravel, when something bright among the white-grey pebbles caught his eye. He was sure it hadn't been there the day before.

He bent down without dismounting and picked up the orange leatherette case. It turned out to contain much more than a phone. Out slid a brand new silver candy bar loaded with buttons and the biggest display screen he had ever seen on a personal digital assistant. An inscription in slanting characters screamed, "5 megapixels." Six hundred retail, he guessed, minimum. How could a company charge that much and not make available anything better to carry it in than this flimsy sleeve with a loose belt clip? For organized crime, electronics companies had bikers beat. He wondered whether he'd seen this Day-Glo rig on the waist of one of the joggers or mountain bike riders he'd encountered in the past week, but they rarely came here. No, he couldn't place it. It felt warm to the touch, as if it had been on only recently. Well, finders keepers. He could use the camera, a video camera it looked like, but that wasn't the half of it. Multimedia player, Web browser, e-mail—this baby was loaded with features beyond the basic contact and appointment management functions of his old PalmPilot. With luck it would have no more than basic password protection, and the Dark Arrow they called Virus could show him how to do a hard reset that would let Walter in at the negligible cost of erasing the previous owner's data. A PDA wasn't the status symbol a bike was, but Walter could still count on turning the brothers a little green. Surely his hard work over the past month had earned him that much.

He wondered briefly whether to take his find back home before heading off to the lab, but he wasn't afraid of losing it as its last owner had. He zipped it into a cosy inside pocket of his black leather jacket before resuming his circuitous cross-country path to the house where his chemicals and pill press sat waiting.

*   *   *

From 4:45 on, Ted's Corolla was parked in a shopping plaza in Applewood Heights. His eyes were glued to a map on the screen of his cellphone. There it was, the bait PDA just where he had left it in the vacant lot.

Five o'clock, and the marker still sat at the same map coordinates. Whichever route he took subsequently, Walter always seemed to pass this spot. With reason. Bouncing over the rough—in places muddy—terrain behind the chain link fence would effectively shed following cars right away.

It hadn't been easy to decide what colour the case should be. The more conspicuous, the greater the danger that someone would pick it up before Walter got to where Ted had dropped it. The more muted the shade, the greater the danger that Walter himself wouldn't see it. The sun was setting early these days, just after five, and a drab colour would be easy to miss in the twilight. In the end, Ted had bet on the loneliness of the spot at that hour. Joggers preferred the parks and footpaths.

At five past five, the marker still hadn't moved. Even if Walter picked it up, he might not take it to the lab. But why not? If he was at all suspicious that the device was equipped with a global positioning system, he should still feel confident that the GPS was inactive so long as the juice was off. Off was exactly what it appeared to be. On was what it was. Using the power button would restore or suppress all the expected lights and sounds—Steve had seen to that brilliantly. An elegant bonus: Steve's handiwork would expire in a few hours with the current battery charge, leaving no trace for the bikers' computer nerd to discover tomorrow. What Steve had of course not been able to do was to keep the device from generating heat as it transmitted its position. If the temperature made Walter suspicious, he might drop the gizmo back in the gravel or shy it into the bushes.

At 5:08, the marker started to move. Ted rubbed his eyes. The orange dot crept out of the lot and down the creek lane, depositing a trail of yellow breadcrumbs between it and its original position. Was it Walter who had taken the bait?

At 5:15, the cellphone was heading north on Cawthra Road. The dotted trace line ran through two paths too narrow for cars, but the marker had travelled too far too fast to be with a jogger or anyone on a pedal bike. Walter—it had to be. Ted turned the key in the Corolla's ignition, slid the shift lever into drive, and pulled out of the parking lot. As darkness fell, he followed the breadcrumbs up Cawthra and to the east, checking his phone's display only as traffic allowed. The 5:45 check revealed no change from 5:40. The marker had come to rest in a subdivision northeast of Pearson Airport. Ted drove around and wrote down the address of the townhouse complex. The GPS transmitter wasn't precise enough to tell him which unit it was in: a police stakeout would have to deduce that from the traffic. For their secret drug kitchen, the Dark Arrows had chosen not—as Melody had suggested—a cabin in the woods, but rather a blindingly ordinary dwelling in the jungle of Toronto's sprawl.

Ted closed his eyes in the parked car and felt a moment of joy for the first time since August.

*　　*　　*

"Hello, Ted. Good to hear from you." Detective Rodriguez's voice came through the ether with a friendly warmth. "That sounds like traffic noise where you are. You're not phoning and driving, are you?"

"No, I've pulled over." Ted pushed down the accelerator a little further and swerved around a black Audi. Traffic on the westbound Queen Elizabeth Way was moving well for once. Pity to waste the momentum. "Look, I've got something on the Dark Arrows. I haven't been able to get a hold of Nelson."

"Yeah? The Crown has something for you too. A deal."

"A deal on what?" The needle was crowding 130. Better slow down.

"A plea bargain. Someone from Mr. Szabo's office is supposed to be calling you, but since I've got you on the line... Shawn's pleading guilty. There won't be a trial. You won't have to go on the stand and go back over that night for the benefit of a jury."

There were red brake lights up ahead, but still far in the distance. Time to get past this bus taking all the gamblers to be cleaned out in the Niagara casinos. Meanwhile, Rodriguez sounded pleased, and that was good, but Ted still didn't understand exactly what she was saying.

"Pleaded guilty to first degree murder?" he asked.

"No, manslaughter."

"That's bullshit, Tracy."

Shawn was a murderer. A confession to having caused Karin's death sealed it for Ted. He braked late and hard to avoid rear-ending the Ford Focus in front of him and got a three-second blast from the Audi's horn. Okay, it was time to pull over.

"They call it a plea bargain, Ted. Each side gives a little. He'll still go to jail."

Ted's car came to rest on the paved shoulder, only just out of traffic. A four-metre high wall protecting a subdivision from highway noise prevented his pulling over any farther. The Corolla rocked in the wind every time an eighteen-wheeler passed. If Ted had tried to open the driver's side door, it would have been sheared off and booted past the next interchange. He clicked on his four-way flashers. The pulsing arrows on the dashboard pointed in both directions at once. The sky was dark.

First Karin had been taken away. Now the hope of justice was being taken away too. Manslaughter? The medical evidence must be lining someone's birdcage. Ted felt ill.

"Are you still there?" asked Rodriguez.

"Detective," said Ted, "have you read the post-mortem?"

"The Crown makes these deals, Mr. Boudreau, not the police."

"I thought I heard applause from your end."

"Could have something to do with closing one case so I can work on two others and come home here to my daughter before she goes to sleep. Look, I understand you're acquainted with Mr. Szabo. If you don't like what he's done, I suggest you talk to him."

"Okay," said Ted. He fancied he could hear childish warbling in the background.

"So what was it you called me about?"

"What? Oh, sorry. Nothing important."

*　*　*

When Ted got home at six thirty, there was a phone message from Markus asking if he could drop in during the evening. Ted ordered in a large pizza. On locating a bottle of good Valpolicella Karin had bought one sunnier autumn, he drew the cork to let it breathe. He thought he might get Markus mellow before breaking the news of the plea bargain, then found himself blurting it all out as soon as his father-in-law walked through the door.

Markus professed not to be surprised. "It's not about justice, Macduff. It's about clearance rates. Productivity."

Over supper, they tried to talk about music. Markus had brought a cassette he'd made of Karin playing her own transcription of the stirring anthem "Va, pensiero" from *Nabucco.* "Fly thoughts, on golden wings": a song of banishment and longing—for the land of Israel within the context of the opera, for a future single nation in Verdi's fragmented Italy. Ted recalled a concert performance of *Nabucco,* at the end of which this chorus had been repeated as an encore. The singers put their whole hearts into it. He'd been close enough to see in their faces radiant belief in whatever promised land each held most dear. Karin had been in the pit, her face hidden, but Ted saw it too—then and now—as he heard her play. "My homeland so beautiful and lost."

The tape made both men quiet. At length, Markus took it on himself to toughen them up.

"We mustn't idealize her," he said. "Karin could be damned annoying to live with. I've never known anyone so

201

capable of taking the last cold beer without popping another in the fridge, or taking the last Kleenex without getting another box from the linen closet. You could extend that right across the board. She'd take the last bit of soft butter without pulling more out. She'd forget to thaw meat from the freezer. She never seemed to notice when supplies were getting low and should be added to a shopping list. That was always her mother's job, even long after her mother died. The worst was when she took the last sheets of toilet paper without replacing the roll and I was caught short in the middle of the night. Did she drive you crazy that way too?"

As the examples piled up, Ted was half afraid Markus was going to accuse Karin of dying without leaving a replacement of herself.

Ted could think of his own examples of her improvidence, but wasn't interested in playing this game. The better he knew Karin, the more he'd adjusted to being the one who added windshield washer fluid to the car, both cars, or liquid soap to the kitchen dispenser. He'd never wanted to be married to a maid. And what did running out of cleaning supplies matter anyway, compared to running out of her company, of her love?

When Markus tired of criticizing his darling, his face became solemn and he excused himself to get something from the car. Presently he returned with a long black nylon case. Out of it he drew a rifle of an old-fashioned design. Around 1900, Ted thought.

"Markus—"

"It's a Swedish Mauser. You won't find a better-made gun. Because of Sweden's neutrality in both world wars, there were never any wartime production shortcuts. The army used this right through to the 1950s. The metal parts are Swedish steel—machined, not stamped, for the most part."

"Markus, put the gun away," said Ted.

Markus zipped the Mauser back into its case. "Don't you want to heft it?" he coaxed. "Nine pounds—heavy, but not too heavy. Relax. I have a permit."

"I doubt if it authorizes you to titillate yourself with it in my kitchen."

"Fine, Ted. The gun was just a prop. What I came to tell you is that until that boy is sentenced, he is working every evening in the front of a store with big plate glass windows. I don't have to keep myself out of jail. I have no family left."

This is the week, thought Ted, the first week in November. His father-in-law had been a widower ten years. That didn't make him any more likely to kill Shawn, though, did it?

Markus was a playful man, but serious about his play. He liked to use jokes in his work. When he'd gone out west in his teens, he'd played in jazz and rock groups—deadpan, to hear him tell it, but laughing all the while at the performance he was giving. He'd said he felt so many possibilities in himself that until he had a wife and daughter, he'd doubted that any rôle would ever feel like it was really him.

"If they lock me up for shooting the guy," Markus continued, on his feet and as earnest now as Ted had ever seen him, "it won't be for long. Incarceration is so costly and so unfashionable, they'll probably just look at my grey hair and send me home with an ankle bracelet."

"And then," Ted countered, "you'll be qualified to join a gang and make a career of settling scores."

Markus was ready for this charge. "Ah, there's a difference, though," he said. "The gangster demonstrates his organization's power by whacking you and will feel cheated if the state hangs you first. The vigilante—a different animal altogether." The older man dropped onto the kitchen chair across from Ted.

Leaning forward, he lowered his voice. "A vigilante like me wants the state to punish you, but is willing to step up to the plate himself as a last resort. To see justice done, and to get lawmakers to address the retribution deficit. Now, in Shawn's case, the beauty of it is there's zero risk of my executing the wrong party. By accepting the plea bargain, he's acknowledged he killed Karin. Think of it, my friend—capital punishment without the possibility of judicial error. I don't need your permission, Ted. Just don't be surprised."

Twang! Bang! It was all bluff and puff for Ted's money. A rock performance with fireworks. Still, pointless to call it. "Let me talk to the Crown, Markus. Maybe something can be done that won't land either one of us in the dock."

*   *   *

It took Eliot Szabo from Friday to Tuesday to return Ted's phone call and another two days after that to find a time when they might meet. Not in the Crown attorneys' office on the fifth floor of the Brampton courthouse. With all the security measures in place, it wasn't convenient to receive members of the public there. Szabo suggested the Liberty Bar in East Side Mario's—just across Hurontario Street, six p.m. on Thursday.

Ted made use of the week to study the *Criminal Code,* to work on his Victim Impact Statement, and to shop at the Handy Buy at times when Shawn was alone there. These visits always required a great deal of self-control. Ted rehearsed carefully. His breathing, his walk. He practised his lines. These were nothing more than asking for a particular item the first two times. But on his third visit Wednesday night, when he'd got his change, he placed a piece of paper on the counter and asked for directions. He pretended he had to find an address near where the Whittakers lived, a twenty minute drive from the shop. Shawn looked at Ted's sketch map and made a mark with Ted's pen. He was cool, Ted gave him that. Less exuberant than previously, more settled, graver. He was growing out his dark hair. But Ted thought Shawn looked nervous too. A vein in Shawn's forehead was pulsing in a way Ted had never seen before. Was Shawn going to ask him what he was coming around for or tell him to get lost? He did neither that night, and Ted didn't intend to give him another chance.

Next day Szabo arrived on time for their drink, but Ted was there before him, already perched on a tall chair at one of the tall tables, sipping a large Coke with ice. The lawyer ordered a Heineken, to which the barmaid replied that there was none on tap.

"A bottle's fine, my dear. A better size for me, in any case. Our problem, Ted, is this. We can prove Shawn entered your house and stole your computer, but we can't prove that he killed Karin, or was even in the house when she died."

"Did the detectives give you any reason to think anyone else came in that night?"

"No, but they can't prove someone didn't. This character Scar, for instance."

"But manslaughter, Eliot? That's a logical impossibility. Whoever killed Karin either meant to cause her death or meant to cause her bodily harm likely to cause death and was reckless as to whether death ensued or not. That's what the pathologist's report shows, and that's murder—not manslaughter. Furthermore, irrespective of what you mean or how reckless you are, if you kill someone in order to facilitate the crime of break and enter or in order to get away afterward, that's murder. Not manslaughter. Let Shawn plead not guilty if he likes, but whoever is guilty is a murderer."

"That's the letter of the law, but you want to get yourself an annotated version of the *Code.* That section about homicide in the commission of an offence has been modified by the Supreme Court." The height of the chairs made them impossible to tip, but Szabo leaned back as best he could and patted his bald spot. His beer and a frosted glass stood untouched on the table in front of him. "You and I can agree to call it murder between ourselves, but why should we care what the court calls it? I told you I put murderers in jail, and that's exactly where Karin's killer is going."

"For how long?"

"Natasha and I have agreed on a joint recommendation of six years."

"Six?" Ted hadn't thought he had any breath left to take away. "This kid—this man is dangerous."

"Most killers never kill again," Szabo pointed out.

How often had Ted surprised his students with this very statistic? "Shawn could be one of the exceptions," he now argued. "Break and enter is a high recidivism crime. Another chance encounter with a householder could well mean another death."

"Well, six is just a submission. There'll still be a reading of the Agreed Statement of Facts, followed at some point—the same day or later—by a sentencing hearing. You'll get to read your Victim Impact Statement. The judge could give him a longer sentence."

"Or a shorter one."

"Right," said Szabo. "There's no minimum unless a firearm is used. Frankly, I'm surprised Natasha went as high as she did."

"Eliot! Doesn't six years mean he can apply for full parole after two?"

"Yep."

"And in any case—unless he screws up—he gets statutory release after four, right?"

"That's about it." Szabo looked as if he were ready to pour his beer at last, but—perhaps to get through it quicker—started drinking from the bottle instead.

"What would it take," asked Ted, "to open this deal up again?"

"That would only happen now if Shawn were to change his lawyer. Are you sorry you didn't take me up on my offer to recuse myself?"

"I don't know," said Ted. "I'd like a copy of this Agreed Statement of Facts."

"You'll get to hear it read in court."

"Before then—today."

"We're still finalizing the wording," said Szabo. "It's too late to change anything anyway."

"Eliot, you just contradicted yourself."

"I guess I did." Szabo grinned self-deprecatingly.

"So?"

"We can't give it to you in any case."

"If you think the judge won't want the document out in the world before it's presented in court, how about letting me read it in your office, no photocopies?"

"Afraid I don't have time."

No time to deal with Ted's emotional reaction, perhaps, but Ted suspected darker considerations.

"Ted," said Szabo, "what is it you really want?"

"I want to see what selection of so-called facts could possibly support the deal you've reached. Did you promise Shawn's lawyer not to let me see it?"

Eliot Szabo was slow to answer. "I can't stop you from thinking so."

Such a compact was pretty much what Ted had expected to find when he picked this particular scab, but the poison was still bitter. Everything he discovered about the system of criminal law seemed calculated to weaken his sense of obligation to it.

"I'm glad you're a man of your word," he told Szabo. "Can you get me a copy of the post-mortem?"

"We're not filing the p-m as an exhibit, so there's no need to go over that with you. We never give out copies."

"Need or no need," Ted insisted, "let me have a look."

"I don't have it any more." Szabo finished his beer and wiped his lips on a cocktail napkin. "You can try the detectives if you like."

Ted did not point out that Nelson was already in trouble for what he'd told him about Karin's injuries.

"You're giving yourself a lot of torment over this, Ted. Call me a jerk, but I thought a criminologist would understand the process."

"Most criminologists never lose a loved one to crime."

Szabo left a sympathetic interval. "That must be rotten," he said. The tone of his voice and the expression on his face seemed sincere, if a shade remote.

Ted nodded slowly. "Rotten. Are you married, Eliot?"

"Divorced. My son and daughter mean a lot to me, although we've never lived much together. Look, Ted, I don't want to preach at you. But will it really lighten your grief or ease your dead wife's soul to see Shawn Whittaker punished more rather than less?"

"It will show that in the eyes of the community, the life of one citizen counts for something. Yes, that's important—to me and to Karin's father as well. He's suffering cruelly, as you can guess."

"Then you have to get your impact statement in, so we can

get copies distributed. The hearing is less than two weeks away. If you're having trouble writing it, I can help you."

"I can write it, Eliot. Where I'll need your help is in getting permission to read it."

"Say, can you get the check if I leave you some dough? As long as you don't criticize Shawn, make specific sentencing recommendations, or talk about the crime rather than its effects, you'll be allowed to read your statement. Not ad lib, mind, read—exactly what you've written. That's what you're owed."

"And you'll see to it that's what I get?"

"Sure." Szabo stood up and stacked a few large coins in front of Ted. "Least I can do."

*   *   *

"You're a hard man to get hold of."

It was Saturday morning, the morning of Remembrance Day. Nelson had just emerged from the Derry Road building where Major Crime was based and was about to get into his unmarked black sedan when Ted pulled into the parking lot. The Emil V. Kolb Centre had the reassuring look of a civilian office building, evidently dating from before the bunker era of police architecture.

"Yeah, Ted," he said. "I've been avoiding you."

"Can I buy you coffee?"

"Naw, I got to be somewhere." The detective zipped up his jacket against a nasty wind, glanced at Ted, and relented. "Come sit in the car for a minute if you like."

"Let's sit in mine," said Ted. "It'll be warmer."

Nelson packed himself into the Corolla's passenger seat, which he slid all the way back. His knees still rose well above his lap.

"Tracy thought you'd be relieved you don't have to testify," he said. "But I knew you wouldn't like this deal, and I didn't want to have to pretend I did. Yeah, it closes the case, but it leaves a bad taste." He grimaced, as if he really had something unpleasant in his mouth.

"Thanks for saying so, James. I'm trying to move on. I've written a Victim Impact Statement." Ted handed Nelson a single page. "I've faxed a copy to the Crown as well. I'd appreciate it if you could have a look before you stuff it in your pocket."

Nelson, who had already folded the document in three, opened it reluctantly. Maybe he was afraid soap opera sentiment about the dear wife was going to gush out from it and drown him. His eyes got bigger as he read.

"Now this is different," he said. He read without further comment to the end. "You're pleading for leniency for Shawn Whittaker."

"Correct, detective."

"On the basis of information he supplied about a motorcycle gang called the Dark Arrows, including the location of their secret clubhouse and the lab where they turn out ecstasy tablets to peddle to teenage ravers."

"That's what it says." The ring of confidence Ted heard in his own voice belied his one big doubt.

He might yet have to withdraw his Victim Impact Statement on account of the danger represented by Scar. Scar alone knew that he—Scar—had told Shawn nothing of the Dark Arrows or their assets, but that as Shawn's recruiter and mentor, he'd be held responsible for any snitching the gang believed Shawn to have done. To save himself, Scar would have to hunt down the true source of the leak. However reckless Ted's grief made him of his own safety, he had to recognize that the trail that would bring the quiet-spoken biker to his doorstep one evil night would most probably run through Layla and Melody.

"Who exactly did Shawn supply this information to?" Nelson wanted to know.

"Could it have been to you, James?"

"I didn't hear anything like this from him."

"Then it must have been to me."

"When? Where?"

"At the Handy Buy, in the last week or so. If Wednesday's security tape hasn't been recorded over, you can see him marking a location for me on a map."

"Why would he do that?"

"Perhaps to ease his conscience."

"Puh-leeze, Ted."

"Or perhaps in the hope that I'd put in a good word for him in my Victim Impact Statement, although I hasten to say I offered no inducement and made no promises."

"You realize you can be cross-examined. Shawn's lawyer will shred you up so fine, the judge will need an microscope to see the bits."

"As long as the judge lets me read it, James, I don't care. It's not written for His Honour. My intended audience will recognize the substance of the revelations as true, and they already doubt Shawn's discretion."

"I'm not going to pretend the accused told me any of this."

"I respect that," said Ted. "Let's say he told me. Here's a second page with all the juicy details and addresses." Ted passed Nelson everything he'd discovered about the drug lab and everything Melody had heard about the clubhouse and its security. About Chuckles's police work he revealed nothing. Nor, despite his warning to Dwayne, did Ted mention the

211

burn Shawn suffered during a visit to the store by Chuckles and Scar. "What I'm asking," Ted continued, "is that you take this information to your superiors or to the province's Biker Enforcement Unit, or to whoever is in a position to mount the appropriate raids. So the Dark Arrows don't get a chance to just move operations somewhere else."

"I've got no problem with causing those racists some grief. You want them hurting by the time you finger Shawn."

Ted said nothing. He didn't want Nelson thinking too much about this part of the plan. Nelson, however, could cope.

"By the time you deliver this," the detective continued, "Shawn Whittaker will be under the watchful eye of the court. From the sentencing hearing he'll go straight to prison, and we know inmates are perfectly safe in those places." He nodded ironically.

"Perfectly," said Ted. He'd read, and had no reason to doubt, that during the 1990s, the number of people murdered while in custody in Ontario was sixteen, more than one a year.

"Yeah," said Nelson. "Safer than on the street, in fact. So all you're doing is giving Shawn an incentive not to apply for early parole."

"One more thing." This was no time for Ted to be squeamish. "Tell whoever mounts the raids to be especially on the lookout for Scar Hollister. If ever there were a man too dangerous to be given the benefit of a warning shot..."

"I sure as hell won't put it in those terms," Nelson chided. "Officers respond to what they're given."

"Fair enough, James."

It sounded to Ted as if Nelson would know how to handle the Crown if Szabo had any questions.

Chapter 13

By five on the morning of the last Friday before his court appearance, Shawn Whittaker was feeling sleep-deprived, bored, ripped off and virtuous. He sure as hell shouldn't have been spending any part of his last week of freedom working, but Dwayne—with a truly brilliant sense of timing—had come down with a flu that sent his guts straight down the toilet and left no question of his being able to hold down his usual graveyard shift. So Shawn was pinch-hitting. At least he'd leave his family with a good impression of him.

They'd been strange since the plea bargain had been struck at the start of November. No, Dwayne had been strange for much longer. For over a month, Dwayne hadn't exchanged a word beyond "Pass the butter" and "Your lawyer phoned." Well, Dwayne owed Shawn for tonight. For the rest, if Dwayne disapproved of his brother, that was his problem. It would be up to him to come round.

The change in Cliff and Meryl, however, was more recent. Following the bail hearing, they had been affectionate—almost clinging. Shawn wanted to tell his father to get a grip.

"I could turn down a few runs, son, do your shifts in the store instead. I'd like to give you the time you need to sort things out. And then, with me home, you and I'd have a chance to talk more."

"Thanks, Dad. You just keep doing your job. You can help me most by being strong." Saying these words gave Shawn a sense that he was the man of the house. Nothing built character, he decided, like being an outlaw.

His mother was more resourceful. More intrusive—though Shawn could always bring her into line by playing on her insecurities.

"It all takes so long," she'd say. "It wears you down. But we kept you out of jail in October. We'll do it again."

Both parents had thought the trial would clear Shawn. The plea bargain hit them hard.

Now they had to hear their son say he had caused the death of an innocent woman, a customer, someone they knew. It knocked the stuffing out of them. They felt they had to go back to the drawing board and figure out how to love a killer as a son.

"It's not an admission," Shawn had tried to tell his mother when she barged into his bedroom in her bathrobe late one night. He had been lying on top of the bedclothes, still dressed and looking through the friends listed on his cellphone for one whose conversation wouldn't bore him too much. "It's just a move in a game. If we went to trial and I pleaded not guilty, they'd probably put me away for longer."

"Then we could go to that association," said Meryl, "the one that helps the Wrongfully Convicted. Maybe we still can, but *this*—this bargain will be hard to explain." She sat on the edge of the bed. "Better start by explaining it to me. Did you kill Karin, Shawn?"

"If you don't like the deal, Meryl, you should have hired Eddie Greenspan to defend me," he replied icily. "I guess you were saving your money for something closer to your heart. Let's talk about that 'cause I'd like to know what it is."

That had shut her up. The longer he kept her from deciding he'd done Karin, the longer he'd benefit from her doubt. She wanted him to be innocent, would believe so as long as he let her. She should thank him, really, not nag. Shawn was thinking of getting a skull tattooed on his lower arm so she'd never again ask him to wear a Handy Buy golf shirt.

Despite the Greenspan crack, Shawn wasn't disappointed with Natasha. A plain little mouse, but scrappy. He'd expected some jail time, not looking forward to it, but seeing it as a rite of passage. Toughen him up. He had a lot to learn about not minding being hurt. Where he thought he might be ahead was that he already didn't mind hurting other people. Even people he liked. If he saw the necessity of killing Natasha or even his brother, he'd do it, and there'd be no one in prison he'd feel as close to as Dwayne.

Dwayne, whose deadly dull shift he was doing at the Handy Buy.

Shawn had tried to put some games on the company computer, but it was hopelessly limited to inventories, revenues and a few letter templates. Forget about Internet. The magazines the supplier filled the rack with seemed to publish the same articles every two months. The weeklies featured the same movie stars every issue. Then there were the customers. Tonight they had been few and boring. Most seemed genuinely oblivious to the fact that the clerk behind the counter was out on bail. One or two had the air of knowing and of trying to act normally. A woman who came for cigarettes after three a.m. appeared to be wearing only nightclothes under her car coat and really had quite a decent figure, as well as a husky voice and a friendly manner, but was so wrinkled that she might as well have been wearing a hazmat suit and speaking Klingon. Shawn actually found himself looking forward to the arrival of the day's newspapers at five thirty. Maybe something there would catch his interest.

Something did, and how! He ordinarily didn't read much

beyond the headlines, but these weren't ordinary headlines—

"Secret motorcycle gang raided."

"Police bust clubhouse, ecstasy lab."

"Broken Arrows."

"Biker killed, cop bitten in fray."

Shawn pieced the story together from various accounts. At eight the night before, police had simultaneously raided two alleged assets of the secretive Dark Arrows Motorcycle Club. At a townhouse in the Malton area of Peel Region, ingredients and equipment for producing MDMA or ecstasy were seized, along with over fifteen hundred finished tablets with a street value of over forty thousand dollars. Meanwhile, SWAT teams had captured a heavily fortified biker clubhouse outside the village of Pebbleton in the Caledon Hills. The raids were timed to coincide with the Dark Arrows' regular Thursday night meeting. A dozen bikers in custody now faced charges of drug trafficking, possession of unregistered firearms, obstruction of justice, and attempted murder. Only one fatality resulted from the raid. A Doberman pinscher belonging to the bikers nipped an officer's hand, causing his gun to go off, with the result that the dog's handler was fatally shot. The victim's name had not yet been released.

Shawn tried to picture a SWAT team member, body armour head to steel-capped toe, not wearing gloves. What next?

Ontario Provincial Police spokesman Earl Fischer, who admitted that the gang had been very successful in flying under the radar of the Biker Enforcement Unit, professed himself satisfied with the raids. Asked whether the BEU had infiltrated the motorcycle club or been tipped off by a member-turned-informer, Constable Fischer declined to say anything that might help identify their source. Despite the large number of arrests, he admitted that a small number of

Dark Arrows remained at large, and there was a real risk they would be looking for revenge.

Shawn flexed his left hand. The scar tissue didn't look too bad, but he disliked the tight feeling when he moved the fingers. He guessed that would pass if he kept working on it—but in the meantime, it was a reminder of the last time he'd been made to feel small. No list of those arrested had yet been published, but he hoped that when it was, it would include Scar Hollister.

Two days later, the police released the name of the dead biker. This was more payback than Shawn had counted on, or truly wanted.

When Ted read the news, he breathed a huge sigh of relief. At the same time, he was quite clear that Scar's death was no lucky break for Shawn.

*　　*　　*

Natasha Cullen had not been practising law many years, but more than enough to remember Eliot Szabo as a member of the defence bar. He took on the most banal petty crooks and made them happy by pretending to negotiate the sentence the judge would have given them anyway. He knew the odds and made them work for him. Natasha, by contrast, was always striving to distinguish herself by taking on the extraordinary cases.

This time the roles seemed reversed. Shawn wasn't complaining about the six-year sentence Natasha had negotiated for him. She herself let him think he was pulling a fast one, despite the lack of direct evidence that he'd done the killing. The problem was that he simply wouldn't co-operate by taking the stand and fingering anyone else. Maybe he was suffering from a romantic notion of honour among thieves.

Meanwhile, the highly predictable Eliot Szabo had become a man of surprises. Never had she seen anything less ordinary than the Victim Impact Statement that tumbled out of the envelope from the Crown counsel. As soon as she could get him on the phone, she gave him a blast. "Mr. Boudreau can't read this in court, Eliot. In the first place, it contains untruths. In the second place, it's not a Victim Impact Statement in that it doesn't confine itself to the effects of the crime or crimes on the victim. In the third place, it puts my client's life at risk."

"Natasha, my learned friend, you have me mixed up with the judge. His is the ear you should bend."

"Cute, Eliot, but the judge won't know my client didn't tip off the BEU."

"Nor do I," Szabo put in. "If Mr. Boudreau isn't telling the truth, you'll have the chance to catch him out when you cross-examine."

"Eliot, don't forward this to the judge. If you already have, I suggest you ask him to set it aside."

"Are we done?"

This wasn't like Szabo at all. Natasha Cullen wondered what had got into him. "You aren't thinking you're still a defence lawyer, are you, and regarding the victim as your client?"

"In that case," Szabo replied, "wouldn't I have had to get Ted Boudreau to approve the plea bargain that you and I and Shawn Whittaker struck behind his back?"

"We no more struck a deal behind Mr. Boudreau's back than I brushed my teeth this morning behind his back. He simply has no rôle in the process." Natasha Cullen stopped for breath. "I think you've just admitted my point, Eliot. I'll be moving to have this hearing conducted in camera. Any objections?"

"Certainly not. We wouldn't want anything to actually happen to your client."

"Does Mr. Boudreau know he won't have an audience for his little piece of theatre?"

"I haven't said anything to him about it. I like a quiet life. Heck, he studies crime for a living. Let him figure it out."

*　　*　　*

Wednesday, November 22—the day had arrived. Markus drove Ted to the Brampton courthouse early. After lending their keys and coins to the Linescan X-ray machine, walking through the magnetometer arch, and having their outlines traced by scanning wand, they were admitted as weapon-free. From the information desk in the foyer, they discovered which third-floor courtroom to wait outside. When they got off the elevator, they found windows all down one wall flooding the corridor with natural light. Fixed metal seats distributed in front of this glass faced inward, away from the outside world. The seats were perforated with closely-spaced holes. Like a colander, Ted thought, tentatively resting his butt on one next to where Markus had already plunked himself down. It was surprisingly comfortable.

More so than the conversation. Ted hadn't told his father-in-law what he intended to say, responding to every inquiry with a plea for patience. Markus felt he was too old for patience and was having a hard time getting his mind onto any other topic.

"Have you replaced your television?" Ted asked him.

"What would be the point? All the films that aren't about killing are about divorce or adultery or intergenerational conflict."

Ted was on the point of asking if Markus had ever considered subscribing to the golf channel when a wheelchair rolled off the elevator. In it, wearing a purple muumuu patterned with butterflies, sat the diminutive Martha Kesler. On recognizing Ted, she flashed him the broad, white smile that once again, as at Convocation Hall, cancelled any impression of fragility. Her chair today was pushed by an older, fleshier, seedier man, who wore a pink breast cancer ribbon pinned to his black turtleneck.

"Professor Boudreau, I was hoping to catch you before we all go into court. My deepest sympathy."

"Thank you, Ms. Kesler. And what brings you here?"

"Oh, research. I want to see how plea bargains further or frustrate the aims of therapeutic justice."

Ted thought he must still have looked curious, for she went on.

"And—naturally—this case meant more to me since we'd met. Kyle, Ted Boudreau was the very able moderator of the panel discussion I told you about. Ted, Kyle is bravely allowing me to tell people he is on parole for trafficking heroin and cocaine and is receiving therapy for his own dependencies. He also gives lectures on just saying no."

Ted shook hands with the chair pusher. Deciding it would not be tactful to ask whether Tyler, Kyle's predecessor, had finished serving his sentence or had violated its terms and was back in custody, he introduced Markus.

Martha Kesler looked from father-in-law to son-in-law. "You two must have been going through it. Mr. Gustafson, I'm a victim of violent crime myself, and I'm a parent as well, but all that those experiences together can do is give me the barest inkling of your suffering. And I know how isolating suffering can be. Even good friends don't want to know us when we're in that much pain."

"That's kind of you, Martha." Markus allowed his face to crinkle pleasantly. "It's true that my friends won't talk to me." A piercing glance at Ted. "But there's always intoxication. And

I also find great comfort in imagining Shawn Whittaker's severed head on the top of a pole."

"Markus." Martha laid a thin hand on his wrist. "We both do counselling for a living, and the community is not so big that word doesn't get around. I know you help many people in life-changing ways. Let me help you by assuring you that you can dream bigger dreams than retribution and revenge."

"I look forward to dreaming them just as soon as Shawn has breathed his last."

Kyle shifted his weight and made a throat-clearing noise.

"Ted, Markus," Martha Kesler interposed quickly, "look after each other. Which of you is delivering the Victim Impact Statement?"

"I drew the short straw," said Ted.

The news seemed to ease Martha's spirit. "I'm sure you've given it a lot of thought. We'll be listening with interest. Kyle, shall we go in and get settled?" She grinned at Ted and Markus. "Before someone else grabs the last wheelchair parking spot in the court."

The next people to get off the elevators were the accused, his parents, and his lawyer. Ted hadn't seen Natasha Cullen since the bail hearing, and only at a distance then. And yet he almost felt he'd had her as a student, so vividly did he recognize her type. The type that would eat her lunch in a lecture or seminar to save precious study minutes. She'd take few notes and ask incisive questions. She'd usually excel. When things didn't go her way, she wouldn't whine—though she might fidget. For court, she wore a black vest with trousers, black robes and white tabs hanging from her throat. Shawn's suit was navy blue. By contrast to its shaggy appearance two weeks ago, his longer hair was now styled and parted. A young businessman look. He was clearly trying in his demeanour to express modest confidence, to steer a course between cockiness and fear. Meryl too wore a suit, charcoal grey with a narrow skirt. Her back was straight, her arm laced through Shawn's as they walked towards the courtroom. She avoided catching Ted's eye. Of the four in the party, Cliff was the only one the least bit rumpled. His suit was blue like his son's, but far from new, and the shoulders looked as if the jacket had sat too long on a hanger of the wrong shape. The trousers plainly hadn't kept up with Cliff's waistline and appeared savagely tight. When he saw Ted, Shawn's father broke away from his party and came over.

"Mr. Boudreau," he said, "I'm sorry for your loss."

"And I for yours." Ted stood and took the offered hand. It wasn't easy, for Cliff didn't yet know what shape his loss was to take, but there was Markus too. "Mr. Whittaker, I'd like you to meet Karin's father."

"Oh, sweet Jesus," breathed Cliff. "I don't know what to say to you."

"Come on, dad," Shawn called from the courtroom door.

"No need for words," Markus assured him. "Your coming over says a lot."

Cliff swallowed and nodded before returning to his family.

* * *

At work, in his incarnation as a prisoner escort officer or PEO, Charles Godin was never known as Chuckles. Nor was he known as a biker. He drove a twelve-year-old Lumina minivan, which gave him the aura of dignity and frugality becoming to a special constable. At night, his wife used it to get to her work as a cleaner of professors' offices at the University of Toronto. Godin had been trimmer and more agile when he had started his career in court security more than a decade before. His vision had tested then at 20/20. He was disciplined in his use of cannabis and only slightly less so in his consumption of Jack Daniel's. He held a high school diploma and was qualified in First Aid and CPR.

To this day, Charles Godin had no criminal record, or even an unpaid traffic ticket to his discredit. His utility to the gang depended on his respectability, and he was still resentful that Brother Scar—rest in peace—had picked him to seal Thorn's lips. Whackings were supposed to be left to the strikers, as tests of gang-worthiness. But of course, Thorn was the only dude striking for the DA at the time, so logic required that a full-patch member help him out. Godin had used his PEO cuffs to secure Thorn to his Ford's steering wheel while the CO gas was wafting over him. The note hinting at erotic bondage was supposed to explain the chafing on Thorn's wrists, while the padding Godin had taped over the chain had prevented scratches on the wheel itself. Still, the business didn't sit easy with him.

Godin's day job, which paid $17.54 per hour, was neither onerous nor unpleasant. It consisted mainly of cuffing prisoners, shuttling them to and from court, and supervising them while they were there. The hardest thing was getting assigned to the prisoners and courtrooms that interested the Dark Arrows. He was employed by Peel Region, where the Arrows' drug kitchen and clubhouse were both located. He would be usefully placed when charges arising out of the latest raids came to court. That the scene of Shawn's crimes was in the same region was an extra opportunity, which Godin had used all his skill at juggling schedules to grasp.

Shawn's party came through the doors at 9:55 and dispersed itself—his parents to the public gallery, his lawyer and Shawn to the table reserved for counsel. Shawn was paying no attention as yet to the prisoner escort officers, under whose control he would soon have to place himself.

"Order in court," the clerk bellowed. "All rise."

The woman in the wheelchair apart, all in the gallery rose, including her helper, the accused's family, the victim's husband and father, ten to fifteen members of a high-school law class with their male teacher, two girls—underdressed for late November—of an age to have been part of the class, but who sat apart, three reporters, and a couple of subdued-looking men, who might have been waiting for the case after Shawn's to come up.

The judge flapped his way to the bench. These judges never introduced themselves and were never addressed by name, so Godin had given them private nicknames, some based on the Seven Dwarfs, some on the Teenage Mutant Ninja Turtles. Today they had drawn Happy, a blond pretty boy, and surely as young as you could be and still be a Superior Court judge.

*   *   *

The first stage in proceedings was the Crown's reading of the charges against Shawn Whittaker pertaining to the events of September 1; namely, breaking and entering, theft under five thousand dollars, and manslaughter. The judge took a good look at the defendant before asking him to say how he pleaded. The crucial first impression. Remorseful but dignified—that was how Shawn flattered himself he appeared and that was how he intended to act.

He rose and said, "Guilty, Your Honour."

The plea was the signal for Eliot Szabo to rise and ask that bail be formally revoked and that Shawn enter the glassed-in prisoner's box—where Godin stood waiting to receive him.

"Chuckles!"

"Quiet," Godin whispered. "You've never seen me before."

Shawn barely managed to nod. Shock gave way to fear, a rushing fire in the blood. Could he ask to consult counsel? Straining on tiptoe, dignity forgotten, he tried to make eye contact, but his lawyer was looking down at her papers. Chuckles hissed at him to sit. Shawn could do nothing—except sit and think, *Natasha had better demolish Ted's statement.*

Next came the presentation of the Agreed Facts. Eliot Szabo, in black gown, stood at a lectern and read aloud in a clear, flat voice a white document stapled at the top left corner. Ten to twenty pages, Ted estimated. He had not been given a copy.

"Sometime before ten p.m. on Friday, September 1, 2006, the defendant, Shawn Whittaker, unlawfully entered the family home of Ted Boudreau and Karin Gustafson located in the City of Mississauga and stole a computer and several disks. While the defendant Shawn Whittaker was in the house, Karin Gustafson returned home. Her body was found at the foot of the cellar steps by her husband when he returned to the house between eleven fifteen and eleven thirty that evening. The following are the facts and circumstances surrounding the death of Karin Gustafson and the liability of the defendant Shawn Whittaker."

There followed some background, an orientation to the Boudreau house, and details of the police investigation. The pathologist's report was paraphrased imprecisely as having found "more than one" trauma to the back of Karin's head. Nothing else in these sections misrepresented what Ted knew. Then came the defence admissions, beginning with a claim by Shawn that, on one of her visits to the Handy Buy, Karin had told Shawn that her husband had a new computer, and that from that moment Shawn had formed the intention to steal it. Ted did not believe Karin would have said any such thing.

While in the Boudreau home, Shawn further alleged, he had picked up whatever CDs came to hand in the hope that either the music or the data on them might have some resale value. To identity thieves, for example, in the latter case. These were Shawn's ways of writing the Dark Arrows out of the story. Ted had expected their absence and took it in stride.

He sat on the edge of his seat, however, when Szabo came to the admissions concerning Karin's death.

"...The defendant admits that when he came upon Karin Gustafson in the back vestibule of 19 Robin Hood Crescent, he pushed her out of his way to facilitate his escape from the house. As a result of this push, Karin Gustafson fell down the cellar steps, striking her head against the concrete floor at the foot of those steps."

Nonsense, thought Ted, but he wasn't alarmed yet. This story clearly wouldn't square with what Nelson had told him of the pathologist's findings.

"Subsequent to Karin Gustafson's fall," Eliot read on, "the defendant proceeded to the bottom of the cellar steps to ascertain her condition. He raised her head from the floor to inspect her pupils and to see if she was breathing. On failing to detect any vital signs, the defendant was agitated and allowed Karin Gustafson's head to slip from his grasp. From this mishap resulted a further crack to the back of her head on the concrete floor.

"The defendant admits that pushing Karin Gustafson was an unlawful act. However, in pushing her, he did not intend either to kill her or to cause her bodily harm. His sole purpose was to remove her from his path and keep her from blocking his exit. He accordingly pleads guilty to manslaughter..."

So four blows to the head had through legal alchemy become two.

A cry of protest rose in Ted's throat. Getting ejected from the room, however, formed no part of his plan. His outrage merely strengthened his resolve. He'd already written and distributed his Victim Impact Statement: it was too late for him to change a single syllable. And yet, when it came time to deliver it, his nerve might have failed him. Now he knew it wouldn't. His sense of betrayal would sustain him.

The last part of the agreement consisted of the Crown's self-congratulation on having avoided a trial that "risked causing distress to the victim's family"—at which point Ted heard stifled choking sounds from Markus. Ted hoped his father-in-law was not allowing himself to become too distracted, for the next sentence was even richer. "The defendant's guilty plea and admissions are a public recognition by him of his responsibility for this crime and of his remorse."

The judge thanked Szabo pleasantly, reviewed what he regarded as the salient features of his presentation, and said that, in view of the facts admitted to, he thought the pleas appropriate. His Honour announced his intention of now proceeding to the sentencing stage.

This was the point at which Shawn's lawyer got to her feet. Her voice, despite the lack of inflection apparently *de rigueur* in officers of the court, was crisp and carrying.

"Your Honour, we have been given a copy of a Victim Impact Statement filed by the deceased's husband, Mr. Ted Boudreau. We submit that this statement is improper in content and should not be read in court."

The judge made a show of looking through his papers without settling on any one of them. "On what grounds, Ms. Cullen?" he asked.

"It alleges facts not in evidence."

"Oh, I think you can trust me to disregard any improper material. I'd like to hear what Mr. Boudreau has to say." The judge couldn't have been more than ten years older than Natasha Cullen, yet his position allowed him a paternal air.

"In that case, Your Honour, may I request that the sentencing hearing be held in camera? The allegations Mr. Boudreau makes could, if believed, endanger the safety of my client."

"Would a publication ban meet the needs of the defence, Ms. Cullen?"

"In camera, Your Honour. The parties that would wish to harm Mr. Whittaker as a result of Mr. Boudreau's allegations are unlikely to rely on media reports."

"Any objection, Mr. Szabo? Very well. So ordered."

Proceedings were suspended while the special constables cleared the media and spectator benches. Charles Godin reflected that Shawn must really have something to hide.

The in camera motion surprised Ted less than, to deflect Markus's ire, he pretended. He told Markus not to feel obliged to wait around, as Ted could take a taxi home. Markus was furious with this new lawyerly trick to test his patience. He snarled that he would prowl the corridor until the conclusion of the hearing. Ted had better be prepared to give a full accounting.

Nor was Ted surprised when Szabo failed to oppose the exclusion of the public. The Crown counsel was full of sunny promises and unspoken reservations. He'd never had a jury verdict go against him? Of course not, because he plea-bargained rather than take a dubious case that far. Szabo would see to it that Ted got to read his statement? Yes, that was the promise, but he'd also collaborate with the killer's lawyer to make sure no one was listening.

Hardly anyone. Ted had already spotted, filling out a PEO uniform, a pair of broad shoulders he'd last seen covered in biker's black leather.

The Crown did petition successfully for Ted's right to remain for the entire drama and not just be summoned for the part of it in which he was to speak. There was an air of untroubled naïveté about the young judge that depressed Ted even as it suited him. His Honour wanted to explain the mysteries of the law to his lay audience, which the lawyers had between them reduced to Shawn and Ted.

Eliot Szabo was once again first to speak at the sentencing hearing. He said that the break-in on September 1 was a serious crime resulting in the death of an innocent woman. He dwelled on this without departing from the fairy tale account of the death already presented.

"In the other pan of the balance," he said at length, "we find that Shawn Whittaker has no adult criminal record. As a young man of only twenty-two years, with a supportive family, he is a good prospect for rehabilitation—providing we do not make the mistake of locking him up for too long with incorrigible criminals. It is with all these factors in mind that the Crown and the defence are making a joint recommendation that Shawn Whittaker be sentenced to a period of six years imprisonment. I would point out that, based on survey data from the nineteen nineties, this is slightly above the average length of a custodial sentence for manslaughter."

"Thank you, Mr. Szabo," said the judge. "When the Crown and defence make a joint recommendation of this kind, it is my custom to attach considerable weight to it. Now, before I ask if Mr. Whittaker has anything to say, was there a Victim Impact Statement?"

"Your Honour, yes," Szabo said. "To be read by the deceased's

229

husband, Mr. Ted Boudreau. Your Honour should have a copy of it."

"Yes, of course, Mr. Szabo." The judge smiled at his own absent-mindedness. "That's why we're in camera. Is it attached to the Agreed Statement of Facts?"

"No, Your Honour, a separate piece of paper."

The judge pursed his lips as he pawed through his pile of documents yet again. Ted thought he might be looking for the standard four-page form, which Ted—as was his right— had not used.

"Ah," said the judge, "just one page. Is this it? Yes." His Honour lifted the page and turned it over, with the air of politely making a new acquaintance he didn't expect to be with for long. "Mr. Boudreau?"

"Yes, Your Honour."

"Do you understand that you must read your statement exactly as it is written?"

Ted said he did and was called to the witness stand. From here, he had a clear view of Chuckles's face. It was a wide, cold face, wearing a respectful courtroom expression. Ted had been given more than he could have counted on, as much as he'd dared to hope.

What he'd counted on was that the biker/PEO would learn the contents of Ted's unusual statement, through courthouse gossip at worst. What more he got would depend on Chuckles's skill at rigging duty rosters. Chuckles would naturally prefer to work Shawn's sentencing hearing himself—no less to hear first-hand what was said than to remind Shawn to behave himself. All the same, Chuckles's presence had been no sure bet. Ted had lucked out.

At a signal from the judge, he read:

"The death by criminal violence of my wife Karin has had a

huge emotional impact. Without claiming that my heart is tenderer or worthier of consideration than that of any other husband, I'll mention four circumstances that have aggravated my pain. First, I am by training and occupation a criminologist, which means I have been conditioned to believe that murder is a statistically negligible rarity. I'd have done better to prepare myself with the knowledge that it can happen to anyone. Second, some people don't particularly value their life. Karin loved hers, including a musical career still on the upward trajectory. Her death is a loss to her and to all the friends and strangers deprived of the sweet strains of her cello. Third, some husband-wife partnerships are more affectionate than others. Some have gone stale or even toxic. I've never heard of, or indeed imagined, one happier than the partnership I shared with Karin. After eight years of living together and seven years of marriage, we were still head over heels. Fourth, and this is a circumstance I have told no one, at the time of her death Karin was expecting our much-wanted first child. Conception wasn't easy for us. To reach this point, we worked through every medical procedure. Some caused Karin considerable discomfort, which she endured with nothing but gratitude to modern science. Now all her pain is for no gain." Ted felt his voice starting to wobble; he took a moment to steady himself. "And I have lost my child and my child's mother along with my wife."

Ted saw he had the judge's attention. He forged ahead in a reassuring courtroom monotone.

"If these were the only consequences of Shawn Whittaker's homicide, I confess I'd be thinking vengeful thoughts. However, there is another side to the ledger. Information he has provided since his arrest inclines me to plead rather for leniency. Shawn Whittaker's tips enabled police to raid the Dark Arrows' clubhouse and ecstasy lab last Thursday..."

Ted looked up just in time to see Chuckles shift his considerable weight on his wooden chair and draw back his broad jaw in surprise. It was unlikely anyone else noticed, however, for Shawn was conveniently creating a distraction.

"That's a lie, Judge," he called out, jumping to his feet. Because Ted's statement had been provided in advance to his lawyer, Shawn was not blindsided as Chuckles was, but was simply panicking. How could he let a slur so damning go unchallenged? Especially when a goon from the brotherhood he was accused of ratting on was sitting not a metre to his right.

Chuckles glared at him savagely.

"Mr. Whittaker," remonstrated the judge, "we do not heckle in a court of law. You are represented here by counsel, who may request the opportunity to cross-examine Mr. Boudreau when he is finished reading. In addition, you will have an opportunity to speak for yourself before sentence is passed. Please continue, Mr. Boudreau."

"...Shawn Whittaker has no doubt saved the lives of some teenagers that attend raves and are tempted to experiment with drugs. These lives should be weighed in the scale against the lives of my wife and child. Shawn has impressed me as someone who is not destined for a long life of crime. Although I know I am not supposed to make sentencing recommendations, my heart tells me that justice would best be served by a short custodial sentence for Shawn Whittaker."

During the latter part of this statement, Natasha Cullen had been softly tapping her teeth with a yellow stick pen. Now she got to her feet with it still in her hand.

"Your Honour, Mr. Boudreau has introduced facts not in evidence. I'd like the opportunity to cross-examine him."

"By all means."

"Under oath, Your Honour."

The judge raised no objection, and Ted was duly sworn. His mouth was dry. This wasn't something he'd expected, but he didn't despair of keeping his head. He was plainly less rattled than Shawn.

The person from whom Ted would have had the most to fear was dead. Ted's story made sense only if Scar had leaked gang secrets to Shawn. Was it, Ted wondered, too much to hope that Chuckles had resented Scar's position of authority within the gang and would be happy to believe that the enforcer of discretion had himself been indiscreet?

"Mr. Boudreau—" Natasha Cullen addressed Ted for the first time, her voice flat and bored-sounding. "What makes you think that Shawn Whittaker is the source of the tips used by police in their raids on the Dark Arrows?"

"He told me."

"You mean he told you he'd tipped off the police? Because none of the officers he spoke to heard anything like that from him."

"No, I mean he told me, and I passed the information on to Detective Nelson."

"Why would—no, *how* would my client have any knowledge of where these two facilities of the Dark Arrows Motorcycle Club were located?"

"The break-in Shawn committed," said Ted, "was instigated by the Dark Arrows."

"That is not in the Agreed Statement of Facts, Mr. Boudreau."

"Nevertheless. He was paid for his services in part with the ecstasy tablets found on him in Niagara Falls. A gang member named Scar Hollister approached Shawn Whittaker at the gas bar/convenience store his family runs and recruited him for the job. Shawn became a friend of the club and was entrusted with certain information."

"Not true," Shawn yelped.

Chuckles leaped up and, unlocking the prisoner's box, cast a questioning look at the judge. His Honour shook his head, waved the PEO back to his seat, and bestowed a kindly smile on Shawn.

"Mr. Whittaker," he said, "your behaviour strikes me as perverse. Mr. Boudreau is not seeking to malign you. On the contrary. And yet you are reacting as if you were being slandered. The only explanation I can find is that you fear some reprisal from members of this motorcycle gang. If so, rest easy. At your counsel's request, we are in camera here. There is no one present that wishes you harm. Now please contain yourself. I wouldn't want to have to ask the constables to remove you from the courtroom, but you have had your last warning."

Natasha Cullen turned to catch Shawn's eye and, to reinforce the judge's words, held her yellow pen to her lips.

Meanwhile, Shawn was squirming on his bench. It occurred to Ted that even if under normal provocation he was, as Dwayne said, "not a squealer," fear for his life might still cause him to denounce Chuckles. There was no saying how that would play out.

"Have you further questions, Ms. Cullen?" asked the judge.

"Your Honour, yes. You are alleging, Mr. Boudreau, that Mr. Whittaker told you certain secrets of the Dark Arrows Motorcycle Club. Is that correct?"

"Yes."

"Did he say why he was speaking to you and not the police?"

"Karin and I have been acquainted with the Whittakers for a number of years. We watched Shawn grow from adolescent to adult and have always been on good terms."

"You're not answering the question, Mr. Boudreau."

"Perhaps he thought he knew me."

"I'm not asking you to speculate as to what Shawn Whittaker thought, Mr. Boudreau. I'm asking what Shawn Whittaker said."

Ted took a deep breath. In for a penny, in for a pound.

"He said, as it says in the Agreed Statement of Facts, that he had not meant to kill Karin. He said that he was sorry and wanted to make some amends."

So the cross examination petered out. Natasha Cullen could not shake Ted out of his ridiculous story, and the young judge looked as if he were lapping it up. Then His Honour turned to Shawn Whittaker. "*Now* comes your turn to speak. Do you have anything to say before sentence is passed?"

"I'll do my six years, like the Crown said. But no one should believe I gave anyone information about biker facilities—'cause I didn't. I couldn't have told anyone. I never knew about any of that stuff. The only thing I told Ted Boudreau was where the Wal-Mart is in Meadowvale. Honest."

All this, as far as Ted knew, was true.

"Do you shop at Wal-Mart, Mr. Boudreau?" asked the judge.

"No, Your Honour. I don't." Equally true.

"Didn't think so," said the judge with a twinkle in his eye. "Well, Mr. Whittaker, this case demonstrates very clearly how crimes against property may lead to crimes against the person. Your recklessness has led you into a situation where a woman's life has been lost. Even if you did not intend Karin Gustafson's death, you are responsible for it.

"Now the question is: does your behaviour subsequent to being charged give any grounds for hoping that you are turning your life around? The facts appear to be in dispute, but I intend to give you the benefit of the doubt. That is, the benefit of the good deed which you now deny. In the light of

Mr. Boudreau's very interesting Victim Impact Statement, I am reducing the recommended six years to four.

"Do not despair. If you behave yourself, you may apply for parole as early as sixteen months from now, and in time you may even secure a pardon. This is not the beginning of your life of crime, but the end of it."

Chuckles drew his handcuffs from their case on his belt.

That's when Shawn lost it. He turned his face to the bench as the cuffs were being clicked on him and started yelling. "Judge, this officer is one of them—the Dark Arrows. He's going to kill me. His name is Chuckles—" A second constable moved quickly in and helped Chuckles restrain him. "Judge, you have to listen. I'm dead if you let him take me."

From behind, Chuckles got his right hand clamped onto Shawn's shoulder right up against the neck. With the biker's left hand in the small of Shawn's back, the prisoner was propelled towards the door. The other officer pulled on Shawn's right upper arm in such a way that if Shawn did not advance, the pressure on his manacled wrists would tighten painfully.

"Put me in protective custody at least."

"One moment," called the judge. "Prisoner Escort, a moment please."

The officers paused. Ted held his breath.

"Thank you," said the judge. "Mr. Whittaker, you will be evaluated according to the Custody Rating Scale and assigned to a federal correctional institution of a security level appropriate to the risk you pose. If you have safety concerns, by all means raise them with your case management officer. I wish you well."

So Shawn was dragged away—not to the corridor where his parents would be anxiously waiting, but out the side exit in the direction of the holding cells. Immediately after that, the judge ordered a recess. Everyone had to rise for his withdrawal, along with that of the clerk and the court reporter. Natasha Cullen gathered up her few papers and, without a glance in Ted's direction, hurried out, presumably to brief Meryl and Cliff.

There remained only a constable charged with clearing the courtroom—and Eliot Szabo. The Crown counsel patted his head and packed his briefcase. He stood up and pulled down on his black vest. With evident reluctance, Szabo finally met Ted's eye.

"You proud of that, Ted?" he asked. "I'm not. But I predict I'll forgive myself for my part before you will for yours."

Ted's heart was not pounding. His pulse was not racing. It occurred to him that he was a cold-blooded killer. "Forgiveness is overrated," he said. "Or haven't you been paying attention?"

Chapter 14

When Ted Boudreau stepped out of the late winter drizzle into Dr. Ornstein's waiting room, receptionist Sally Lee was showing red-headed girl-and-boy twins how to connect pieces of railway track from the office toy box. Ted smiled and dropped into a chair, where he could keep their progress in view between perusing articles in a news magazine. It bore a date of March 22, still three days in the future, so he imagined it couldn't be more than a week or two old.

There was a brief mention of the first of the Dark Arrow biker trials, the one involving the drug lab. Or as it had to be reported, the trial of Walter Reid—for the Crown had been unable to establish a sufficiently strong link between the ecstasy kitchen and the gang. Walter had his shoulder tattooed with the black arrowhead dripping blood, but he claimed that dated from his reckless early twenties and that he'd had nothing to do with the gang for five years. In the townhouse unit that contained his chemicals and pill press, Walter kept no firearms or weapons of any kind and no club documents or paraphernalia. He was convicted of various offences under the Controlled Drug and Substances Act and drew a six-year sentence, but was not perceived to be high-risk, and upon classification was sent to the same medium-security facility in the Kingston area that housed Shawn Whittaker. Ted had already heard this news on the radio and read it in the daily press, but it bore repeating.

"Oh, train wreck," Sally laughed as brother and sister drove their locomotives into one another.

A father with babe in arms emerged from the inner office to collect the twins.

"No train wrecks today, please," said Dr. Ornstein from her door. "My schedule is too full. Come in, Ted. How are you? You haven't exactly been cluttering up my office in the past six months, so you've either been fiercely independent or seeing someone else."

"I'd rather be thought fierce than disloyal." Ted shut the door behind him. "There just hasn't been much to talk about. The sleeplessness, the flashbacks, the avoidance behaviour— all gone. I've even decided to go on living in the house."

He had considered putting it up for sale after Meryl had asked him not to shop any more at the Handy Buy. But then the Whittakers themselves had moved to Kingston to be nearer where Shawn was incarcerated, and Ted broke off talks with the real estate agent. In February, he had moved his study upstairs to Karin's practice room, where there was more of her than anywhere else. He'd rehung there the photo borrowed, and eventually returned, by the police. The one thing he hadn't yet managed to do was to eat a Friday night dinner at the Bouquet Bistro.

"What about the pain of loss?" asked the doctor.

"Raw, fresh. Like it happened—not yesterday, but last week."

"That's normal. The illness passes; the grief goes on. Believe me, I understand... And work? Courses must be just about over for the year. Will you be back to a regular schedule next fall?"

"Ah no," said Ted. "I have changed horses. I've jumped from criminology to history—specifically the history of crime, criminal justice and criminal organizations. Have you ever heard of the Brook's Bush Gang that killed a Canadian member of parliament in 1859? It seems a subject less freighted with dogma."

"Sounds like you lost your religion," said Dr. Ornstein with a grim smile. "Also, this historical steed transports you to an era when crime was punished more robustly. Take off your shirt and let me listen to your heart."

On the way out, after Rebecca Ornstein had checked all his vital signs, Ted stopped at Sally's desk and waited till she had finished leaving a reminder of an appointment on a patient's voice mail.

"How did Dr. Ornstein's husband die?" he asked, too softly to be heard by the waiting patients.

Sally Lee hesitated, then seemed to decide Ted was someone she'd have permission to tell.

"Drunk driver," she said, while keying in the next number. "Hello, is Mr. Peter Narayan there?"

*　　*　　*

Next morning, Ted was breakfasting in silence when the hordes descended.

He had already listened to the CBC radio news at six and found it not much changed as far as domestic content went from the midnight broadcast, which he had listened to on the way home from Markus's. He had done a lot of listening over the course of the evening, which made the morning peace especially precious.

Markus had talked as much as a man in love. He didn't admit to being in love, but he wanted Ted to know that he was dating. Martha Kesler, of all people. She had made an impression on him when they'd met in the hallway on the day of Shawn's sentencing hearing. Markus had phoned her up to continue the discussion. To invite her for a drink, to invite her to dinner, and give old Kyle the night off. Martha was a sweetie. Even, Markus wanted Ted to know, physically demonstrative. From where Martha sat, it seemed that a bloodthirsty Viking was almost as cute as a pirate, and she found Markus's driving thrilling enough without the Jolly Roger eye patch. Give her this: she'd got Markus's mind off Shawn by and large. She took her message of victim/offender reconciliation everywhere. Markus was accompanying her to more and more of those appearances —Las Vegas next week, Copenhagen in July—to see how much he could find in it. And frankly, just to be with her.

Fine and dandy. Ted was happy his father-in-law had found his own way to cope. As long as Markus was following the wheeling evangelist, he wasn't waving antique rifles around. And he wasn't—thank goodness—advising Ted to start dating too.

The last of his morning coffee dripped from the filter into the pot. Ted filled a mug and sat at the kitchen table. Pulling towards him the fourth volume of Blackstone's *Commentaries on the Laws of England,* he took a large bite of bagel smeared with cream cheese. That's when someone planted a finger on his doorbell and left it there.

He padded down the front hall and peered out through the sidelights. A van painted in the colours and bearing the logo of a local television station was parked in front of the house. On the doorstep stood two individuals, a man in baggy clothes with a camera and a fashion mannequin with a microphone. Ted recognized her without a name coming to mind. The station newbie, he thought, still waiting for her first big assignment. This must be some sort of survey—what culinary specialty should be named for Mississauga? What's your personal way of dealing with spring fever? Idiotic, but harmless. He disarmed the alarm system and opened the door.

"Mr. Boudreau?" said the woman. "I'm Jennifer Malcolm. Could we just get a comment from you on Shawn Whittaker's death?"

"Excuse me?"

The reporter's carefully manicured hand beckoned the cameraman to start shooting Ted's reaction as she filled him in.

"Perhaps you haven't heard," she said. "It's just gone on the wire in the past hour. Shawn Whittaker was found dead in his room at the Bath Institution this morning."

Ted leaned against the door frame. He was surprised to find himself this surprised. Effect was so remote from cause as to seem coincidental, though it was no coincidence at all. Or was it? Whatever he must look like to the TV camera, he didn't close the door in the crew's faces because he wanted to know more.

"How did he die?"

"Correctional authorities aren't saying at this time, but there are rumours of heroin overdose. One of the men that lived in the same cottage found a syringe by Mr. Whittaker's bed. Do you think we could come inside, Mr. Boudreau, where we could sit down and all be more comfortable?"

"This is okay, thanks, Jennifer."

Ted pulled himself together. Junk was a possible murder weapon. Shawn could have been conned into trying what he thought a beginner's hit—or, if uncooperative, held down and gagged while the needle went in and until he lost consciousness. The authorities had never managed to keep drugs out of even maximum security prisons, and Bath wasn't one of those.

"Was Shawn Whittaker to your knowledge a heroin user?" asked Jennifer Malcolm.

"No—but I haven't seen him since he was sentenced."

"Mr. Boudreau, Shawn Whittaker admitted to breaking into your home and killing your wife. He was given only four years. You didn't do any interviews at the time, but did you think four years was long enough?"

Other media vans and cars had pulled up on the crescent. Other microphones were being shoved in front of Ted's face when he made his reply.

"It's turned out to be a life sentence, hasn't it, Ms. Malcolm?"

"Are you happy he's dead?" another reporter yelled.

"Happy, no... I'm afraid that's all I have to say."

Ted closed the door, turned the deadbolt, and reset the alarm. Paying no attention to the doorbell, he went down to the basement and sat on the bottom step. He looked up at the window opening into which he had fitted laminated glass and a set of metal bars. Then he forced himself to look at the concrete floor just in front of the step.

If we had happiness—the words came to him in Quirk's voice—*we wouldn't need justice.*

Epilogue

After the movie, Simon took Melody to a real old-style Ontario beer hall, where you didn't have to order food with your pitcher—and, if you departed from the limited draft offerings, you wouldn't get a glass with your bottle unless you asked for it. The smokers' patio, already in use this cool May evening, was new. But the inside, where the couple had a wobbly table and two unsteady chairs, seemed to have last been redecorated before either of them had been born. Melody tried not to look too comfortable. She could have told the freshly-minted lawyer that if he was hoping to shock the student summer hire, he'd have to do better than this. She *could* have, but decided not to until she knew him better.

On a trip to the washroom, Melody recognized a leggy blonde in a leopard-spotted miniskirt—a slightly older woman who'd lived a hard life. For the moment, the two had the narrow space to themselves. Layla was trying to reglue a nail extension on her right thumb, a task for which she'd had a drink or four too many.

"Let me help. Why don't you rest your hand on the counter here and hold it still so we get this sucker on target."

Without giving her more than a glance, Layla did as Melody suggested.

"Thanks, honey. You know after all these years I'm beginning to think I'd rather be touched by a woman than by a man."

"Do you remember me?" Melody ventured when she had

got the cap back on the cyanoacrylate adhesive. She didn't know if Layla would blame her for Scar's death but was curious enough to chance it. She took off her steel-rimmed glasses and, when that didn't jog Layla's memory, unbuttoned her blouse to show Layla her snake-shaped navel ring—a keepsake of her weeks and months of undercover research. "I'm the server that scooped you out of a toilet stall two summers ago."

"At the Grey Mare." Layla smiled widely. "Ancient history. I don't do horse any more—and from the way you're dressed, I don't guess you're still waitressing."

Melody shook her head. "Should I offer condolences—you know, about Scar?"

"Scar? Oh, he was cooler than cool and a real sex machine, but if he hadn't got killed that night, I'm betting Chuckles would have arranged an accident for him."

"Why's that?"

"The gang blamed Scar for the leak that tipped off the cops. I can't see it myself. Chuckles was jealous of the dude, was mostly what it was. Too bad old Chuckles couldn't have been nabbed with the rest—he's nasty—but really I don't care any more. I've given up bikers."

Layla apparently didn't remember telling Melody gang secrets. The content of those sisterly confidences had faded into a haze of intoxicant-based amnesia.

Melody had always known that Ted Boudreau must have used what she'd given him to trigger the clubhouse raid. The prof had said he didn't want to disclose her data until there was someone other than her to pin the leak on. Still, she didn't see how he'd managed to put Scar behind the eight ball. She'd have to work that one out later.

"No more black leather," Layla continued. "No more getting called 'Ol' Lady.' I've come up in the world. As a matter of fact, I've got a young professional waiting for me out there tonight, so I'd better be getting back."

Melody could count on the fingers of one hand the number of dates she had been on in her life; it was a thrill to be able to say to Layla—

"Me too."

Author's Note

As of 2005, Peel Regional Police was the third largest municipal police service in Canada. In real life, many more officers would have been involved in the investigation than are portrayed in these pages. To make the story easier to follow, I have assigned the work of various units to a fictitious Major Crime Unit, such as might exist on smaller forces, and have consolidated numerous investigators into the two named detectives Tracy Rodriguez and James Nelson. These and all other characters appearing in the novel are products of my imagination: none should be identified with actual persons living or dead. As for the place and street names, some are real—such as Mississauga and Cawthra Road. Some, like Robin Hood Crescent and Pebbleton, are invented. The University of Toronto's Centre of Criminology should not be identified with my made up Department of Criminology.

Acknowledgements

It's a great happiness to be able once again to thank Carol Jackson for her love, friendship, and timely advice over many years and, more particularly, during the gestation of this book. The work has also benefited from the professional skills of Lesley Mann, an editor who sees both the forest and the trees. Many corrections were made as a result of consulting Crown Counsel Ian D. Scott, who generously read and critiqued an early draft. He can in no way be blamed for any court details I still have wrong. Writing a realistic novel with a contemporary setting has presented research problems for an author whose previous mysteries have been historical. The information I needed was not all to be found in libraries or on the Internet. Many thanks to Constable Kathy Weylie of the Media Relations office of the Peel Regional Police. I'd also like to express my gratitude to the following friends and relations, who allowed themselves to be quizzed on subjects touched on in the preceding pages: Lisa Armstrong, Doug Childs, Peter Duivesteyn, Liz Estall, Neil Forsyth, Ric Jackson, Ron Langevin, Shing-kan Lee, Stephen McCann, John Pepall, and Miranda Sorensen. Daniel Camball not only advised me on motorcycle lore, but allowed his Kawasaki Ninja to be photographed for the cover. Thanks lastly and hugely to Publisher Sylvia McConnell, Editor Allister Thompson, and Graphic Designer Vasiliki Lenis at Napoleon & Company; no writer could have finer folk to work with.

Victorian Canada provided the setting for Mel Bradshaw's first crime novel. *Death in the Age of Steam* was shortlisted for an Arthur Ellis Award and was *ForeWord* magazine's choice as best mystery novel of the year. His second historical mystery, *Quarrel with the Foe*, featured Toronto in the Roaring Twenties. Various journals have published Mel's short stories. He has also written on military history for *The Canadian Forum*.

Mel was born and grew up in Toronto, where he took his B.A. and was film editor of *The Varsity*. He holds a postgraduate degree in philosophy from Oxford University. His non-writing career is teaching English, which he has done in Canada and Southeast Asia. Currently, he lives in his native town.